The Master of Monterey

The Master of Monterey

a novel by Lawrence Coates

UNIVERSITY OF NEVADA PRESS

Reno & Las Vegas

Western Literature Series

University of Nevada Press, Reno, Nevada 89557 USA

www.unpress.nevada.edu

Copyright © 2003 by Lawrence Coates

All rights reserved

Manufactured in the United States of America

Design by Barbara Jellow

Library of Congress Cataloging-in-Publication Data

Coates, Lawrence, 1956–

    The master of Monterey : a novel / by Lawrence
Coates.

    ISBN 978-0-87417-529-5 (pbk. : alk. paper)

    1. Jones, Thomas Ap Catesby, 1790–1858–Fiction. 2.
United States. Navy–Officers–Fiction. 3. Americans–
Mexico–Fiction. 4. Monterey (Calif.)–Fiction. 5. Ship
captains–Fiction. I. Title. II. Series.

PS3553.O153 M37 2003

813'.54–dc21   2002015362

The paper used in this book meets the requirements of
American National Standard for Information Sciences –
Permanence of Paper for Printed Library Materials, ANSI
Z/39.48-1984. Binding materials were selected for strength
and durability.

The first and second chapters of this novel originally
appeared in *The Journal,* a publication of Ohio State
University, in a slightly different form.

This book has been reproduced as a digital reprint.

For Kimberly

➤➤ ◄◄

In 1842, Commodore T. ap Catesby Jones, U.S. Navy, under the mistaken belief that war had been declared against Mexico, seized the port but withdrew after three days.

–Monument at Monterey State Historical Park

California seems to me an illegitimate child, an illustration to a fairy tale about Johnny the Fool, or one of the tricks history plays constantly in order to mark the distance between the way it works and our ideas about it.

–Czeslaw Milosz, Visions from San Francisco Bay

CONTENTS

PROLOGUE

IN THE EARLY YEARS OF HIS REIGN, Emperor Felipe IV, ruler of Spain and the New World, decreed that California be occupied. A century and a half later, after the emperor's line had crumbled into decadence, a small Spanish ship finally arrived, carrying twenty scurvy-ridden soldiers and two friars ready to deal. In return for surrendering their land and freedom and swearing fidelity to an invisible monarch, the Native Californians were offered immortality. Many took the trade. The Spaniards in California called themselves "people of reason" to distinguish themselves from their converts.

In the 1830s, more enlightened men granted liberty to the indigenous people and freed up the vast tracts of land and countless head of cattle formerly controlled by the church. They then took the liberty of granting the land and cattle to themselves. These men believed in progress, and so they progressed to a mode of life last seen in Europe seven hundred years earlier. They lived in baronial ease and counted their land in leagues while Native Californians pondered the minor differences between life as a neophyte in the primitive church and life as a serf under feudalism.

Then, in 1842, Commodore Thomas ap Catesby Jones of the United States Navy mistakenly conquered California with one ship, forty-four cannon, and six hundred men. Commodore Jones, the true subject and object of this rare history, had been aboard ship since the age of fourteen. Like many sailors – ship's officers and common seamen alike – he stayed at sea because of love.

PART ONE

Chapter the First

→►- →►- →►-   -◄◄- -◄◄- -◄◄-

Young Tommy Jones returned home to Boston from his first cruise as a midshipman, determined to ask the beautiful Louisa Darling to marry him as soon as he had been elevated to lieutenant. He had been at sea for three years, hoping for a war to make him worthy of her love, a hope that made the officers praise him and the common seamen despise him. He had promised her that he would do great things in her name, that he would make history. A long and vexing peace had spoiled his chances of returning wreathed with glory, but as he took a carriage from the landing to the mossy family manse, he hoped to find Louisa as pure and devoted as when he had left her.

Tommy had been sent to sea by his father, a wheelchair-bound banker who had read Filson's biography of Daniel Boone and who constantly praised the country's relentless movement westward. Old Mister Jones had brought his eldest son into business with him, but he desired that his younger son take up the noble exercise of arms and further the country's expansion.

— You cannot limit this realm of freedom and democracy, he said, any more than you can say to a young boy that he is big enough, and must not grow any further.

Tommy, however, thought more about the virginal Louisa

than the virginal Mississippi River basin. Louisa Darling was the favored daughter of a prominent shipping family, which had made its fortune transporting live cargoes chained hand and foot. She and Tommy had exchanged letters while he was at sea, and though she had never written that she loved him, she always ended her letters with a request that in whatever he do, he think of her. So he thought of her while he scrambled up the masts with the ordinary seamen, and while he exercised the guns and sent broadsides booming into the inoffensive ocean, and while he watched the sea glow green at night about the ship's bow wave. And in his thoughts, she grew impossibly lovely. Louisa Darling came to have white arms strong enough to fold in all the world's restlessness and quiet it with her embrace, her hair was gold to make men despise the base gold of avarice, her purplish eyes, set a little close together, could answer any question simply with a deep look of love. Even her teeth, which always stuck out a bit despite Tommy's most sweaty and fevered imaginings, were incomparable to anything except the most flawless pearls. He thought her the very incarnation of the love that would bring endless joy and contentment, and he knew that if he joined with her he would want for nothing more throughout his life. She was the only virgin territory he truly dreamed of settling in.

He alighted from his carriage by the old manse and walked up the steps in his blue uniform with a sword at his side, and he felt himself taller and stronger than he had been when he left at the age of fourteen, weathered and tested by years on a man-of-war. He opened the front door for himself, before a servant could open it for him, and strode down the marble hallway.

Little had changed — the same silver candlesticks on top of the same Chippendale tables, the same portraits along the walls. But, in his mind, he had changed, and he walked the hall as though he were coming into his own.

He turned into the parlor, and he saw his brother embracing a woman draped with a long white dress. Young Tommy smiled.

— Let me wish you joy, he said. Brother, are you to be married?

— Tommy! his brother shouted. Yes, you know my fiancée.

The woman, still in his brother's arms, turned her face toward Jones and gave him a sweet and pitying smile. It was Louisa Darling. Tommy's brother had made a number of shrewd ventures over the years, especially investing in ships flying the Darling flag after the invention of Whitney's cotton gin. And her father had pointed out that glory is fleeting and uncertain, but there was nothing uncertain about a diamond. When Tommy's brother proposed marriage to her, it wasn't difficult for her to weigh things up between the brothers and favor what the older brother offered.

She turned her face away again. Tommy Jones drew his sword, desiring to wash away with blood the scene before his eyes, so that he would never have witnessed his pure and untouched beloved in the arms of another, so that he would never have known the divine Louisa Darling to prefer another. But before he could advance, a spidery hand clutched his arm and the heavy wooden wheels of his father's chair squeaked.

— Come with me, his father said.

In the study, Tommy went down on one knee and confessed his anguish. He didn't understand why he and his efforts to make history had been rejected, while his brother, who grew rich protected by Tommy's strong right arm, had been favored.

— If she's being forced into marriage, he said, I'll challenge him to a duel.

His father shook his head. — If you raise your hand against your brother, even in a duel, you will be banished forever from her company. And mine.

— But I'll lose her forever if I see her married without trying to stop it.

— You'll lose everything if you try to stop it.

— Then what shall I do? I love her.

Old Mister Jones creaked his wheeled chair forward to where his son kneeled and laid a bony hand on his brow.

— You'll have to leave, he said. And as you sail, you'll have to love your country above all. Serve her, increase and grow with her.

On the day of the wedding, Tommy Jones dressed in his pressed blue uniform, clapped his sword at his side, and waited across the way from the Second Church in Boston. He drew himself to attention when a closed carriage drawn by four horses clattered onto the stony street. The carriage halted before the church's granite steps, and ushers and bridesmaids issued from the open church to greet it. The carriage door was opened, and Louisa Darling, splendid in her wedding gown, descended. As she walked up the church steps with her father at her side, she gave one unforgettable glance over her shoulder to where Jones stood, and their eyes met.

Then the church doors closed behind her, and Jones was left with a vision of her, white-crowned and eternally beautiful, glancing back with an expression he would come to interpret as regret. He shipped out that day, determined to fight for freedom and democracy and to avoid any duty that would ever carry him back to Boston.

During that very voyage, outward bound from Boston, Jones began to develop the remarkable curvature of the spine that would distinguish him for the rest of his life. He continued to grow taller while at sea, as though his father's blessing had been a curse, and he had to walk with a constant stoop to avoid hitting his head whenever he was belowdecks. The stoop soon became permanent. As he grew, his body seemed to elongate itself into a thin, sinuous curve above his pipestem legs, ending in his long, sharp nose, so that he looked much like a walking question mark and could only with difficulty raise his gaze above the horizontal.

In New Orleans once, years after he had watched Louisa walk white-crowned toward the brother he wanted to kill, Jones secured a living reminder of his lost love, who, although she was now drab-haired and sallow-faced and exhausted after giving birth twelve times in her years of wedded bliss, still remained in his mind a white-crowned virgin. From the quarterdeck of his own ship, he saw sailing into harbor a ship fetid and foul-smelling and groaning with human misery. As the ship rounded to anchor, he saw the ship's figurehead, a half-naked mermaid holding up a torch, her firm, proud breasts cleaving the air. Then on the ship's broad stern, the magical name: *Louisa Darling*.

Breathless, Jones recognized the flag of the Darling Company at the mizzenmast, and he hastened to see the ship's cargo unloaded. There, he found himself irresistibly bidding on a hungry-looking African boy who had come out of the bowels of the *Louisa Darling*. The boy's name was written down as Hannibal, and he had already learned some English, which made the bidding go to eight hundred dollars before Jones finally prevailed.

He decided to set Hannibal free with the condition that the African become his personal steward, serve him aboard ship, sail with him wherever duty might take him, and generally be at the Commodore's beck and call, for a nominal wage to be paid twice yearly, or whenever he remembered. Jones presented these terms to Hannibal as eminently reasonable, offering cogent and irrefutable arguments on the advantages of such a position.

— And you will partake of the glory of the United States Navy, he ended, and join the making of history as we expand freedom and democracy across the continent.

Hannibal accepted. Commodore Jones discovered on the bill of sale that Hannibal had no last name. The trader told him that a black boy didn't need one, but the Commodore replied that everyone did who signed on to a ship in the United States Navy. He asked Hannibal for his surname, and the African responded with the long genealogy he had heard at the time of his circumcision, listing his ancestors back to the beginning of Creation, in a hoarse, windswept voice and a language that neither the Commodore nor the trader could understand, but that brought tears to the eyes of everyone else who had no last name. The Commodore asked him to translate.

— I speak memory, Hannibal said while the people around wept.

— Very well, said the Commodore. Put down his name as Hannibal Memory.

They became inseparable. Wherever the tall, thin, curve-backed man in a blue coat with gold buttons and fringed epaulettes was seen, he was followed by the short African wearing dungarees and a white shirt open at the collar. They paced the seas together, sailing the trackless oceans which Jones assured Hannibal would all someday belong to the United States, even down to the plants and shells and primeval mud on the ocean floor. Jones treated his steward with the utmost kindness. He spent idle hours teaching him to read and write, first in English, then in Latin, and he delighted in having him read aloud from Livy's *History* or Caesar's *Gallic Wars*. He also impressed upon him the memory of Louisa Darling, which he was to share, a pure being cloaked in white, standing high above them and inspiring every noble action. In time, he came to think of Hannibal as a true companion, a son almost, and it eased him to know that when he thought back on Louisa Darling his faithful Memory shared his thoughts.

— Louisa Darling, the Commodore would say with a hand over his chest. It makes my heart ache.

— Mine also, sir, Hannibal would reply.

Hannibal always listened carefully when the Commodore, unable to raise his gaze from the horizontal, looked to the west and told him they had to make history, and expand freedom and democracy, for Louisa Darling. But he couldn't forget that *Louisa Darling* was the vessel in which he'd made the Middle Passage, the awful mother who had swallowed up him and his people and then birthed them out dead or starving onto a new continent and into a history where they were written down as slaves. That history had begun for Hannibal when he and the young girl he desired for his bride were stolen by slave catchers and herded in a coffle to the coast, then kept in a barracoon until they were loaded into a ship's sunless hold with scarce eighteen vertical inches to turn in. The young girl Hannibal desired was chained beside him, and they talked of the dear place they had left behind, their desire to return. When the ship ran into a three-day storm, the sailors sealed the hatches, and the slaves slowly began to starve to death. The young girl's voice grew weak and then disappeared, and Hannibal had to talk alone in hopes that his stories might sustain her. He continued to talk to her for a day after she died, until the storm let up and the hatches were opened and she was thrown to the sharks that escorted every ship from Africa to the New World.

Hannibal arrived in America with a fearsome hunger which he would never lose, no matter how much he ate, and an equally fierce desire to keep alive and continue his story of generations. He had accepted the Commodore's offer because he had heard in the barracoon about plantations where masters named Carothers McCaslin begat children on African women, then begat children on their own daughters, and masters named Le Gré forced African men to whip and scourge the women they would love, or be whipped and scourged themselves, and yet other masters named Wall sold away the children who might remember their roots. Hannibal decided that Commodore Jones might be a means to escape Le Gré, and though he wanted no part of history, as what he had had of it was enough, he had already thought that if their intention was to make history, perhaps they would voyage to a region where history did not yet exist.

He studied Latin eagerly, to understand the origins of the history he would escape. He looked at it as a magical language that gave power to those who mastered it, containing the sacred stories of the whites. But he was dumbfounded when he read Livy and Caesar and Sallust, and it seemed impossible that there could be so many white men in the world when, according to what he read, they had spent most of their days killing each other off rather than begetting new generations.

The Commodore himself was also an enigma to Hannibal. He conquered lands, ruled ships that brought fire and destruction wherever they went. Yet he had no woman, no children. He had only Louisa Darling, who, Hannibal presumed, spurred him on with her continual absence. One thing Hannibal noticed about the Commodore as he studied him was that he continued to grow, long after a normal man would have stopped. He grew long and serpentine, a slender blue line, and would have reached seven feet in height if not for the curvature of his spine.

Hannibal continued to grow as well over the years, though not in the same manner as the Commodore. His endless hunger, conceived in the dark hold of the *Louisa Darling* when his beloved one starved while listening to his voice, compelled him to consume vast portions of salt pork, and boiled potatoes, and duff pudding. He ate mounds of his own food, and also ate everything left at the Commodore's table, as the Commodore was a light eater and sometimes barely touched what he was served. In time, Hannibal grew from a short, hollow-chested boy to a short, squat man with broad shoulders and a great round belly in his middle.

As the ships they served on over the years saw action, Hannibal attended the Commodore on the quarterdeck while bullets whistled around the thin figure from sharpshooters high in the rigging of enemy ships. At key moments, the Commodore asked him to give the sailors and marines a rallying cry, inspiring them with a message from his beloved. Which Hannibal, with a different meaning than the Commodore intended, was eager to do. He cupped his hands around his mouth and shouted in a millenary voice:

— For freedom! From Louisa Darling!

When Jones was named Commodore of the Pacific Squadron and ordered to ready his flagship, the *National Intention*, for sea, a story of impending war with Mexico began to gather form. The story grew from speeches on the floor of the Senate, editorials in New York newspapers, published dispatches from the pathfinder John C. Frémont on the western marches. Words attracted words, one story birthed another story, until war over Texas and the shapeless lands beyond was imagined whole and complete, though it had yet to take place. The story grew tangible aboard the *National Intention* when an emissary from Senator Thomas Hart Benton took brandy with Commodore Jones one evening on the quarterdeck of the flagship.

The man wore a dark cloak, and a broad-brimmed hat that shadowed his eyes, and a heavy gold ring with a curious Egyptian symbol colored his left hand. — I've heard from the senator, he said.

— Yes?

— If war broke out, an American commodore might seize the capital of California, Monterey.

The Commodore stalked restlessly about the quarterdeck, still eyeing the horizon.

— Might raise the American standard. Bring the territory under an enlightened form of government.

— Yes, the Commodore said, half to himself. Expand freedom and democracy.

— Fulfill the obvious destiny that Providence has pointed out to us.

The Commodore, curve-backed and questioning, turned toward the man. — Is this just story? he asked.

— Just story . . . can become history, the man replied. If men of will choose to make it so.

— Tell the senator . . . , the Commodore began.

— I don't have to tell him, the man said. He'll read your report.

After the man had gone, the Commodore sent Hannibal for charts of California and repaired to the wardroom. The African came back carrying rolls of old sheepskin traced with wavering lines, and charts from which dust-colored moths sprinkled into the air and then fell dead from their first contact with reality in a hundred years, and other charts smelling of nutmeg and clove, and one chart that left a taste of iron in the mouth just to look at, on which California was traced out in blood and called Nova Albion by Sir Francis Drake. Jones and Hannibal looked at the charts together, and they saw that California had changed size and shape many times since the sixteenth century. At times it was an island, and at times it was a peninsula. The Northwest Passage appeared and disappeared from its northern border, and the Río Buenaventura sprang from the middle of the continent and a cartographer's pen to empty into the Bay of St. Francis. The land sometimes grew fat and serrated as a pumpkin, and at other times was thin and wavy. It changed position, migrating to the north one century and to the east the next century, dodging around the ocean, hiding behind a foggy curtain.

The Commodore saw opportunity. — This land is adrift from history, he said.

— Is there any chance, sir, Hannibal asked with guarded hope, that if we arrive there, we'll be adrift from history as well?

The Commodore shook his thin head. — We'll never be adrift from history, he said. We bring it with us. We can make it with every one of our forty-four guns.

Chapter the Second

➤➤ ➤➤ ➤➤ ◄◄ ◄◄ ◄◄

The *National Intention,* Commodore Jones's flagship, was under the command of Captain Rafael Rafael, a man ready to take a ship over the edge of the world as long as he didn't have to promise to come back. When the Commodore brought him in to go over the charts of the voyage, and he saw the land drifting lost in the Pacific, he asked what they were going to do there.

— We're only going to carry out orders, Commodore Jones said.

— And what are our orders, sir?

The Commodore looked at him in wonder at such naïveté on the part of a captain in the United States Navy.

— We don't have any, he said.

Captain Rafael Rafael couldn't have been more pleased. He wanted to sail outside the already ordered regions, he wanted to find an untouched place, he wanted another shot at Eve and the Garden. Rafael Rafael had been born with three testicles, the gift God gave Adam to console him for never having had a mother, and his eyes were shaded like fragile blue china, the very color of which made women cry and wave lace handkerchiefs in delicate hands after his ship while it crossed the bar.

His first encounter with women came at the age of twelve, when the fabulously aged yet still enchanting Pearl Prynne spread tarot cards to uncover his true nature. Pearl Prynne, the heiress to the Chillingsworth fortune, had recently returned from Europe and was a houseguest in the Rafael manor in Manhattan, and she gave a reading for her hosts, beginning with Rafael's father (material success and bitterness), Rafael's mother (loneliness and gemstones), and Rafael's older sister (early joy, followed by a great transformation). When she came to Rafael Rafael, her black elfin eyes seemed to glitter above her enormous scarlet dress, which ballooned over half the divan. She laid out the cards in the shape of a mirror, smiled at her young querent with every one of her perfectly sharp teeth.

— Thou shalt seek harmony in many women, she said. But be thyself always at one remove from fulfillment.

Rafael Rafael couldn't sleep that night. He felt the black eyes calling him from his bed, and he finally stood up and wandered through the hallways until a rumor of something like lavender mixed with the smell of unwashed chickens wafted from under a door, stopping him in his bare feet. The door swung open, and he walked into the candlelight with an anxious fear that attracted him irresistibly. Pearl Prynne sat at a low table in front of a moon-shaped mirror, and she was running silver brushes through the long, milk-white hair lying loose about her shoulders, but she was still dressed in her elaborate crenellated dress.

— The door, she said.

He closed it, and she slipped a hand under his nightgown and felt with a knowing smile his third testicle, his Adamic gift, and as he leaned back against the closed door and panted, he looked into her century-old face and her young bright eyes and young-feeling hand and he wanted to marry her. She let him undress her, and it took forever, both because of his haste and inexperience, and because of the thirteen layers of dress, undergirdings, whalebone, laces, trusses, and silk undergarments that lay between Pearl and the world. When he finished, what remained was, miraculously, a young girl with boyish hips and no breasts, with no testicles at all but a use for all of his. He felt larger than her for the first time since he'd seen her until she pushed him ferociously down on the bed and climbed on top of him. Then he felt cut off from this world, adrift in a place where nobody else existed except for himself and this other who could set herself free from time. But he felt, deep within himself, the slow tolling of an inevitable bell, sounding lower until it reached an unbearable bass note, and he couldn't go lower without going as high as he was able, and then ending. And he found himself back in his bedclothes, alone in the hall with sadness and ashes in his mouth.

When he saw Pearl Prynne the next day, she was again covered over in her thirteen layers of silk, iron, ruffles, and bone, and he couldn't see through them to the mystery that had been revealed to him. Then she smiled with her perfect sharp teeth and glittering eyes, and he suddenly felt naked and hid from her sight all day long. But that evening, he was drawn again irresistibly to her door by the odor of lavender and rotting earth, and he felt decades drop from her with every layer of clothing and her voice became as young as an elfin child in the candlelight.

Pearl Prynne had been a wanderer on earth, ever since she left that bounded world of Salem to which her mother had returned, and on the night she told Rafael Rafael he would never see her again, he begged her to stay, claiming he would never know peace if she were to leave. He told her he would marry her, and she laughed her young girl's laugh, which was also the laugh of an aged woman who had heard many such declarations and knew each and every one of them to be absolutely sincere. She told him the story of the Dark Man, who met people by the brook near Salem and wrote down their names in a book with an iron pen and blood, and had the names of thousands upon thousands in his book, who came to him at night to dance and despair. Young Rafael Rafael, a child of the nineteenth century, that century of progress and noble ideals, said that such things were just in one's head.

— And be they not true for that? Pearl asked.

— Have you seen the Dark Man? Rafael Rafael asked, suddenly fearful.

— Have I not, Pearl declared. Many times have I seen him, and to dance for him takes delight from all else in the world, but it brings no contentment, for one of his names is Desire.

— I never want to see him, Rafael Rafael said.

Pearl laughed again, and now her laugh began to creak and groan like an old door swung on its hinges by a cold wind. He drew away from her, sat froglike in a corner of the bed and watched.

— 'Tis too late, she said. Thou hast seen him. Look in a mirror over thy left shoulder come the dawn.

Then she whispered in his ear that her mother had returned

to Salem because she thought it was the only place the Dark Man would leave her in peace, but she had been mistaken. The only place he would leave you in peace was a place you remembered in the past to which you could not return, or a place you dreamed about, where you could never arrive. Rafael Rafael declared that he would so arrive there or go back there, and Pearl laughed as a young girl again, and drew him under the covers with her, over her and under her, and because it was the last time, he felt the smell of her more strongly and knew in a way he hadn't before that the immemorial motions of the heart and body he felt now would in the future become a memory, irretrievably in the past, and before he could ask Pearl how she had learned to keep her body beneath its scarlet shrouds and veils young and smooth, she whispered a final secret to him.

— I too am always dissatisfied.

Her voice came to him like a siren song, urging him on to finish it off, which he did with a sweet violence, drawing from her cries that would haunt him with their absence. In the morning, she was gone, and he looked into a mirror. There over his left shoulder, he glimpsed a shadow like a face, leering at him. At first he thought it was Pearl's own face in a dark veil of mourning, not gone at all, but come back to devote herself to him and cut herself off from all other men for the rest of their lives. But when he whirled around, he found himself alone. He turned back to the mirror and looked at his own face, and he found he could only see the dark shadow out of the corner of his eye, never when he tried to look at it directly. He pressed his nose against the mirror, as though melting into it, to try to get a closer look at the Dark Man. The face receded as he pushed closer, but it was impossible for Rafael Rafael to see just himself. He spun quickly around again, but found himself still alone.

He began searching for a mirror in which he could see only himself, but it proved impossible. Every mirror he tried, from the gilt oval looking glass in the front hall to the polished silver salt shaker at table, yielded the elusive floating face accompanying his own. He felt time speed up, the days crumble quickly into nothing, as though the time before he met Pearl and saw the Dark Man had passed sweetly and slowly, all of a dreamy piece, and now each unit of time was something that disappeared, never to be recovered.

On the grassy grounds of his father's estate, there was a single still pool ringed by the draping arms of weeping willow trees and rustling green leaves of beech. Rafael Rafael stole away there at various hours of the day, trying to surprise a special combination of light and atmosphere where he could see himself in the unbroken water surface without the Dark Man haunting the edge of his vision, and simply lose himself in himself, as had been possible before he had known Pearl. The Dark Man always accompanied him, and sometimes he seemed to hear the Dark Man's laughter inside his head, and it sounded weirdly like the cries of Pearl urging him to hurry to his death.

His tutors despaired of him, and his father threatened to send him to sea a midshipman if he would not begin acting like a man, while his mother, feeling that her boy's affections had been twisted away from her, adorned herself with diamonds and wandered splendidly through the hallways of the house, hoping to have him come across her unexpectedly and be dazzled. Only his older sister felt sympathy for him and began to follow him down to the glassy pond to keep watch over him. One day when he seemed to have fallen asleep on the grassy sloping banks, lying on his belly with his face toward the water's edge, she came quietly up behind him, kneeled by his side, and folded both her hands over his eyes.

— Guess who, she said.

— Who? Rafael Rafael asked.

— Me!

— Me?

He opened his eyes as she unfolded her hands and saw his sister's face above his left shoulder, reflected on the water, just where the Dark Man's face usually floated. Her face looked like his own, the same brow and flaxen hair, the same fragile blue eyes. Rafael Rafael was suddenly ravished by the sight. He rolled to his back and looked up at his sister's face framed against the blue sky, and he felt that as long as he could gaze at her, the Dark Man would not be able to call him on.

— Oh me, he said. Oh, sister, oh me.

Rafael's sister was already promised to a safe man, a Wall Street lawyer who had business connections with John Jacob Astor and did a snug business among rich men's bonds and mortgages and title deeds. But she saw something in Rafael Rafael's eyes that made her fiancé seem a poor creature diminished by his daily contact with the affairs of the world, worn down at the edges by the rules of conduct he followed so scrupulously. She began to neglect her artist's palette and her piano to pass her time at the pool with Rafael Rafael, who now no longer looked in the water but rather at her.

They passed days and weeks and months that way, ignoring the mirroring pool and gazing at each other with such fearsome intensity that they grew thin and pallid together. When the fiancé of Rafael's sister came over to dine, she barely noticed him, even when he spoke about setting the date when she would make him the happiest of men.

— As soon as I'm ready, she said.

— Which will be . . .

— Several years.

Mr. Rafael now thought both of his children had gone mad, and because he knew that he had done nothing wrong, he dismissed all the house servants and would have dismissed his wife as well, were it possible to do so merely by giving notice and hiring a replacement. Mrs. Rafael, for her part, determined that the best way to control her daughter was to get her involved in putting together a trousseau. But when she brought her daughter to buy silks and furs and more emeralds, her daughter seemed merely to pine for her place near Rafael Rafael. So Mrs. Rafael spent most of the time trying on the items from her daughter's wedding wardrobe, to inspire her she said, and parading around in dresses far too small for her, even wearing her daughter's wedding crown on occasion and telling her that she would have to become more a woman and less a child to deserve it.

The fiancé was willing to let the engagement lapse. He had looked at his bride as another strand binding him to the comfortable, monied world, because of her good breeding and accomplishments. He didn't desire to have her upset the cozy niche he'd found for himself. But Mr. Rafael still insisted that he keep his promise, while pledging to up his bond business with him by 25 percent per annum, and at the same time speaking of increasing the fiancé's trade to John Jacob Astor. That august name, rolling roundly from the tongue, clinched the deal that Mr. Rafael had cooked up.

He'd decided that the only thing that would turn his daughter around would be for her to have three children in as many years, and while he doubted that the fiancé was up to the task, there weren't any other options. He set a marriage date, to be a private ceremony conducted within their home in two weeks' time, and announced it as a fait accompli, not to be gainsaid.

Rafael Rafael was in tears, fearing the loss of his sister and sure that the Dark Man would return. He went to the side of the pond alone, but was afraid to look at his reflection until his sister came and touched his hand. She was trembling. Slowly they bent over the still water, holding hands, and saw at last over both their left shoulders, a dark face leering at them.

— Oh, sister, Rafael Rafael sighed. I'm to blame.

— Father's to blame, she said, still trembling. He took her in his arms to comfort her and found that she was pressed all against him in a way he remembered perfectly from Pearl Prynne.

When he came to her that night, he found that she was waiting for him, sitting up under the covers with her eyes pale as his own in the candlelight. They grappled with each other frantically, struggled both toward and away from each other. Rafael Rafael found no thirteen layers of clothing, but rather a simple shift between him and her naked beauty. When he finally succeeded in working the shift up over her head and gazed upon her, he felt himself transfigured, as though she were a part of his body that he had lost and that he wanted to meld with again. She reached out to his Adamic secret and touched it, suddenly tearful and gentle.

— This is what they hid from me when you were a baby, she said.

She became his partner, drawing him toward her and surprising him with her primeval knowledge. The candle flame guttered from the heat of their joining, a molten heat from when the Earth was young and smoldering and humans roamed the land with four arms and four legs, powerful as gods. Then she cried out.

— This is the only crown I wanted.

And they grew still together, slowly as still as the center of a spinning disc, each certain that they had arrived, blissful and invincible, together.

The next day, Rafael Rafael found himself a midshipman under Captain Armstrong, a friend of his father, weighing anchor for the South Seas. The servants had discovered him with his sister in the morning and said nothing, of course. They had allowed Mrs. Rafael, dressed again in part of her daughter's trousseau, to discover them together and shriek the word that led to their definitive separation.

Two years later, in the antique port city of Tripoli, two letters caught up with him. In the first, his sister pledged her undying love forever. In the second, his father informed him that his sister had died in childbirth slightly less than nine months after she had wedded her fiancé. The child also had died.

Rafael Rafael rose quickly in the service in the years that followed, because whenever his ship was in combat, he exhibited extraordinary bravery, heedlessly putting himself in harm's way to gain victory. Yet through some secret decree of fate, he was never touched by ball or cutlass, not even scratched. He was promoted to lieutenant, commander, captain, and finally named captain of the Commodore's flagship.

While he was ashore, he searched for a woman who could take him back to a place he remembered in the past, or forward to a place he had only dreamed about, but he never found one. The women who came to Rafael Rafael, drawn by his fragile blue eyes and sensing his Adamic gift, left him feeling only sad and empty, alone again with the leering face of the Dark Man weighing heavily upon him. He abandoned them all, wanting only to get back to sea, letting them cry and wave lace handkerchiefs in delicate hands after his ship while it crossed the bar.

At sea, he began to read the journals of Christopher Columbus, and was intrigued to find that the old Admiral of the Ocean Sea had decided that the world was not quite round, but rather was shaped like a woman's breast with a nipple. The Terrestrial Paradise, Columbus believed, was to be found on the tip of the nipple, as being closest to the heavenly sphere, and he had decided the great freshwater rivers he found gushing out of South America must originate at this Edenic fountainhead. This made a certain kind of sense to Rafael Rafael, and he understood the drive that made Columbus sail west again and again into lostness. Rafael Rafael also read Milton's *Paradise Lost* repeatedly, but he always stopped midway through Book IV. He had read it through once, and he feared that no matter how many times he read it, no matter what desire he brought to the poem, it would always end in exactly the same way.

When the Commodore told him to ready the ship for California, he was thirty-five, in the middle of some road or other, and he hadn't looked in a mirror for more than twenty years.

Chapter the Third

Merry Jack Chase, maintopman and seaman extraordinaire, looked down from the peak of the main mast at the antlike activity on the deck as the *National Intention* made ready to sail west and achieve the apogee of our country's glory. Stevedores brought salt pork in such quantities that a whole nation of hogs must have been sacrificed in order to ensure that the voyage would enjoy the favor of the gods, and they brought shot and powder enough to convince any heretics who might believe that the gods had other intentions. A picked crew reported aboard: young men thirsty for glory, and blooded marines with a taste for combat, and others equally desperate. Jack Chase looked down on Commodore Jones, pacing the quarterdeck unquietly, as though already seeking the horizon, and round Hannibal eating the Commodore's duff pudding, and Captain Rafael Rafael overseeing the loading while ignoring the women crying on the dock.

When a new midshipman came aboard and looked up at the ship's intricate rigging in a dazed stupor, Jack Chase came halfway down the ratlines and bid him welcome aboard. The midshipman asked with a tremble in his voice whether he would really have to learn the name and uses of every line.

Jack Chase said he would, and the boy firmed his lip, though his eyes watered

— *Possunt, quia posse videntur,* he said.

This was William Waxdeck, a fifteen-year-old who could trace his ancestry to the Pyncheons of Salem, Massachusetts. His second cousins, thrice removed, owned vast tracts of land in the north and west that had not yet been discovered or explored but that formed the basis of their fabulous wealth. William's own branch of the family had been less fortunate, and when his father went bankrupt investing in the lead mines of the Upper Mississippi, William was plucked from the Albany Classical School and forcibly embarked on a career as an officer and a gentleman. He arrived on board the *National Intention* with more books than foul weather gear, a fact that made Jack Chase laugh.

— *Possunt, quia posse videntur,* Jack repeated. 'They could do it because they imagined they could do it!' Why, you're a scholar, not a sailor. But welcome aboard, for this will be a most literary voyage.

Indeed, when the Commodore heard that a Latin scholar had reported aboard as a midshipman, he called Waxdeck aft and ordered him to suspend his duties amid the masts and riggings and common sailors and marines and serve instead as the Commodore's private secretary. Waxdeck's first and last duties would be to compose an epic poem in heroic couplets on the theme of a ship carrying out the intentions of a great nation to spread freedom to the very logical ends of the continent. The hero of the epic should be shown sacrificing his own personal good in order to serve the destiny of the nation, and the whole work should be dedicated to the always virtuous and ever beautiful Louisa Darling.

At this statement, the Commodore drew himself up to his full, curved-backed, question-mark height. Midshipman Waxdeck looked at him through watery eyes.

— I will treat your orders as though they came from the gods themselves, he said.

The allusion pleased the Commodore, and he ordered that Waxdeck be given all the paper and ink he should ask for as soon as the ship got under way.

This order was given with such high priority that Keyes, the yeoman, unloaded barrels of salt pork and ship's biscuit, and filled the space with paper of the highest quality, and quill pens and bottles of India ink, and pencils manufactured by a Concord firm. Keyes had a face bloated and round as a beet, and was the best-fed man aboard ship. He hated to see the pork taken ashore, and he hated an order to give anyone as much as they wanted of anything. He had spent most of his career giving out as little food as possible to the common sailors while making sure the officers had plenty. By skimping on the sailors' food and embezzling only half the money saved, he had gained his reputation as an able administrator. Keyes thought that offloading pork and taking on words was a dubious idea — salt pork, no doubt, was a more dependable commodity in systems of exchange.

Jack Chase saw the stevedores taking off food and stowing writing materials in its place, and he laughed and asked Keyes what they were going to eat when they were becalmed in the doldrums. The yeoman answered through clenched teeth.

— We'll eat verse.

Major McCormick, head of the marine contingent, was drilling his troops on the dock, and Jack Chase called out to him what he thought of offloading food in favor of words. McCormick winked at the handsome sailor and said it didn't matter. For with powder and shot, he could win food well enough, and words couldn't stop grapeshot to the best of his knowledge.

— But I've got no great use for poetry, he added, pulling on his crotch. For I can neither read nor write.

When the sails were unfurled and the anchor weighed, a contrary wind came up out of the prophetic east and held the *National Intention* in port. Captain Rafael Rafael tried to work the ship through Hampton Roads and across the bar, but for a week they were buffeted and blown back. Commodore Jones was beside himself. He told Hannibal that it was unnatural that anything as insubstantial as a wind should oppose the will of the country, which was founded on principles of freedom. Hannibal agreed with him, while taking note of possible weaknesses in the history forty-four guns could make.

Waxdeck was sent for, and he eased the Commodore's mind by reminding him of the classical precedents for contrary winds at the beginning of a glorious conquest. Agamemnon, for example, had to sacrifice his own daughter in order to start the Trojan War, but his fame endured for thousands of years.

— If I had a daughter, the Commodore declared, I'd sacrifice her in a minute.

Hannibal said he didn't have a daughter either, and the Commodore tried to conjure up some other expedient.

Hannibal was thinking of starting a daughter somewhere in California who might remind him of his beloved and mend the thread of his story of generations broken by the *Louisa Darling,* but he didn't mention these reflections to the Commodore. In the meantime, the ship clawed out to sea and was blown back into port a couple of dozen times.

The last time the *National Intention* returned to the dock, a young boy stood there, frail and wan, with the skin of a lamb wrapped about his shoulders. The boy was Jimmy F. Bush, the forgotten child of the Ishmael Bush clan, and he and his family had been part of that band of pioneers who were opening the way for the march of the nation across the continent. Every year, Jimmy's father would throw his rifle over one shoulder and his axe over the other and strike out west, striving to stay a little ahead of the frontier. But every year, he would discover that the frontier had caught up with him, and that other families had settled into river bottoms near him, and county clerks had already begun to blaze trees and set boundaries, and the earth was no longer empty and free for him to claim like one of the sons of Adam. They would move again in the spring, abandoning the land that they had broken to a more placid wave of immigrants behind them. And when they had driven their ox-drawn wagons to a place beyond the sight and hearing of other white men, they set up their ragged tents, felled the trees they would use for fuel and forage, broke ground for a crop, and began to kill the buffalo and antelope in the surrounding areas.

— The 'arth was made for our comfort, Ishmael Bush often said, while he ate roasted hump from a pointy stick and his brood gathered around the fire using the shoulder blades of deer to dip beans out of a blackened pot.

Young Jimmy Bush was an afterthought in the family, the runt of the litter, a small, frail child of his parents' age. While his older brothers Asa, Abner, Enoch, and Jesse hunted with their father and learned to swing an axe, Jimmy spent most of his days among the few cows and sheep that the Bush clan brought with them. He fetched milk in the mornings for his mother and sisters to use for biscuits and butter, and gathered wool for them to card from time to time, and otherwise he was ignored unless an animal turned up missing, in which case he was whipped until his back was bloody. Jimmy grew up talking to animals more than to humans, at times telling them to please not get lost, so that he wouldn't be beaten, and at other times telling them to please get lost so that he wouldn't be ignored.

When it was time to pull up stakes in the springtime and once more endeavor to leave the frontier behind, it became Jimmy's custom to take one spring lamb and hide with it in a dry stream bed or a nearby hollow. He had learned that his father and mother would seek him out before they left, and greet the discovery of his hiding place with cries of relief that the lamb was safe, while he would be beaten and kept without food until sundown. For the rest of that day, his stomach growled and caved in on itself, and he could hold clearly in his mind the tender, joyful sound of his parents' voices.

In the spring of 1841, while Ishmael Bush was complaining about the Prairie getting *crowdy,* dissatisfied that he could no longer safely fell every tree he could view from the flap of his tent, an astonishing sight arrested the entire Bush clan. They were loading their gear for their annual migration, and a small line of wagons appeared from the eastern horizon, slowly pushing west on a route that had been described in books by authors who had never left New York, a route marked out only in the most passionate of humanity's dreams. Ishmael Bush watched dully as the wagon train passed by. Men walked beside the slow-moving oxen carrying rifles, or built road over a shallow creek so that the wagons could cross. Women walked beside the men, some carrying children in their arms up steep hills. What grieved Ishmael most was that he sensed that this wagon train was forever pushing the frontier ahead of it. That dividing line between Savagery and Civilization was suddenly advancing at a frightening pace. Ishmael looked back east, along the route the wagons had traveled, and he saw that Civilization had already arrived; all the trees had been felled in the wagon's wake, and all the wild animals had been killed. He saw, as in a vision, endless lines of wagons following him, and fences built across the oceanic Prairie, and the hated county clerks along with the fences.

In a dull panic, he drove his sons and daughters to finish piling their rude furniture, iron pots and plows, powder and shot, and barrels of flour into their two wagons. While his sons hurried to slop grease onto the axles and kingbolt, old Ishmael shouted at the oxen and cracked a whip over the shoulders of the lead yoke, and they creaked off to catch up with the frontier, barely able to see the crude sign on the rear wagon ahead of them which read CALIFORNIA OR BUST, forgetting young Jimmy, who was hiding out in a dry oxbow with a soft lamb smelling of shit and urine hugged to his chest.

At twilight, surprised and hurt that he hadn't been beaten, Jimmy emerged onto the Prairie and found that his family was gone. While the young sheep bleated for its dam, Jimmy walked around in circles, finding only gnawed bones and tree stumps to tell him that this had once been his home. He hugged the lamb tightly, as it would be the offering he would present to his father and mother to be welcomed back, and he tried to orient himself to go straight where they would be. But the vastness of the plains confounded him. He felt suddenly lost in it, his way home blocked by the very openness of space all around him. He wandered in the gloaming until he came upon what seemed to be a linear track marked by tree stumps and buffalo carcasses, and he began to follow it, unaware, as his sense of direction was never very good, that he was following the wagon train's trail back east.

Jimmy staggered easterly for days with the lamb clutched to his chest. He petted the lamb, called it his friend and brother, told it they soon would arrive, while its cries for its mother grew fainter. When it died, Jimmy wanted to bless and bury it. But driven by hunger and cold, he skinned and ate the animal and wore its fleece over his shoulders, certain that in doing so he had committed some horrible crime for which he would have to be punished. And to sufficiently punish him, only his mother and father loved him sufficiently.

For a year he doggedly kept his path through a welter of moving humanity, coming across stagecoaches, and keel boats, and great white sternwheelers taller than all the trees he had ever known, and railroads that moved faster than the fires of the Prairie. He found land broken by his family ages ago, now tenanted by strangers who would sell it to strangers and move on. He was briefly taken into the company of men who used him and cast him aside in their hurry, cared for by women who called him an orphan and coaxed him to tear off the lambskin he clung to, until they abandoned him as one of the abandoned. Down the Missouri, the Mississippi, up the Ohio River, along the National Road, he moved against the tide as though he might intersect with his parents at some unremembered point of origin, until he came to the edge of the sea, face-to-face with the *National Intention*.

Jimmy stood confounded by the sight of so much water, confounded by the terminus it seemed to place on his search, until Jack Chase called down from the maintop and asked him what he was looking for.

— My mother and father, Jimmy Bush said.

— Where are they to be found? Jack Chase asked.

Jimmy struggled to think. — They were heading west.

— Come aboard, then. For we're going as far west as can be, and you can meet your mother and father when they arrive. You'll seek no more on your present course, unless you can walk across the sea.

As soon as Jimmy set foot aboard ship, the Commodore had him seized. He was asked when he had left the crew. He said he had never been part of the crew, and this was put down as an offense because everyone was part of the crew. He was asked why he had come back aboard. He said because he thought he was lost. This was a graver offense, because nobody was permitted to be lost aboard the *National Intention*, especially not lost and heading east. He was asked how he would plead. He pleaded with them to give him a little bread. The Commodore ordered him made a spread eagle, and he was bound hand and foot to the rigging, while all hands were mustered to witness punishment.

Jimmy was flogged three times for being a deserter, once for being hungry, twice for letting on he was hungry, and five times for saying he was lost. Then he was cut down and sent belowdecks, not altogether unhappy. Being beaten and hungry reminded him of his mother and father, and he felt he was on his way home.

The next day, while women waved lace handkerchiefs from the dock in delicate hands, the *National Intention* cleared Cape Henry and sailed for California with a crew of glory-hungry warriors, would-be merchants, homesick children, lovelorn men, all under the command of the restless and questioning Commodore Jones.

Chapter the Fourth

They sailed on the same route that some years later would be followed by an endless line of hulks, scows, barges, carrying hoards of desperate-eyed goldseekers to the mother lode. And while the ship rolled south, the Commodore's private secretary and official bard of the voyage lay sick in a canvas hammock spilling a continuous string of green bile from one corner of his mouth into a bucket lashed to the deck. However, the stream of bile, varied at times by fits of vomiting, did not stop William Waxdeck from beginning the first canto of his epic, which at times he wished to entitle the *Jonesiad,* and at other times the *Californiad.* Jones himself had suggested *The Spread of Liberty and Louisa Darling.* However, they finally decided on a title of *The Conquest of the West by Sea, with special Attention to the rôle of Commodore Jones of the National Intention, in honor of Louisa Darling.*

Waxdeck described the eagle that flew toward the sun when the ship set sail, and the comet that fell toward the earth when the ship took departure, and then began to recount the battle across the adverse seas of fortune, as the *National Intention* battled hurricanes, Pampano winds, waterspouts, and sea monsters. Waxdeck didn't actually see anything he described, since he spent the whole voyage belowdecks. He just depended upon the other midshipmen to tell him what happened, and then exaggerated it and put it into meter, as he understood the basic aesthetic principles of the epic to demand.

Several times a week, the Commodore had Hannibal Memory carry Midshipman Waxdeck aft to his cabin to recite his latest heroic couplets, which he did between retchings. Then, after a glass of sherry, the Commodore had Hannibal carry him back again. It didn't bother the Commodore that Waxdeck was describing things he hadn't actually seen. After all, he reasoned, Homer himself had never seen the Trojan War, and yet he wrote the *Iliad*. The Commodore also ordered his faithful Memory to make out a copy of Waxdeck's work as it progressed, so that one copy could remain with the poet, while the other copy could be in his hands.

At night, Commodore Jones would mount up to the quarter-deck with a sheaf of poetry in his hands and pace from port to starboard. He knew that Louisa Darling lay always behind him, but the poem told him without allowing for any doubt that he would make history by going forward, and the poem also told him that the highest service he could render to Louisa Darling was to make history in her name. So he would peer into the brass binnacle and see the glowing disk of the compass, then gaze out at the dark horizon with a hand over his breast. Often, he would read a canto or two aloud by oil lamp, to ease his heart.

Whenever Hannibal carried Waxdeck back to his hammock, he emptied the bile bucket over the rail, then returned to Waxdeck with the empty bucket in one hand and some blank sheets of paper in the other hand, so that both could be filled.

He had been mulling over the difference between history and memory, and had decided that one important difference was that history was written down. Indeed, according to a Latin translation of Plato, writing destroyed memory. This confirmed what had happened to his people and his story of generations once the *Louisa Darling* had come to take them on the Middle Passage. Written history had overcome memory. What he wasn't yet sure about was whether history had to be written about the past. At times he had the odd feeling that it was the poem that determined the course of the ship, rather than the ship that determined the course of the poem. And when he copied over Waxdeck's cantos, it seemed to Hannibal that the bard had already determined the end of the story, in which Commodore Jones triumphed.

Then the *National Intention* sailed past Argentina and below Cape Horn, and it was battered by the same endless hump-backed swells that had battered Magellan three hundred years earlier, and it couldn't make any headway. They tacked far to the south, then far to the north, then far to the south again, and they ended up in the same position in which they had begun. They put the helm up, and put the helm down, and shortened sail, and braced the yards, but they could not double Cape Horn. Hannibal noticed at the same time that the poem was not progressing. Rather than sing of bringing freedom and democracy to the ends of the continent and rendering service to Louisa Darling by making history, the unheroic couplets began to go in circles, pondering whether the march of the nation across the continent would increase human happiness, and putting into question the very ends of the voyage.

While the *National Intention* struggled, the Commodore grew more displeased with how the poem would sound to Louisa Darling, and he sent Major McCormick, head of the marines, to investigate. The Major found that all the other midshipmen hated Waxdeck as a malingerer and had stopped speaking to him after he had refused to write a canto for each of them that they could later use to attain glory and a promotion. Waxdeck had nothing to write about until he began to question Jimmy F. Bush, who brought him his meals, about what was going on topsides. Jimmy told him of his plans to go west to meet his mother and father there, even if it meant heading east once he arrived, and had in fact asked Waxdeck why it mattered to bring freedom and democracy to the end of the continent.

— Will freedom and democracy help me find my mother and father again? he asked.

Waxdeck had trouble explaining that freedom and democracy would bring about untold benefits for all, when their progress across the country seemed to be the cause of Jimmy's losing his parents. As he tried to explain it, he grew confused, and when Jimmy asked him whether he himself wouldn't really rather be home in Albany with his own mother and father, Waxdeck burst into tears.

The Commodore found Jimmy's intervention a serious breach of aesthetic principles, and he had the malefactor brought before him. While the ship pitched and rolled in the icy white hands of the Great Southern Ocean, the leader of the Conquest of the West by Sea lectured Jimmy on Aeneas's shield in Virgil, and the prophecy of Tiresias in the *Odyssey*, and of course the foretold fall of Troy, stemming from Paris trying to decide between bribes.

— In summary, the Commodore said, an epic presentation of an endeavor presupposes the ultimate rightness of that endeavor. Questions that lack answers are not admitted.

Jimmy wondered how the Commodore, who seemed to carry a questioning in the shape of his own body, could see himself as an epic hero. But he admitted the charges, guilty of poetic insubordination, and at an order from Commodore Jones, all hands were called to the mainmast to witness punishment.

Jimmy stripped off his shirt and laid aside his lambskin; his rack of bones shoved pitifully through his skin, and his skin glowed pale as the ghostly great albatross that shadowed the ship, save for the purplish stripes remaining from his last flogging. A grating was lashed to the mast and Jimmy leaned into it, pressed his chest upon it, and stretched his arms over his head. An old quartermaster bound his feet together, then trussed his hands to the crossbar.

While the crew watched, Major McCormick took a new cat-o'-nine-tails from a green bag, combed out the tails so that each would strike separately, and then swept them in a long arc onto Jimmy's back. Fresh lines of blood rose from the gelid flesh. The Major shook the tails loose again, then whipped his arm back and then forward again to bring the whips onto the body of the boy. Jimmy surged against the bindings that held him, like a fish twisting at the end of a hook, crying out involuntarily for his mother and father. And all the men of the crew witnessed something of themselves there as the cat fell, witnessed their desire for home whipped out of them, saw their own homelessness punished in Jimmy's body, then saw themselves wielding the cat. McCormick struck again and again, scribing lines over lines into Jimmy's scourged skin, until he had made up a dozen. Then he took a knife from his belt and cut the boy down from the grate.

— There, he said. *That* will keep the ship on an even keel.

After Jimmy had been cut down, the Commodore ordered Major McCormick to talk to Waxdeck every day when the watches were dogged. So McCormick sat beside the green-faced youth with the string of bile sliding from his mouth and began to recount in a long voice all the exploits of his endless soldier's career, beginning with Andrew Jackson's battle for New Orleans, protecting the National Road in Ohio, invading Spanish Florida in order to sign a treaty, escorting Cherokee and Choctaw beyond the Permanent Indian Frontier just west of the 95th meridian, helping enforce the Tariff of Abominations against smugglers. After a few of these talks, he began to call Waxdeck "sweet boy" and "dear boy" and to chuck him under the chin when he made a point.

— My motto is, always, go forward. Never take a step backwards, sweet boy.

Waxdeck was enthralled. He began to write heroic couplets filled with progress triumphant, requesting more paper and ink from Yeoman Keyes, who grumbled that they would run out of food in the Southern Ocean before they would run out of writing materials. Waxdeck began to clean himself up and slick back his hair and be sitting up and alert at the times when Major McCormick would come to tell him what was going on above decks. When he shyly asked the Major to read some of the latest couplets, written with the influence of his tales, the Major declined with an amused shake of his head.

— Can't read or write, dear boy. Your marks there are as foreign to me as the Cherokee chants I heard on the way to Oklahoma.

— You're a representative of the oral tradition, Waxdeck said.

— If you say so, dear child. But I can't read. And I can write my name well enough with my gun, he added, pulling on his crotch.

As the poem again began to advance, the *National Intention* began to fight its way out of the icy reaches of Drake's Passage. The Commodore noted the progress on a chart after a noon sighting of the sun.

— Hannibal, he remarked, this voyage will make history.

— Indeed, sir, Hannibal said. And *you* will make history. But Hannibal had begun to have the uneasy feeling that history was making the voyage. He had begun to wonder how he would escape from the history in which his people were written down as slaves if he found California already won and dedicated to Louisa Darling in Waxdeck's narrative before the *National Intention* even made landfall.

Then the wind and seas slacked enough for the ship to double the cape and head north, and they rode the current that had been set in motion by the hand of God and the drawings of Baron Alexander Von Humboldt up the coast of America, crossed the doldrums, and headed north for the Sandwich Islands.

In the starry evening, while the *National Intention* sailed lonely on the blank and limitless ocean, seeking out a new place on which to bestow the blessings of liberty, Jimmy F. Bush took off his blue serge top and wrapped his fleece around his waist to let the pus dry from his suppurating back, which seemed to crawl with yellowish, phosphorescent creatures from the middle of the earth. He stood on the ship's forecastle with Jack Chase, that handsome sailor, and looked out at the horizon line while darkish waters flashed from time to time about the ship's bow wave. The other sailors had left Jimmy alone with the marks of the latest flogging, but Jack Chase accepted them with an equanimity born of decades spent aboard the warships of the world's navies.

Then Hannibal Memory mounted up a ladder to the forecastle. He knew he was out of place. Sailors muttered and looked away as he walked by, opened a path for him as he went forward and closed in behind him. But Jack Chase greeted him with a wink and a smile, as though he had been expecting him.

— Why here's another one who, I expect, knows the taste of a cat-o'-nine-tails.

Hannibal nodded. Although he had never been flogged since becoming the Commodore's steward, he had been whipped in the coffle and the barracoon, and also while on board the *Louisa Darling*. When his beloved had been taken away and thrown to the sharks, he had continued to chant his story until a mate grew sick with language and beat him until he was too weak to speak aloud.

— I too have been guilty of poetic insubordination, he said.

He asked Jimmy to turn around. The boy leaned over the

rail, and Hannibal carefully rubbed into his back an ointment he had learned of some decades ago, made up of beef fat, cobwebs, and ashes. He laid it in gently along the yellowish stripes.

Jimmy stood up, already feeling some cool relief from Hannibal's hands. — I don't mind getting flogged if it helps the ship on its way to the West, he said. That's where my mother and father are. And Major McCormick says it will every time he cuts me down after beating me.

Jack Chase laughed and danced along the ship's rail.

— Why, he speaks truer than he knows. If it weren't for men being beaten, no ship would sail. Every ship you see crossing any ocean in the world is only afloat because of the backs of men striped with a colt, or a cat-o'-nine-tails. Sure, if it weren't for your back, the *National Intention* would never have left port, or would have foundered off Cape Stiff. Seamen have backs and captains have lashes, just like children have bums and fathers have flat open hands. We'd all be shivering in caves if we hadn't been beaten out of them. The world moves forward because people are beaten. Without you, we'd have sunk long ago. Why, look you. There's McCormick, and the Captain, and the Commodore himself. And belowdecks Midshipman Waxdeck penning his lines like ranks of soldiers. What are they all dreaming of but arriving at a land where beating is at an end? And what are they doing but bringing powder and shot there?

— And a story, Hannibal said. They're bringing a story.

— Oh, that old story. We'll all be happy there, sure as Louisa Darling is the true spirit of freedom and democracy.

Jack smiled, as though he knew what Louisa Darling meant to Hannibal.

— That's reasoning from false premises, he said.

— A logical fallacy, Hannibal said.

— Aye. But fallacy or not, we're carrying forty-four guns. Do the guns bring the story, or does the story bring the guns? Possunt quia posse videntur.

— There's more than one story to bring, Hannibal said. More than one way to imagine.

— To be sure, Jack said. Jimmy's bringing a story where he finds again his mother and father. And they love him. But what if his parents fetch up in California after the *National Intention*, and they see the Stars and Stripes flying. Will they think they've come someplace new, or crossed the continent just to end up where they began? And will they love Jimmy if they are in the same place where they began?

Jimmy shrugged his shoulders into the quartering wind. — I don't want someplace new. I want to go back. . . .

— *Back* to where they *will* be? Jack laughed. And you, Hannibal, if we come to California and you find it's the same place you left behind, what will you do?

The ship's bow wave rumbled about the forecastle, low and insistent. Hannibal wondered whether he could ever again remember his story of generations alone and authentic, remember it as he had remembered it before it was in contrast to the history in which he and his people were written down as slaves. And he thought about Waxdeck's epic, sailing out ahead of the ship, weaving the land they would find into its narrative demiurge.

Chapter the Fifth

After he finished copying Waxdeck's latest pages for the Commodore to take up to the quarterdeck and read aloud while holding a hand over his heart and gazing at the endless horizon, Hannibal Memory took over a corner of the cabin to begin his own poetic insubordination, to oppose the official bard, to trouble the entrance of California into that history. Although he knew he couldn't contend with forty-four cannon, he could contend with imagination and words.

Waxdeck had begun to give Hannibal some instruction in poetics when the steward picked up new cantos to copy, and he told him that the heroic couplet was the form that in English best approximated the quantitative verse found in Greek and Latin epic forms. For instance, Waxdeck said, consider Pope's translation of the *Iliad*.

Achilles' wrath, to Greece the direful Spring
Of Woe's unnumber'd, heavenly Goddess, sing!

That wrath which hurl'd to *Pluto's* gloomy Reign
The Souls of mighty chiefs untimely slain.

His own beginning, he said humbly, had aspired to emulate the great cripple.

That restless hero who with mighty Hand
Brought his BIG SHIP to moor in Virgin land

That Brave one who with ardent Martial toil
Did plant our FLAG into the Yielding Soil

That Jones who brought to *California's* Breast
The blessings of our Destiny Man'fest

Who casts out tyrants, to VACANT land would bring
Democracy and Freedom, Goddess, sing!

Hannibal pondered the magical form of the heroic couplet, which gave such power to words on a page. The beats of Waxdeck's pentameter sounded on the inside of his skull, and as he sat down with an empty piece of paper and a full bowl of potatoes and pork in front of him, it seemed as though he had no choice but to write in the same meter. Besides, if his narrative were to wrest power from Waxdeck's, perhaps it needed to be in the same form. Hannibal ate several quick spoonfuls and began.

Sing, O Gods, of that well-rounded man
Who brought his endless story to new lands

Who used the restless curve-back'd Commodore
To ferry him beyond baleful HIST'RY's shore

Who fled the *National Intention's* slavery
For *California's* lush fecundity

Who left the ship to sink without regret
A new child and a new line to beget.

He studied what he had written, somehow dissatisfied. The words seemed very abstract, distant from what he had to relate. If he were really to mend his broken story, he would have to tell the death of his beloved on the *Louisa Darling*. But as he gnawed his pen and thought, the heroic couplets refused to come together and describe the terror and stench of hundreds of starving men and women chained below battened hatches while an overladen ship fought a storm. He looked hard at the paper, and the face of his beloved paled in his memory before the hard-edged presence of words.

He also reflected that Waxdeck had begun earlier and had already worked the ship around Cape Horn and into the Pacific. He didn't know if he would ever catch up if he had to write in heroic couplets. The events and their meaning might already be fixed before he had even had a chance.

The Commodore came belowdecks and found Hannibal tapping his fingers on the armchair while his portable writing desk rested on his lap scattered with different piles of paper.

— More copying? the Commodore asked.

— Aye, sir.

— Good, good. The Commodore paused, and Hannibal was suddenly terrified that he might come over and see what he had just written. But the Commodore merely asked a question.

— What do you think of Waxdeck's work, so far?

Hannibal replied circumspectly that the epic poem was sure to add luster to the Commodore's career, and that while heroes needed poets to make their names famous, poets equally needed heroes about whom to write. The Commodore nodded and sighed.

— You're a faithful man, Hannibal, he said.

The Commodore sighed again and put his hand over his heart.

— Louisa Darling. It makes my heart ache.

— Mine also, sir.

Hannibal melted in relief when the Commodore left. He decided then he would have to continue in expedient prose, as it would be the only way he could write rapidly enough to catch up with Waxdeck in the odd moments he would have free. Despite the fact that he was afraid that he too would participate in killing memory by writing history about what would happen in the future, he forged ahead to combat the epic in which his *Louisa Darling* would never sail. He ate while he wrote with prophetic force, and finished his food at the same time he finished the passage . . .

And while the National Intention *carried Hannibal beyond the land ruled by history where he and his people were slaves, a screwworm began boring a hole deep in the bilges of the ship, so that it would founder when it came upon the new place, and nevermore carry Hannibal back again, but rather leave him there to thrive with his memories again in force and his story to be continued into all the tomorrows of the world.*

When the ship anchored in the crystalline green waters off Honolulu, Commodore Jones found stories of war and a British squadron floating around the harbor. The Commodore was invited aboard the flagship of Rear Admiral Thomas, but he learned nothing. The Admiral, long seasoned in empire building, was amused by the Commodore's anxious desire to discover the truth concerning international relationships. The Admiral was convinced that the truth about international relationships depended mainly upon the number of cannon aboard ship at any one time.

— My esteemed Commodore, he said. You're concerned about whether a state of war exists or does not exist between Mexico and your country, so that you can take the necessary action (which I won't presume to guess at). Yet let me pose the question, for you to consider: If you take the necessary action, won't a state of war then exist?

— Perhaps, said the Commodore.

— Perhaps, the Admiral smiled. Perhaps you are being overly nice about a mere question of temporality, whether the state of war exists a priori. The French are not so scrupulous. If La Pérouse were here, he would tell you himself.

— Are the French in the Pacific? the Commodore asked.

— I've heard the French fleet just sailed from Valparaiso. Destination unknown. Hadn't you heard?

The next day, the Admiral himself took his three ships out to sea, courteously saluting the American. He hadn't mentioned to the Commodore that he was sailing so soon, nor where he was sailing.

Commodore Jones was in despair. He feared that he would find the flag of some other nation already flying in place of the Mexican flag in Monterey. Even though war was only rumored, he trembled to think of the Russians or the French or the English beating him to the prize. He followed the Admiral's fleet out to sea, but it had disappeared.

The *National Intention* sailed north of the Sandwich Islands, into the band of prevailing westerlies that would take it into the continent's west coast if the Commodore so ordered. It was local apparent noon, and the sun swung up to its highest point of the day while the Commodore paced restlessly on the poop deck, a thin, moving question mark surrounded by rumors. The first lieutenant waggled a sextant, taking the noon sighting for Captain Rafael Rafael. The ship's bow scared up a school of flying fish, which shot like silver stars across the ocean's choppy surface, pursued from below by tunny and from above by swooping frigate birds. There wasn't a cloud in the sky. The Commodore thought of Louisa Darling, and he suddenly felt lonely, homesick for land he could name Darling Land.

The first lieutenant stood before Captain Rafael Rafael and saluted. — Noon reported, sir.

— Make it so, the Captain affirmed.

Make it so, the Commodore repeated to himself. *Make it so.*

— Captain Rafael, he said aloud.

— Aye, sir.

— Set course for Monterey. Do it now.

While the *National Intention* squared sails and rode the wind with a bone in her teeth toward the coast of California, and the Commodore gazed at the line that divided sea from sky as though it were a seam that would yawn open and display a new land ready for the shape of his desire, Captain Rafael Rafael immediately stowed all the old charts they had brought along and determined to make landfall using only his own inner compass, since he was certain that the place he was seeking could not exist on a chart. He rolled up all the old flat parchments that showed California floating in different positions every century, and he swore he would have no new charts drawn up, fixing the land's position once and for all. He felt in his heart that if California were charted definitively, it would never be that place Pearl Prynne had told him about, a place he dreamed about where he could never arrive. He walked to the bows of his ship, looking for some sign that the Earth was inclining upwards, as old Columbus had thought of South America, looking for some sign that they were sailing toward that favored spot on the Earth that swelled up like a woman's breast to a nipple, closer to the heavens, looking for some sign of fresh water that spilled down from that place and sweetened the sea.

A sign was not long in coming, though it was not the sign the Captain had wished for. The following day at dawn, young Jimmy F. Bush from the maintop spotted a long, black, loggish object floating thickly from the direction toward which they were sailing, strewn with seaweed and starred with limpets and barnacles. Young Jimmy always looked keenly to the west, because he hoped to see his father and mother waiting for him there, happy to have him with them once again. Then he saw the floating thing like a half-submerged island in the gray chopped waters, and he sang out:

— Object sighted one point off the starboard bow!

Captain Rafael Rafael changed course to bring the object alongside and ordered it to be brought aboard. The red-capped boatswain swung a grappling hook round in the chains and snagged the object with a perfect toss. The line was taken to a block and tackle, and seamen from the starboard watch began to heave away as the ship's sails shivered in the wind.

A horse rose dark and dripping with salt water toward the yardarm, a dead stallion gutted through the rib cage by the treble hook, stiff as stone in death, its long masculinity standing out rigid in rigor mortis between its splayed legs. The horse twisted slowly below the block and tackle, its eyes closed as though still dreaming of running a herd of mares in season, as though the six-foot-long nerve that ran down its spine to its hindquarters were still vibrating with life. And the odor of earth still came subtly from traces of dirt clinging to its inner ears, just enough odor to make each man who hauled on the line sorry he had come to sea.

Major McCormick, that man who never looked backward, drew his saber and shouted to Captain Rafael Rafael on the quarterdeck.

— Shall we cut her loose, Captain, before she infects the ship?

The Captain looked sadly at the horse and drew his hand down with a slashing motion. McCormick nodded and swiped at the line, but the ship took a roll to starboard and instead of cutting the line, he slashed off the horse's long, erect penis. Then the hook tore through the rest of the horse's rib cage, and the beast splashed into the sea with a gash over its heart and fell astern in the wake of the *National Intention*, seeping blood into the white wash of the water.

The crew moaned in despair at the falling horse, and McCormick turned on them fiercely.

— No moaning, do you hear? I thought we beat that out of you. Next man who moans loses his!

Major McCormick was really concerned about how his dear

boy Waxdeck would take the event. Although the Major was still illiterate, he was learning something about the great tradition from his talks with the bard of the voyage. The relationship between Patroclus and Achilles, for instance, and their oral tradition in the Greek heritage of warfare. And he knew something of the importance of signs and portents to Waxdeck, even though he didn't quite grasp how they were tied to later events. Yet Waxdeck had told him of the Roman general who had stumbled while disembarking from his ship in Africa, and how badly it might have turned out if the general had not turned a bad omen into a good omen by taking up fists full of sand and shouting: See, Africa, how your conqueror grasps you.

McCormick sat beside the green-faced youth at the time of dogging the watches, as always, and he stroked his hand before telling him what had happened. Midshipman Waxdeck had still not been topside during the entire voyage, and had not seen a single thing that he was writing about. Yet he had no trouble at all reading the horse as a good omen. The horse might stand for the profligate nature of the Spanish dons who now controlled California but were not using the land to its full potential. Or it might stand for the backward system of government that currently held sway over the land, keeping the people in ignorance of the blessings of freedom and democracy. Waxdeck said he would have to see which interpretation was easiest to express in heroic couplets. Horse's Penis, for example, might rhyme with Warrior's Genius, almost. At any rate, Waxdeck assured his Major that he had struck a blow for either liberty or greater economic expansion.

Hannibal Memory also wondered how to interpret the horse

for his narrative of bringing generations to a land outside the history in which he and his people were slaves. The horse had been black, and McCormick's mighty blow had made him moan loudest of all. Hannibal wondered whether, if he just left the horse out of his narrative, it would disappear from his memory, and so not influence future events. He wasn't certain. But he knew that Waxdeck had taken the liberty of inventing certain good auguries at the ship's sailing, so he decided to take the liberty of leaving out an augury that he could not interpret, and he redoubled his narrative efforts to unleash the screw-worm into the ship's wooden hull.

As the *National Intention* sailed eastward, Captain Rafael Rafael spotted more horse corpses floating on the feminine emerald-green ocean. They were like a long curving line of buoys guiding him into Monterey without charts, but not the kind of guide he had thought would be waiting for him at the portals of Eden. He wondered what they meant, wondered whether the horses meant that in approaching his goal he was approaching death, and then wondered at his wondering. In the land he hoped to reach, signs shouldn't *need* interpretation.

In fact, the horses were merely the latest expulsion from California. They multiplied quickly and took rangeland away from cattle, and the Californios determined to slaughter them. But they discovered that they didn't have enough bullets in the entire territory to kill the horses, and not enough shovels to dig a hole to bury them all. So they stampeded the wild horses over cliffs into the sea, which they did with great dispatch and skill, driving eight thousand three hundred and twenty-seven horses past the surf line. The horses thrashed the ocean white until they drowned, and then they floated out to sea. Some old men from the Ohlone tribe walked the beaches and pushed back out to sea the horses that washed ashore. They floated out like a long, beautiful finger pointing the way to the capital city of Monterey, and the Captain followed them.

On the bright morning that the *National Intention* was climbing the last crest of ocean, which would bring landfall on California, the first screwworm was discovered by Chips the carpenter. Chips lived in the bilges. He was the only member of the crew who could hear the thick voice of the ocean crying at the wooden planks and not go insane thinking that only two inches of tree stood between them and the starry depths where monsters with eyes on the sides of their heads waited to kill them with their vision. Chips was a cave dweller, a troglodyte, with a long black beard rank with algae, and skin the color of mottled milk, and black eyes sunken under bushy brows. On top of his bald head was a plate of silver the size and shape of a butterfly, which replaced the part of his skull smashed away by a shattered oaken spar at the tail end of a forgotten engagement during the War of 1812. Chips oversaw the keel and the keelson, and the heavy lead weight that kept the ship in ballast. He preferred to speak with the rats and other lower forms of life that lived in the bilges than to speak with the yeoman and gunners and ship's officers who lived above him. Yet he spoke to the rats with great seriousness and conviction of the ship's mission and the role of the bilges in that mission, as a counterweight to the heavy masts and cannon. And that mission was to fight. He sang to the rats the song he had heard just before his ship joined combat.

Hearts of oak are our ship

Jolly tars are our men

We are always ready, steady, boys, steady,

To fight and to conquer again and again

It was only when the ship was fighting that he truly felt happy. He never knew where the ship was sailing, or who it was fighting, or why. So long as the ship was fighting, he was content.

— Fight, he told the rats, fight and conquer. Then he threw some biscuit down to the timbers and watched the rats fight amongst themselves.

On that portentous morning, he found six inches of salt water tainted with horse blood in the bilge, and whole families of rats cowering along the ribs away from the keel. The rats were pointing with their noses at a single spot, so he took some tar-soaked oakum from his pockets and stuffed it down between the keel and the first plank. He mounted slowly up a ladder to the tween decks, still far from the open sky, and he prowled there until he found the boatswain coming down to break out pikes, cutlasses, and pistols from the yeoman's stores.

— Leak, he told him. Man pumps.

— All right there, Chips, the boatswain said as he hurried by. We'll get to it.

While Chips stared stupidly after the boatswain, uncertain why he was being ignored, Jack Chase, that handsome sailor, called out from his dancing royal yard high above the chalk hill of the ocean in a voice known by the Phoenicians three millennia past.

— Land ho! Land hoooooooo-oh!

Commodore Jones, on the poop deck, raised his long glass to his right eye and stared dead ahead.

— Sail on, he cried. And clear the gun decks.

California heaved up over the horizon in awful fecundity and guided the ship in with horse bodies issuing forth from Monterey, the capital of Alta California and cornerstone of Mexican control of the territory. Monterey was a pile of lumpy white buildings with red-tile roofs, haphazardly spread out on a green plain like seeds on a loaf of bread. The buildings generally followed a curving cart path between the Custom House, perched above the rocky landing beach, and the Presidio, squatting nearer the forest edge. Every building there was made from adobe bricks, baked out of clay soil mixed with straw, then whitewashed to keep the bricks from sinking back into the earth. After the winter rains, all the inhabitants inspected their houses to see how much had melted away.

The Presidio was a squarish fort of cracking adobe walls with circular blockhouses on the two corners facing the sea. It was kept up with government funds, and therefore it was the most decrepit building on the green. The native Ohlones in the nearby rancherías had the good sense to live in huts made of sticks covered with bulrushes and grasses. When one of their dwellings began to sink into the earth, they simply burned it down and built a new one. They didn't depend on the government to maintain their buildings.

Chips went below to see if the water level had increased, Captain Rafael Rafael piloted the *National Intention* along the horse corpse buoys, and Commodore Jones scanned Monterey with his long glass, fearing to find the French fleet that had left Valparaiso, or the English fleet from Callao. He found only two small Mexican trading vessels, the *Paz y Religión* and the *Don Quijote* riding quietly at anchor. The tricolor Mexican flag was still hanging limply above the Custom House and the Presidio. He looked for signs of the war between Mexico and the United States, signs that would make all the stories true and all the omens and auguries invented by Waxdeck inevitably and unquestionably right. He saw a small battery of cannon behind a breastworks on a hill separate from the Presidio, which could fire upon the anchorage, but unfortunately nobody was there aiming a cannon at him.

He turned the glass on the Presidio, and with joy in his heart he saw two lines of mounted horsemen, like two processions, making for the Presidio's front gate. He handed the glass to Captain Rafael Rafael.

— Look there, he said. They're bringing reinforcements to the fort.

The Captain saw the same two lines of horses proceeding to the Presidio, but he saw differently than the Commodore did. At the head of one of the processions, he saw with sudden clarity a woman with tears in her heart and a thin chain of gold around her neck, and upon seeing her he felt that any number of dead horses he'd had to follow to get here had been worthwhile.

He did not mention this to the Commodore, only agreeing that they were reinforcements. The Commodore ordered two boatloads of marines to row to the trading vessels and inform them that they were prizes of war. Then, as the *National*

Intention rounded into harbor, he ordered a single cannon readied to fire a warning shot. They backed sails to slow the ship, steadied the helm, and Hannibal gave out his parabolic shout.

— For Freedom! From Louisa Darling!

— Fire! coughed the Commodore.

With a shot not heard round the world, a single cannonball flew from a United States man-of-war into the unfailingly blue Aztlan sky and plummeted down toward the soil of California. Chips, down in the bilges, looked up suddenly from the rising water and groaned in satisfaction at the cannon's sound. Jack Chase, high up on the maintop, laughed at the hundredth invasion of his endless career in the navies of the world. The yeoman Keyes fretted at the use of powder and wondered if they would be able to get the cannonball back in good condition. Down in the tween decks, Major McCormick stroked William Waxdeck's greenish forehead while the youth began to compose a verse describing the flight of the cannonball — the arc up to its apex, he decided, would symbolize American arms and aims triumphant, while the arc down to its impact would symbolize Mexican interests defeated. As the sound of the shot reverberated and the cannonball fell, Captain Rafael Rafael tried to focus in again on the woman at the head of the procession with the long glass at full extension. In the moment before the cannonball struck, Hannibal wondered whether it would bury itself like a seed, the first seed of his story to be planted in this land. Commodore Jones had a moment of misgiving as he realized that he had gone to war on the basis of stories of war. Now that the story was willy-nilly about to become fact, he hoped for the good of his career that American and Mexican troops were already slaughtering each other in Texas.

The shot cracked into the main gate of the Presidio with the precision of destiny and crumpled the wooden doors as a hundred generations of winged termites and grubs panicked into the air. The horses in the processions reared up, and both lines turned and galloped in opposite directions away from the fort. Commodore Jones was stunned. Every rule of war told him that they should rush into the fort to defend it, but he didn't realize as the residents of Monterey did that the decrepit Presidio was the least safe place to be in case of attack, and that its main strength lay in the enemy's ignorance of how weak it was. The Commodore took the long glass with some difficulty from Captain Rafael Rafael and turned it on the broken gate. Two soldiers peered out through the shattered timbers, as though they were looking into the daylight for the first time since Christmas. No answering fire came from either the Presidio or the battery. Yet the Mexican flag still flew over the fort, undaunted. Commodore Jones was resolute. The two boatloads of marines had returned with reports that the captains there were content to be prizes of the great young democracy, which, so it was said, had a great respect for private property. Jones immediately called for McCormick to lead the marines onto shore under a flag of truce and fulfill the ends of the war.

Waxdeck clutched at the Major's hand as the marine rose to his feet. — Go bravely, he said. Let honor be your guide.

The Commodore instructed McCormick to negotiate carefully the surrender of all the land of California, and the minerals under the land, and the roots of plants growing in the land, and the animals that roamed on the land, and the trees that spread branches over the land, and the clouds that passed above the land, as well as the air, sunshine, and rain, including those parts of California that had never been seen and only existed in legend, tall tale, and hearsay.

— Be skillful, the Commodore said. Use tactics. Parlay.

— I can parlay well enough with my gun, sir, McCormick said.

Commodore Jones knew he had chosen the right man for the job. He sent him off with orders to strike the Mexican flag and raise the Stars and Stripes in its place. And he gave him, for the sake of convenience, a newly amended Surrender Form. All that was necessary to complete the Articles of Capitulation was to fill in the dates, the name of the garrison, and the name of the governor and/or commandant general. Article four made provisions for repatriation of Mexican soldiers to Mexico now that the land they stood on was no longer named Mexico. Article one gave permission to the Mexican troops to play music as they marched out of the fort. And Article five guaranteed the right to personal security, property, and religious freedom, to all who agreed to consider themselves conquered. The form was in English, so Jones was certain it would be understood perfectly.

The longboats crawled toward shore, many-legged, like waterbugs. Rifles pointed out between the oarsmen like spikes on a seedpod. The men aboard the *National Intention* watched in sudden silence as the boats rowed their way through the thick beds of kelp that wrinkled the water, through the schools of sardines that would one day give birth to Cannery Row, through the friendly nods of sea otters about to be hunted to the brink of extinction. The men watched the boats always going forward under McCormick's direction, toward the placid shore. The white buildings with red-tile roofs were asleep on the green plain, and two cows appeared on the ridge of the gun battery, chewing slowly and watching with great unconcern the boats plash through the water. The cows were brown and white with large liquid eyes, and frays of hay hung from their mouths. They were the most beautiful cows the men had ever seen.

Then Chips emerged blinking from the leaking bilges into the open air, blood-tainted water soaking his calves, and he groaned incoherently from his tangled mouth at the sight of forested hills and green plain rising from the ocean around him. He scratched his face with his long nails until blood ran, closed his eyes and opened them, and then spoke with a desire for revenge on that peaceful sight that lay before him.

— Fight, he said. Fight and conquer.

The boats bumped against the shore, and marines gathered in good formation and marched up to the broken gate of the Presidio, and everything changed.

PARTE SEGUNDO

Capítulo Primero

When the American cannonball fell from the sky and splintered the gates of the Presidio five paces from the nose of Arcadia Serrano's wedding cavalcade, postponing her oathtaking on the brink of the chapel, she raised her hands to heaven and gave thanks to God and the Mother of God and the angels of God and all His saints for their divine intervention.

— And especially Santa Teresa, on whose day I was born, for this reprieve.

Arcadia had been a virgin since she was three years old. Her mother died during her first day of life, in the warm soup of birthing, and her father died three years later when he attempted to lance a bull from horseback to win the favor of a young woman he hoped to marry. The bull met the lance thrust bravely and shivered the filbert shaft, and one splinter of wood flew straight through her father's heart. Arcadia was given a gold chain to wear around her neck, with her mother's wedding ring and a piece of the broken lance threaded upon it, and she was sent off to live with her uncle José and her aunt Josefina, who were childless. Arcadia's earliest memory of her new home was of her aunt picking her up, turning her this way and that, inspecting her. Uncle José looked on like a man experienced with livestock. Then Aunt Josefina put her down and pronounced her fate and her status.

— She won't be such a burden, her aunt said. Because she is a virgin.

Arcadia had in her name a land grant of eleven square leagues, rich with cattle and wild horses, to be controlled by her uncle until such time as she had proven herself, by a chaste and upright life, to be worthy to pass control of it over to a husband. To help guard her chastity, her aunt and uncle gave her a governess and a servant. The governess, Duenna Recta, was a spinster with prunelike lips who had dressed in black every day for the past thirty-five years in mourning for the husband she had never had. She found the army officers in California too irreligious, while the common soldiers were too crude and lowborn. The rancheros and their mayordomos were concerned only with the increase of their cattle, which struck her as an immodest occupation, while the artisans who had arrived as colonists were too dissolute and hard drinking. And she discovered that with every proposal she turned down, she was more esteemed and respected, so that she gained a good name with every man by not finding any man good enough to marry her. She worked on her trousseau for forty-three years, but had worked exclusively in black embroidery and needlework since the age of eighteen, not so much out of despair but rather out of cold logic; she would surely have out-lived any man she would have married, because of the corrupt earthly influences that govern men's lives, and so her black dress was only an anticipation of the inevitable, without any of the distasteful intermediate steps. Her trousseau nevertheless grew to tremendous proportions, all of the finest materials and most exquisite handiwork, far surpassing the available space in her cedar chests and finally hanging from all the walls and the ceiling of her adobe house like black spiderwebs.

She spoke with no men at all except for Fray Echevarría, and that only because he wore skirts. And she baked him *tortas de maíz* when she wasn't embroidering, corn cakes so dense and tasteless that the good friar was forever befuddled as to how he could thank her without telling a falsehood before God's eyes

For Arcadia's servant, they found among the land and people belonging to her parents a woman born in old Mexico named Magda. Aunt Josefina initially opposed the choice, but Uncle José prevailed, saying, — Who better to keep her a virgin than one who knows men? Magda had shipped up to California in search of the man who had promised to marry her, a friend of her father's who had the tattoo of a rattlesnake winding around his navel. He had taken her virtue when she was twelve, then left Michoacán when she was thirteen, promising to return. With time, Magda's memory of his face dimmed, but not the memory of the tattoo, and when she set out to search for him, she found that most men's faces had something in common with his. Any man she met, she discovered, might potentially be him, and she couldn't be sure until she had met him with his shirt off. She worked her way through the men in the surrounding villages, then through the territory, de-shirting them all. She never wanted for food while her skin was soft, but she never found the man with the rattlesnake around his navel.

Eventually her breasts sagged down and her hips ballooned

out, and she could no longer de-shirt any but the very old and the very young. When she heard of a call for colonists to California, a territory with a shortage of women and a surplus of men, she decided to search on there, although it proved equally futile. But she found a place on a rancho because of her great ability to make dirty linen snowy white, and because she could cure dental problems with the eyetooth of a black dog, complaints of the kidney with radish, broom seed, white wine, and lime juice, and menstrual cramps with aguardiente and raw egg white.

Arcadia spent nearly every moment accompanied by one of her two companions. Duenna Recta took her to church at dawn for matins, wearing a black dress like herself with sleeves to the wrists and a rebozo covering her hair and neck. She taught Arcadia how to bow her head and avoid looking any man in the eyes, because it was through the eyes that temptations of the devil entered. She also taught her to pray to the Virgin Mary to protect and preserve intact her purity.

— These prayers go directly from the Virgin to God, she said. You can see how well they have worked for me.

During the day, she guided Arcadia in using the hand loom, the embroidery hoop, and the needle, to build up her trousseau, for the sad day on which she would have to serve man's carnal needs. She also taught Arcadia how to read and write, because she had to learn the catechism of Padre Ripalda. Duenna Recta regretted having learned to read herself, because there were only eighty-nine books in the territory, and most of them were by heretics like Rousseau and Voltaire, and therefore knowledge of letters was one more avenue through which the devil could enter. If she could forget how to read and write now that she had memorized the catechism, she said, she would.

Between visits to the church and hours spent with the needle, Arcadia took off her black rebozo and rested near Magda. The old woman taught her how to dance the jota, the fandango, the bamba, and the canastita de flores. She taught her how to wear a tortoiseshell comb high in her hair, tied with gold ribbons, and how to let a lace mantilla fall gracefully over her bare shoulders, so that it seemed like she was protecting her modesty while she was revealing her allures. She taught her how to play the guitar, as there were no pianos in all of California, and she taught her the secret of the fan — how to spread the fan in such a way that nobody could know whom you were looking at except for yourself and he who you thought might be the one with a snake tattooed on his belly.

In short, Arcadia was taught to be a perfect nun from one mentor and a perfect coquette from the other. She loved them both, but she enjoyed using the words of each against the other, for their confusion and her pleasure. When Duenna Recta began to discuss with her the qualities of fruitfulness in a well-ordered home which would soon be hers to enjoy, a reward for her chastity, Arcadia began to ask detailed questions about how cooking beef and sewing for her husband would make her a mother of children. Duenna Recta tried to answer her questions, but she only confused matters by expressing everything in negatives and prohibitions. She said that Arcadia shouldn't scream, nor move too much, nor take off any more clothing than absolutely necessary. She shouldn't let it be frequent, as she was a woman of dignity and respect, and certainly never on holy days, Sundays, or the day of her saint. When Arcadia persisted in asking questions, the Duenna grew flustered and said that all she had to understand for now was that she should never touch herself in an evil way, for that would only tempt the devil and make her bleed before her time and be less attractive to her husband. Arcadia then asked Duenna Recta to show her how to touch herself in an evil way, so that she wouldn't be afraid of doing it without knowing it. Duenna Recta turned scarlet, and for answer took her to church to pray in front of a painting of the Virgin Mary. In this painting, the Virgin had her hands together, and a dove fluttered by her shoulder, and some Latin words twisted out of the dove's mouth and into the Virgin's ear.

— There, she said. That's how you become fruitful.

— By putting something . . . words . . . in the ear? she asked. Duenna Recta blushed again, but managed to nod.

— My ear itches, Arcadia said.

— Keep your hands together, the Duenna said.

In fact, Arcadia already knew all about how one becomes fruitful. Magda had told her long ago. She had also told her that there was no evil way to touch yourself. It was good to touch yourself, because someday you would have to teach a man how. That was a skill men weren't born with. But touching yourself, Magda told her, was not nearly so pleasurable as encountering the snake man.

Whenever Magda talked about the snake man, Arcadia noticed, she mainly recounted tales of the misery and woe she had met in her various attempts to locate him. In fact, the tales of woe and misery were told with much more detail than Magda's hazy remembrances of her pleasures, so that the search for the snake man seemed to be in fact a search for unhappiness. Arcadia asked her whether, given her experience, she might not have desired a life of fruitfulness in a well-ordered home.

— *Hija mía*, Magda said, once I met him, I lost my other desires.

The secret was not just in encountering him, she said, which all women might do, but in making him stay. Arcadia's goal must be to meet him surrounded by other men who desired her. Then he would hold her in great esteem.

— And could Duenna Recta be esteemed by him? Since she has turned down more proposals of marriage than any ten women in California?

— She could, Magda said grudgingly. If she had ever learned how to dance.

Arcadia learned to dance from Magda and learned to weave and pray from Duenna Recta, but she didn't want to choose between the two. When she felt her mother's wedding ring nestling close to her heart, and the lance that had slain her father, she wondered why God had had to choose between her and her mother, had seemed to choose that her mother would die and she would live. She wondered why her father had perished, trying to bring death to the bull and bringing death instead to himself. Her own desires were diffuse and unformed, but they began and ended in the hills that were held in her name, where she didn't have to choose. She visited the hills on washdays and all days in between when she could talk the

Duenna into allowing her to ride out in an oxcart with Magda and a single Ohlone oxherd, to gather the herbs Magda needed for her medicine. In the hills, it seemed to her, God had not chosen between this or that. In the hills, she thought, all might live.

One washday, Arcadia was awakened by Magda before dawn, and the two went out into the plaza in front of the Serrano house. There, by torchlight, they joined the group making up bundles of soiled linen to be tied to the backs of horses. An old white-haired Ohlone soaped the oxcart's great axles and yoked the gentle oxen into the *gamella*. Arcadia and other young girls placed lunch baskets into the oxcart, then climbed in themselves, under the green cloth of an old Mexican flag that was used as an awning. Then, with a shout, they began toward the hot springs, some walking alongside the cart, some leading horses piled with linen, all talking happily. Arcadia sat in the cart with her knees drawn up under her chin and watched the day begin dimly over the eastern hills, watched the trees gradually take shape against the gray sky, and then the rocks emerge from the darkness, while the oxen plodded patiently before her and the old Ohlone swung his long *garrocha* over their backs. When the rutted path grew steep, Arcadia climbed out of the cart and walked, stopping to pick flowers in meadows alongside the way.

Their first sign of the springs were wispy columns of white steam rising among a grove of oaks, and the smell of sulfur. Then they descended a little way into a natural bowl, where the warm waters were flowing over a crusted basin, and falling down a worn rock channel to the brook. The sun rose as they unbundled the clothes from the horses, filling the air with a pale light that did not yet warm the air, but brushed a rare cast of color over all it touched.

They hiked their skirts above their knees and waded into the pools with the linen, and they rubbed in homemade soap and then scrubbed it against smooth rocks, laughing and splashing and making a game of it. Then they rinsed each piece of linen until it was bright and stainless, and spread it out to dry, laying a patchwork of white over the green shrubs and golden grasses that surrounded the springs.

The sun was rising toward noon when they had finished. They rested by the pool, waiting for the wash to dry, beginning to eat some of the food they had brought along. This was one of Arcadia's favorite times, when she could run with the other girls, or sit alone and watch the shaggy hills. One girl had brought a leather ball, and Arcadia played catch with her and some others while a woman picked out a simple song on a guitar. Then Arcadia threw the ball off line into a thick stand of shrubs, and as though she had awakened a sleeping monster, the shrubs began to quake and rumble.

The other girls backed towards the oxcart, and the women suddenly stood up and watched the shrubs, calling for the oxherd, who was asleep down the hill. Arcadia stood alone and watched while from amongst the tangled branches, a bull emerged, as though it had grown from the earth itself. The bull was sleek and black, large-shouldered and shining-eyed, and its tail pointed stiffly to the sky. It lowered its massive head toward the women and snorted, and pawed the ground, and targeted them with its curving horns.

Arcadia felt strangely charmed as she watched the bull prepare to charge. Without reason, she felt that this bull was the same that had caused her father's death, a bull charging toward its own sacrifice, but instead placing the man who opposed it on the altar of bleeding hearts. And she understood that, if the bull charged, one of them, or both, would surely die in violence or in retribution.

She took one step forward, toward the bull, and remembered how Saint Francis had communed with the birds and beasts of the savage fields, and Santa Teresa found her soul's home unmediated in the hills she had loved. She wanted to embrace the bull, call it by the same name Adam had called it by, the name it would recognize as its own. She held her hand out to it, took one more step forward.

— Stay, toro, and don't charge. Don't make God choose between us.

The bull lowered its head, pawed the earth again.

— Stay, toro. In the name of Saint Francis and Santa Teresa, and in the name of the Virgin, don't charge.

Arcadia stood with firm knees and saw the bull turn its head left and right. Then its eyes met her own, shining. They gazed across space at each other for a timeless moment, alone and connected. Then the bull snorted once more, and turned away, and trotted back into the brush.

Arcadia was suddenly surrounded by women, touching her and praising her.

— This one is dear to the Virgin, they said. Even Magda, who had long forgotten her own virginity, called it a sign that she was special.

When Arcadia began her fourteenth year, however, she found herself valued not because she was dear to the Virgin, but because she was dear to men. Her aunt and uncle were childless themselves and placed their hopes in her to carry on the family line. They were pleased that she was dear to the Virgin, but only because they wanted to keep both her and her eleven leagues of land intact.

In the spring of that year, Arcadia unwillingly became a woman in the eyes of Don Ignacio Castro during the rodeo, when stock from the endless leagues of Serrano land was rounded up for branding and castration of the young, and vaqueros and families from around the district came to help run the stock and celebrate the springtime with a fiesta. Don Ignacio came from a neighboring ranch for the rodeo, small and spindly on a cream-colored stallion, his head topping a skinny wrinkled neck and his mouth hidden behind a drooping white mustache. He came with his twelve sons, silent and severe, sitting a row of horses behind him, and his eleven daughters chattering in a cart drawn by two oxen, and his third wife buried a week earlier in a grave beside her two predecessors, all dead in childbirth, on his own lands.

One hundred and eighty-four vaqueros gathered to drive the Serrano stock into corrals anointed with bull's blood, where the cows bearing the brands of neighbors were cut out from the herd, and new calves were roped by their two hind feet from horseback and dragged over to receive the branding iron before being let go bawling onto the plain. In three days, eleven thousand five hundred and sixty-three head were run through the corrals, somewhat more than the year before owing to the end of a drought. Don Ignacio himself did not rope or herd or brand. Rather, he sat feebly on his big horse and directed his twelve sons with a glance or a nod of his head. Where he looked, there two or three sons would ride as though they were his feet and hands. His daughters spent the day in the plaza of the Serrano house, where Ohlone women ground corn by hand between two stones and baked tortillas. At mealtimes, two or three daughters brought Don Ignacio tortillas rolled with spicy beef and frijoles, and wiped his chin for him, and rolled him a cigarette made from imported tobacco. He smoked slowly and weakly, the middle of his mustache yellow.

When Arcadia rode out with the cart loaded with food and drink for the vaqueros, Don Ignacio watched her from under his hooded eyes. He took the pulse of his old age, weighing his power to populate this land with more Castros. Since the indigenous peoples had wasted away and died under the loving care of the Franciscans, then dwindled further under the fatherly hand of the Dons, the land had grown empty and silent. Don Ignacio had worked mightily to bring voices back into California, Spanish-speaking voices to name again the nameless mountains and streams and trees that wandered errantly over the earth until anchored by the human word. He had labored to people this vast territory, and with his third wife dead, he had wondered if his labor was at an end. But when he saw Arcadia's grace in the saddle, he wanted her to take the name of Castro, so that he might labor further.

Uncle José decided to slaughter cattle after the roundup because the Boston Trader, Míster Lurkin, had a ship due in Monterey, ready to deal for hides and tallow. Uncle José, like most other rancheros, was in debt to the Boston Trader for the furniture, clothing, and manufactured goods that were not made in California. Six picked men stripped to their shirt-sleeves and took out daggers while other vaqueros herded a number of cattle over to the *calaveras,* the place of skulls. Then the men with daggers mounted up and rode in quietly among the cattle. Leaning over, they plunged their daggers through the spinal cord of an animal behind the head, and as a hot fountain of blood spurted up, the steer dropped dead. They killed dozens of cattle quickly and silently until a misplaced blow caused a bull to bellow and bolt, spooking the herd. Then the dagger men killed on the run, riding alongside terrified steers and leaning over from the saddle and stabbing them through the neck, then springing forward as the lifeless animals tumbled forward to the bloody ground. The other vaqueros hazed the herd back toward the calaveras, while the dagger men danced on horseback among the cattle, yelling in triumph at every body that fell. The herd swirled around their dead companions, stumbling over bodies and bellowing in terror, while they were picked off one by one. As the herd grew smaller, they again bolted for the open plains until the vaqueros turned them once again back to the killing grounds. The cattle fell blood and meat to the green grassy plain, suddenly without any hot life to animate them. Finally a single bull survived alone and upright, tired and panting and spattered with the blood of his kind.

Arcadia crested a hill with the oxcart at that moment, looked over the field of slaughter, and saw the bull standing alone. Again without reason, she recognized the bull as the same one she had charmed by the springs on that washday when she had been found to be dear to the Virgin, and she wished with her heart that the bull live, and live gloriously, and not be chosen.

On a hill opposite her, Don Ignacio contemplated the bull and then nodded to his second son, Fidel Segundón.

Fidel rode up quickly behind the bull, guiding his horse with the four-inch rowels on his hand-wrought spurs, and slashed the bull across the flank with his knife. The bull bellowed and started off at full speed, tossing his horns angrily. Fidel closed with him rapidly and bent toward him as the jingle bobs on his spurs chimed and the silk scarf around his neck shimmered in the sun. In an instant, the six-inch blade dipped in and out of the bull's neck, as though the bull's flesh were water, and Fidel held aloft his red and dripping dagger while the bull fell forward and buried its broad, soft muzzle into the earth. Arcadia watched the bull fail, and wondered if slaughter was the end of fruitfulness, and she thought about her own mother, dead in the blood that had brought her into the world.

Out on the field, Ohlone men belonging to the Serrano rancho were flaying hides off of the dead cattle, while Ohlone women stripped the naked bodies of fat and piled it on green hides to drag to the trying-out pots.

The fiesta to celebrate the roundup began that night at sunset. Duenna Recta didn't want Arcadia to appear or, if she did, to wear black and keep her hair and ears covered. But her aunt Josefina stated that she herself had married at fifteen, although God had not seen fit to give her children, and therefore Arcadia was by no means too young to take part in a dance. While Ohlone musicians played endlessly the guitar and violin and entire bullocks were being roasted over open fires, Arcadia dressed carefully under Magda's direction. She slipped on a white muslin dress with blue flounces and spangles to glitter in the lamplight, and bound the dress around her waist with a scarlet sash. The dress rose into a short-sleeved bodice that left both her shoulders bare. She put on slippers of white satin with wooden heels that would clack when she danced, and earrings of pearl droplets from the Gulf of California. She bound flowers into her hair with golden ribbons, and left small dark ringlets of hair hanging from her temples, and finally she threw a white lace mantilla over her shoulders. Then she opened a fan and looked at Magda in the way she had been taught.

— Remember, Magda said, your goal now must be to attract many men.

The ground in front of the Serrano house had been watered and beaten level, and while musicians beneath the overhanging roof played a waltz, Arcadia joined a group of women just inside the door. Every few measures, her uncle José, dressed in a close-fitting jacket and short breeches fastened below the knee with silver buckles, came through the door and escorted one of them through. Arcadia heard shouts and cries of appreciation, and when the shouts died down, her uncle came for another. The eleven daughters of Don Ignacio were ahead of her, rustling in muslin and silk. Each of them was led out dancing while she waited; she would be the last, she was the youngest. Arcadia wished almost to be praying in front of the Virgin, or alone touching herself in an evil way.

Then her uncle came for her and brought her dancing through the door. Around the beaten earth was a huge arc of men on horseback, rich in silver bridles and high leather saddles, the horses prancing and snorting as the men jockeyed for position trying to force their horses forward. Uncle José danced one measure with her and then let her go, and she twirled alone to the music, her dress sparkling, and looked at the circle of men capering on their horses, wearing blue jackets with red cuffs and collars, and blue velvet pantaloons buttoned down the sides, and black felt hats with silver tassels, their faces flashing in the lamplight as they yelled in appreciation of her, and she forgot her reluctance in the moment of delirium, and she searched the faces to see if she could recognize Magda's snake man.

Don Ignacio, sitting silently on his stallion and surrounded by his twelve sons, studied the young girl. He looked at his sons and nodded.

When the music stopped, Arcadia joined the other women along the front wall of the house. Then men who wanted to dance dismounted from their horses and begged the ladies for the honor of being their partners. After the dance, the men would remount and the women would retire against the wall. At the first dance, Arcadia was claimed by Don Ignacio's eldest son, Ignacio Jovencito.

— I ask you on behalf of my father, who no longer dances, he said, indicating the frail old man on the large cream stallion.

— With much pleasure, Arcadia replied.

The next dance, the second eldest son, Fidel Segundón, asked her to dance, once again on behalf of his father. The following dance, the third eldest son, and the dance after that, the fourth eldest son, always on behalf of Don Ignacio. It continued in succession, down to the twelfth son, after which the eld-est son began again.

At first Arcadia was grateful to be asked, despite the fact that these were the sons of the old man who directed slaughter with a glance. But as son succeeded son, she grew disillusioned with them all — cold, passionless dancers, precise in their steps and distant in their expressions. And yet nobody else stepped up to ask her to dance. None of the men who had shouted for her and who were even now causing their horses to jump and prance had come to ask her to be their partner, perhaps because of the nods and glances of the old man of the cream stallion. She felt it was a horrible trick — the Castro sons had rounded her up, as though she were one more calf.

Finally, her uncle José declared a bamba, a dance the women could do alone. Those who chose to dance took a stone jar filled with water and balanced it on their heads. Then they posed with fists on their hips and their hips thrust forward, and their chin turned to the right over bare shoulders. The music began, guitar and violin and vihuela, and the women danced forward toward the men on horseback, hands still on their hips, wooden heels clacking, jars of water in perfect balance. The men shouted, and one or two horses reared back on their two hind legs and sent dust into the lamplight while the women moved. Then one vaquero threw a handkerchief down at the feet of his favorite. In time with the music, the woman dipped down and plucked up the handkerchief, and tucked it in her bodice, all without spilling a drop of water.

Arcadia, delighted at last to be free from the grip of the Castro sons, danced the bamba with a grace and cunning to catch men's eyes which she had learned from Magda, and which the men in the circle had never before seen. They threw handkerchiefs down to her, and she swept them up, dancing toward the men then away from them with the stone jar perfectly straight and still upon her head. She kept away from the side of the arc where Don Ignacio sat with his twelve sons, and she jutted her hips out at the other men who might desire her.

As each woman lost at last her stone jar, she retired back to the wall with her trophies. The jars spilled one by one as the Ohlone musicians increased the tempo of their playing at a sign from Uncle José. When Arcadia and one other woman were left, a hat was thrown to the ground between them. The other woman swooped down and picked it up with her right hand. Another hat followed, and Arcadia plucked it from the earth and spun around with the hat pinned to her hip. The music reached a frenzy and the horses jostled each other as the men tried to get closest to where the two women were dancing. Another hat was thrown to the dancers, and as the other dancer dipped down, her jar of water wavered, then toppled onto the beaten earth. She left the hat and retired, to shouts of joy and admiration. Arcadia snatched up the hat with the stone jar still on her head and danced holding a hat in each fist.

Then from the other side of the arc, Don Ignacio slowly unfolded his serape in the air and floated it to the ground before him. This was the highest praise a man could offer a dancer, to ask her to do him the honor of dancing on his serape. Arcadia swirled over toward him, the spangles on her dress glittering, and stepped onto the tightly woven blue wool. As she danced wildly, and the men on horseback all around her shouted their approval, her heels stamping the cloth into the earth, she felt the old man's eyes, deep set in endless layers of wrinkles, pierce right through her clothing, a chill look of knowledge and possession. And then there was water in her eyes, tears and the spilling pristine water from stone jar, and she ran off across the space of beaten earth and into the house crying.

Don Ignacio slowly dismounted from his cream stallion, moving one limb at a time like a stiff puppet, and ratcheted over to where his serape lay wetted on the ground. He bent laboriously down to pick it up, but then swept it around his shoulders with unexpected grace. Everyone looked at him as he raised his hand and pointed to the doorway where Arcadia had disappeared.

— That is the one I will marry, he said.

Don Ignacio's great wealth and his cattle without number and the great esteem in which his family name was held made it impossible to say no, even though he had sons, all unmarried, who were older than Arcadia. He came the next day, dressed formally in a short jacket the color of a dove's wing and a high yellow hat of the finest vicuña wool, surrounded by his dozen sons all dressed identically, and asked Uncle José for Arcadia's hand in holy matrimony. If any of the sons had doubts about their father's wishes, they didn't express them. Uncle José, who was impressed that a man of Don Ignacio's age should feel capable of taking on the burden of satisfying a young virgin, resisted the temptation to ask him for his secret and simply accepted with much honor the respectful and dignified proposal of his compadre who would now to some extent be his nephew, although he was twenty years older.

Arcadia didn't want Don Ignacio putting words into her ears, or his anything into her anyplace else, but she wasn't admitted to have a choice in the matter. She was only able to have the wedding postponed until the fall so that she could finish her trousseau and learn what she needed to take on the charges of wife and mother.

In this desire for postponement, she had the support of Duenna Recta, whose respected spinster's voice was enough to sway even Don Ignacio. The Duenna was delighted with the match, of course; with such a husband Arcadia would be a widow that much sooner. She was able to prevail upon Arcadia at last to knit and embroider in black, so as to save time, preparing to be a bride and a widow at the same time, and while she had the responsibility to teach Arcadia the facts of life she would face as a bride, she simply repeated her long litany of negatives and euphemisms, saying that if she would refrain from doing this or that, and do the unspeakable as infrequently as possible, she would be a fruitful and well-governed wife, and all would respect her.

Arcadia listened to the straight, thin voice of Duenna Recta as she bent her head over her black embroidery, and she felt she was embroidering her own shroud. She wondered if she could postpone her wedding by sneaking up at night and undoing her needlework so that her trousseau would never be finished, but she didn't realize that the trick had been tried before. Duenna Recta kept the trousseau locked in a redwood chest and kept the key hanging from a satin ribbon between her untouched breasts.

Magda told her that the only way to hold off Don Ignacio would be if she were to find and keep the snake man.

— Pray to the most holy Virgin, was all Magda could say. That she send the snake man to you. She was blessed among women. She must know how to find him.

As time passed and the hills turned golden with summer and autumn grew closer, Arcadia was wild with sadness. She went frequently out into the hills of the ranch with Magda. The hills looked smooth as potter's clay, strewn with endless grasses all as high as her waist and wispy with seedpods already scattered for the next year's growth. The horizon was broken only by isolated oak trees, standing alone about the golden hills where a hidden spring of water fed their thirty-foot-deep taproots. Here and there they came across bulls watching over a dozen cows, and horned rams, and stallions, and goats with long, urine-stained beards. Once they saw a chestnut horse bite a mare on the nape of her neck, and then cover her from behind. Arcadia watched with pious joy the getting of new life, then bitterly turned away from the sight, a sight to be denied her forever in a marriage created only to cheat death.

On days when she did not make an expedition into the hills, Arcadia prayed before the painting of the Virgin and the twisting words. People thought she was praying for strength to be a good wife, but she was secretly praying for a miracle of God to allow her to seek out as much misery and woe as she had to, even more than Magda had endured, in order to find love.

When the cannonball fell out of the prophetic sky, and Arcadia felt the historic whistle of wind pass between her and Don Ignacio and interrupt her wedding at the last possible instant, she was certain that the American ship had come as a miracle in answer to her prayers. For a moment amid the cloud of sawdust and termites that rose from the broken door, she looked through the very space in which the cannonball had flown, looked toward her bridegroom at the head of the opposite cavalcade. She saw him stretch his hand across the shattered and disrupted air, toward the flowers woven into her white satin dress, toward the gold-fringed sash draped around her neck with which the priest was to bind them together for life. He reached for her, beckoned her, as though he should now be the one to ride her to safety, and she saw in the black eyes sunken in wrinkles the fire of an incurable lust brought on by the nearness of death.

Her horse reared up, and her uncle José, who rode on a bearskin *anquera* behind the saddle, turned her away from peril and her wrinkled bridegroom, who still posed with his open hand held out toward her. They rode swiftly down the grassy plain, and as her satin shoes broke and her bridal crown whipped off her head and her hair fell free, she prayed again that her dearest prayer be answered.

Capítulo II

As the wedding cavalcades scattered, and Major McCormick embarked toward shore, and Commodore Jones looked on from the quarterdeck, pacing and restless; as Captain Rafael Rafael felt his heart yearn toward the shore as toward a forgotten home, and Hannibal roundly thought out how to bring his unbroken story of generations to this New Africa; as Chips half wished for war to break out, and half wished for someone to realize that the ship was leaking, and William Waxdeck was already beginning to compose couplets on the glorious victory of the *National Intention*; as Jack Chase laughed from the maintop, and young Jimmy F. Bush was looking to the east to see if his parents were coming over the horizon — the leading men of Monterey met in the office of the ex-Governor of California, Juan B. Alvarado, to discuss the unprecedented state of being under attack. Don Ignacio entered, still in his wedding finery, just in time to hear the ex-Governor thank God in a loud voice that the newly appointed governor had arrived in Los Angeles.

— I won't surrender, he said. I can't surrender. Let Governor Micheltorena do it.

— Patriotism and our national honor demand we fight, said

Don Bragas de León, the lionhearted. Repulse these would-be invaders of our sacred parts, he said.

— Weddings also are patriotism, Don Ignacio said. Children are patriotism. An invasion shouldn't stop a wedding.

Then Fray Echevarría burst into the office, denouncing the Americans as servants of the Antichrist. who were trying to wrest this land away from those who had first found it occupied only by lost tribes ignorant of the Savior's birth, and who then subdued the land to God's laws, making sure in the process that the tribes understood why they needed a savior.

— ¡Sí, sí! shouted the lionhearted one. God and country! Death to the invaders.

— Como quiera Ud., said Don Ignacio. But what about my wedding?

The Friar began to pray that the fruit of Don Ignacio's wedding should bring a deliverer for California.

— Thank God I am ex-Governor, said the ex-Governor.

Comandante Silva, chief military authority for the territory of California, entered the chambers and brought everyone to order. He stated plainly that he had only twenty-nine men in uniform, eleven cannon that were nearly useless, and the fortifications, which everyone knew were of no consequence.

— I've sent word to Governor Micheltorena, he said. Perhaps he has brought enough men under arms to oppose the invasion. In the meantime, let us see what terms are offered by the Americans.

— I won't surrender, said Don León, because I am a man.

— I can't surrender, said ex-Governor Alvarado, because I am ex-Governor.

— I won't surrender my bride, declared Don Ignacio.

An adjutant brought word that the representative from the American ship was at hand. Behind the adjutant, a large red-haired man in a blue uniform pushed his way in and began to speak in an outlandish, barbarous tongue that none of those present understood but that all recognized as English. They answered him in Spanish, which made the man pull on his crotch and turn red in the face. Ex-Governor Alvarado, an educated man, attempted the language of Voltaire and Rousseau, but this only provoked further outbursts of unintelligibility. The Friar asked in Latin if he would like to sit down, which seemed to infuriate the strange creature. He placed his hand on the hilt of his sword, and with the other hand threw a document down on the table among them. They looked at it carefully and nodded, although they did not understand a word, passing it from hand to hand around the table. The Friar said it was in the language of the heretic pirate Francis Drake, *el Draque,* who tried to claim California for his schismatic queen two and a half centuries earlier. Ex-Governor Alvarado tried to read it in French and announced that it seemed to describe a method for cutting down trees. Don León refused to touch it, sure that it required a dishonorable act, while Don Ignacio puzzled over the words to see if it mentioned Arcadia. Comandante Silva, meanwhile, had sent for Míster Lurkin, the Boston Trader, to act as a translator.

Lurkin arrived with a broad hat lowered over his brow and a heavy gold ring with a curious Egyptian symbol on his right hand, and immediately the room grew quiet. Lurkin was the only citizen of the United States who resided in California. He had lived there twenty years, but nobody could say exactly what color his eyes were. His other countrymen who settled there had married among the numerous daughters of the Californios, taken up Catholicism on Sundays, and embraced Mexican citizenship and land grants of eleven leagues. Lurkin alone remained landless and foreign. He had sent away to Boston for a bride of the purest Puritan heritage, had his sons educated at Protestant missionary schools in Honolulu, and controlled only a store on the waterfront near the Custom House. Yet he was one of the most respected members of the community, always allowed to ignore magnificently the decrees that floated up every three or four years from the capital of Mexico forbidding foreigners from owning land or trading with California. Lurkin held most of the landowners in debt to him in greater or lesser degree, each one owing him so many leathern bags of tallow and so many thousand hides of cattle, in exchange for the silks and silver harnesses and wooden furniture that arrived on the ships he controlled. How would they ever pay their debts, the landowners asked, if he were forced out of business? What of their honor, and new silks for their daughters? So he remained, singular and foreign, landless yet with a line of credit connecting every land grant in the north to him, never appearing without a hat low over his shadowed eyes and a heavy ring of Egyptian gold.

Lurkin picked up the document from the table and announced to all in Spanish that it contained the articles of surrender, and that the man before them was a major in the United States Marines. McCormick pulled on his mustache, uncertain just how much to trust the strange man who, though obviously an American and therefore certainly convinced of the necessity of the *National Intention* to take over California, could nonetheless speak the local lingo and therefore was suspect. Anything but the language of Old Hickory, Andrew Jackson, seemed suspect to McCormick.

— Tell them we want them to give up the works, or we'll blow them to Kingdom Come, he said.

Lurkin translated smoothly. — He requests you sign the documents of surrender he has offered, in the interests of humanity, to avoid needless bloodshed, as your garrison is obviously outmanned.

He rendered the Surrender Form into Spanish, and everyone looked at ex-Governor Alvarado. — They are madmen, he said, or pirates. I can't sign.

— Señor Alvarado claims he cannot sign this because he is no longer governor, the Boston Trader told McCormick. He can't give up the entire territory.

— Well, who *can* give it up? McCormick asked.

— Governor Micheltorena.

When McCormick found out that Micheltorena was three hundred miles away, and wouldn't be available to surrender that day, and moreover was completely ignorant of the presence of the *National Intention* and his own duty to surrender and clear out of the territory, the marine's face grew red and he snatched the Surrender Form from the table and swore to tell Commodore Jones that he'd have to turn the whole town to rubble.

As soon as McCormick left, everyone began talking at once. Don León swore to defend even the rubble from invaders, while

Fray Echevarría prophesied either a return of the warrior saint Santiago from the *reconquista* or a glorious martyrdom for them all. The ex-Governor thanked God he was ex-Governor, while Don Ignacio tried to explain to the friar that he wasn't interested in martyrdom, he was interested in weddings. Comandante Silva announced that he would instruct his twenty-nine men to lay down their arms rather than face a ship of forty-four cannon and six hundred trained fighting men. Don León said that would be an act of craven betrayal. Everyone was about to come to blows when Míster Lurkin held up his hand.

— Gentlemen, he said. This is the nineteenth century. Language can be negotiated.

Aboard ship, Commodore Jones paced restlessly from one rail of the quarterdeck to the other, waiting for the Mexican flag over the Presidio to be struck. He was worried that the city would not surrender peacefully. He was also worried that the city *would* surrender peacefully, but that it would turn out that the United States and Mexico were not at war. He had instructed Waxdeck to proceed with his epic as though the two countries were already at war, and to compose certain triumphal odes in praise of the new land that his strong right arm had brought under the reign of freedom, democracy, and the benevolent influence of Louisa Darling. But he wasn't sure if that was an efficacious way of influencing international relations or not. He had done his utmost now to prove that every story of relations between the United States and Mexico degenerating to a state of war was true, and so he hoped only that relations, if not already degenerate, would be so before news of his actions arrived in Washington.

Hannibal Memory, round and short, walked beside the Commodore as the whole ship waited for a sign of surrender, a sign that the land had fallen into American hands like a ripe fruit. Hannibal was the only man on the quarterdeck, among the officers and midshipmen, who knew that the ship was sinking. He had heard the garbled voice of Chips and understood amid the tangled cries that he had found a leak; Hannibal had heard the carpenter's pained exhortation to destroy the land that would never appear as beautiful as it did now, before they occupied it, and also the plea to save the engine of destruction. All this he heard and understood, as it corresponded with the narrative of the voyage he was writing in prose to combat Waxdeck's heroic couplets, which he nevertheless copied faithfully and presented to the Commodore. He said nothing to anyone, and as he walked beside the unquiet Commodore, he was composing in his head the next sentences he would write down, since his prose work seemed to be having good effect thus far.

After an interminable wait, and without the Mexican flag's being struck, Jones saw the marines march back down the hill from the Presidio, climb into a boat, and row back to the *National Intention*. Major McCormick shouted up to the Commodore through a speaking horn.

— Nobody onshore is authorized to surrender, sir.

Commodore Jones was astounded. — They can't surrender?

— They say they aren't authorized.

The Commodore found himself in a quandary. If they couldn't surrender, there didn't seem to be any way to uphold the honor of the United States and spread freedom in the name of Louisa Darling except by continuing to fire his cannon until the walls of the Presidio had completely crumbled, and then invading with his marines.

The gods seemed to be conspiring against the Commodore, and while Waxdeck, who was seasick even at anchor and still lay in his berth with a bucket of green bile beside him, was making ready to describe the erasure of the pueblo of Monterey, which he had never yet seen, from the face of the earth, the Commodore sadly told Captain Rafael Rafael to have the cannoneers ready their guns.

Rafael Rafael had spent most of the hours since the first warning shot was fired scanning the shore with a long glass, an act that looked like diligence only because nobody realized he was seeking a glimpse of the woman he had seen at the head of one of the lines of horses headed for the Presidio. He heard the order with horror, as the *National Intention* was prepared to destroy the place he had dreamed about, which couldn't exist on any map, before he even had a chance to set foot in it, and he wondered if Pearl Prynne's words were true, that the only escape from the Dark Man was in a place you would never arrive. He gave the orders to the cannoneers to prepare to fire, and while they rammed home their powder and shot and lit their punks and stood poised over the torch holes, he tried to think of a means by which he could persuade the Commodore to change his position. The Commodore stood at the taffrail, that restless, questioning man, thinking in his heart of Louisa Darling and home as he prepared to give the order that would bring Monterey freedom and democracy.

While Rafael Rafael stuttered, Merry Jack Chase suddenly appeared above the Commodore's head, hanging by one hand from the mizzenmast shroud and, while recognizing the Commodore's position as internally coherent, attacked the conclusion on logical grounds. For, he asked, could the Commodore really be said to have *conquered* Monterey if the pueblo no longer existed? Could he be said to have brought freedom and democracy there if there was no there there?

— For while the landmass of California will certainly exist after the cannonade, Jack Chase said while dangling in the air, as it existed before it fell under the control of the Spanish crown, *Monterey* is wholly a human artifice. And if all traces of the artifice are destroyed, can the statement "I have conquered Monterey" be true? Can the statement "I have brought freedom to Monterey" be true? When the truth of both statements depends upon the truth of a prior statement, "There exists a pueblo called Monterey"? As well as the statement "There exists a being called I"? Not to mention the statement "There exists freedom."

Commodore Jones had always done poorly in logic. He sent Hannibal to consult with Waxdeck on the question, while the punks burned lower in the cannoneers' hands and Jack Chase swung lightly in the shrouds. The midshipman had also failed logic, so he based his answer on poetics. In Virgil's *Aeneid*, marriage between a conquering hero and a native of the place is key to successful conquest. In no epic that he knew of was the place destroyed before it was conquered. Moreover, in the American tradition, a place usually kept the name of its former inhabitants, as Connecticut or Massachusetts and elsewhere;

destroying Monterey might trouble that unwritten rule. But in any case, the existence of Commodore Jones could not be in doubt at all, as his name already figured in the title itself of Waxdeck's work, *The Conquest of the West by Sea, with special attention to the rôle of Commodore Jones &c.*

As Hannibal relayed Waxdeck's reply, Captain Rafael Rafael suggested a compromise, in deference to the women onshore and taking into account their possible importance to the poetics of the Great Tradition. Instead of requesting the surrender of the entire territory, the Articles could be amended to request the surrender just of the Presidio and Custom House, where the offending Mexican flag was being flown. Then the Stars and Stripes could be run up, and the honor of the United States could be upheld, and they could wait for Governor Micheltorena to arrive for the rest of California to be surrendered.

Jack Chase laughed and climbed hand over hand back up to his pinnacle on the maintop, and Captain Rafael Rafael wasn't certain if Jack Chase was laughing at him, because he knew his secret thoughts. But Commodore Jones, overcome by logic and poetics, ordered the cannoneers to stand down, and he called to McCormick in the boat.

— Scratch out a line of the Surrender Form, and replace California with the Presidio and the Custom House of Monterey.

Major McCormick pulled on his crotch apologetically.

— I can parlay as well as any man, sir, he said. But I can't read or write.

The form was brought back aboard, and Waxdeck made the

corrections. Then the marines were dispatched once again to shore, and they marched again up to the Presidio.

The entire crew watched the marines enter through the broken gate once more, with the exception of Chips. Disappointed at a possible peaceful outcome, he had begun to recall dimly that the ship was leaking, and he went to the redcapped boatswain and tugged on his sleeve.

— Not now, the boatswain said.

Chips then went to a lieutenant, who, like the boatswain, gazed to the south in rapt attention. The lieutenant also told Chips to wait. He approached the first lieutenant, and the first luff greeted him with the congenial promise to give him twenty lashes if he so much as opened his mouth.

Hannibal bounded down from the quarterdeck to intercept the carpenter before he actually told someone. Chips stood with his blood-and-salt-water-soaked pants, his long black beard hanging with algae, his eyes blinking in the unfamiliar sun.

— Ship is leaking, he told Hannibal.

— They can't see it just yet, Hannibal said. But they will.

In that moment, Commodore Jones heard music float across the indifferent waters of the bay. The tune was "Yankee Doodle." Through his long glass, he saw the Mexican flag slowly being lowered. On deck, his sailors were beginning to sing along with the music. Some of them had begun to dance rude hornpipes, twirl around in each other's arms.

Yankee Doodle keep it up
Yankee Doodle Dandy

Yankee Doodle keep it up
Yankee Doodle Dandy

Then he saw the American flag slowly raised over the decrepit round blockhouse at the corner of the crumbling, defenseless fort. The lieutenant of guns, down in the ship's waist, called out

— Three cheers for the United States! Three cheers for Commodore Jones!

Huzzah!
Huzzah!
Huzzah!

Capítulo III

The glorious conquest was less than twenty-four hours old when Don Bragas de León, the lionhearted one, marched into the hills to form the nucleus of the guerrilla force that would harass the Yanqui invaders until the approaching army of Governor Micheltorena arrived to eradicate them completely, at which time Micheltorena would take his rightful place as the Master of Monterey. The Governor was rumored to have marched from Los Angeles with three hundred men under arms, and Don León rode into the wilds of the San Gabriel Mountains to be ready to meet him. He left early in the morning with seven horses, three Ohlone vaqueros, a sergeant from the garrison named Vargas who had read *Ivanhoe*, and a mule carrying boxes of rifles and powder and shot, which had mysteriously come into Míster Lurkin's hands.

Comandante Silva had led his twenty-nine soldiers out of the Presidio with colors flying in the presence of Major McCormick's marines, and the American flag was run up in place of the Mexican flag above the old fort. The Mexican soldiers were ordered to remain as a unit until transportation could be arranged to Manzanillo. Most of the soldiers had not been paid by the government in years, and so they were immune to Don León's exhortations to join the guerrillas once they found out he wouldn't pay them either. To his talk of honor and glory, they preferred being twelve hundred miles further from a ship of forty-four cannon and twelve hundred miles closer to the National Treasury. Only Sergeant Vargas, who had read Sir Walter Scott's narrative as a literal transcription of reality, and who understood the present situation as prefigured by King Richard's crusade to the Holy Land against the infidel and return home to claim his throne, agreed to meet the lionhearted one at dawn. They rendezvoused at Míster Lurkin's trading house and drank several glasses of pulque, which the Trader carefully noted in his account book, figuring four glasses equaled one cowhide. Lurkin casually mentioned that he had heard that Micheltorena was bringing *four* hundred men, which further inflamed Don León. Without much persuasion, he encumbered his land with more debt to buy the arms he thought he would need, a debt that he was certain the government would make good after the glorious victory.

Major McCormick, ignorant of the nascent threat, was inspecting the crumbling ramparts of the Presidio and attempting to find a cannon that might fire a shot without the breech exploding. He noted with a surly expression that most of the cannon were aimed toward the sea, in the general direction of the *National Intention,* and he ordered them wheeled around and aimed toward the edge of the forest.

— The enemy will come from inside the land, he reasoned.

Then he noticed some mysterious scratchings around the torch hole of the cannon, and he called a younger lieutenant over to confirm his suspicions. The lieutenant stated that the cannon had all seemingly been christened with names, and he read aloud Santa Margarita, Santiago, Santa Lucia. The largest cannon, an eighteen-pounder, was called El Espíritu Santo.

— Popish names! shouted McCormick, pulling on his crotch. We'll fix that.

At his direction, the older names were scratched out with Bowie knives, and he sent to Waxdeck aboard ship to decide what the new names should be. The midshipman and epic poet sent back a list of names: The Democracy, The Justice, The Conquest, The Scourge of the West. The largest cannon, he deemed, should be named The Blessings of Freedom.

— Carve 'em in, McCormick ordered. And when we've got the American names on 'em and they're aimed toward the interior, we'll give 'em all a test fire, so they're ready to shout a salute for the Commodore.

William Waxdeck, lying in his bunk belowdecks, had still not actually seen the conquered land. His seasickness was such that, even while at anchor, the gentle rocking of the ship caused a line of green bile to spill from the corner of his mouth. However, his sickness didn't prevent him from beginning the heroic couplets describing THE ADVENT OF JONES, the first steps the Commodore would take upon the land he had won for liberty and democracy, in honor of the ever-virginal Louisa Darling. He wanted to be sure that he wrote it up before the Commodore actually set foot on shore, to make sure that if events didn't go correctly, they would at least be interpreted correctly. The discovery of the Americas by Columbus seemed to offer a good model for Waxdeck's couplets — although the people of Monterey were not naked, as the

Indians of the Caribbean had been, still, they would surely welcome Jones with gifts in the same manner, and rejoice at the coming reign of democracy just like the Indians had rejoiced at becoming subjects of Ferdinand and Isabella, as Columbus reported them saying. Because Columbus was referred to as the *Christum Ferens*, the Christ Bearer, Waxdeck began to refer to Jones as the *Democratium Ferens*, the Bringer of Democracy. He wrote furiously, so that the meaning of everything that happened would be fixed in advance, and he sent for Hannibal frequently to make copies for the Commodore's perusal and, so Waxdeck thought to himself, for the Commodore's instruction.

Hannibal attempted to keep up with the copying required by Waxdeck and at the same time not let the couplets he had to write over and over again interfere with his own prose narrative. At times he grew confused, and suddenly found himself breaking into prose while copying Waxdeck's epic and accidentally describing his own actions to continue his line and his story in the land beyond that other history. Other times, he found that a heroic couplet had leaked into his own writing, which he then diligently scratched out.

When this happened, Hannibal wondered whether he had made a mistake in taking up writing to achieve his ends, whether Plato was correct and writing did kill memory. He wondered if he would ever be able to keep a story separate and complete, in and of itself, and he had to sit carefully and repeat for himself in whispers his remembered story of generations and the name of his lost beloved. And yet, his prose had been effective thus far. Only he himself, his prose narrative, and Chips recognized that there was a leak in the *National Intention*. And he was already beginning to write of the woman he would join with in California, who would in some sense again be his beloved and mend his remembered story.

When Hannibal journeyed between the midshipmen's quarters and the Commodore's cabin, Chips trailed behind Hannibal and begged him to tell the officers that the ship was leaking. He was working feverishly down in the dark, slime-mold-covered bilges, stuffing oakum between the ship's keel and the planks and wondering if the pumps would ever be manned. Hannibal continually assured him that the officers would see that the ship was leaking in due time, but that just then, they would find it impossible to believe. When Chips grew too insistent, Hannibal finally directed him toward the midshipmen's quarters.

— If you won't take my word for it, Hannibal said, talk to one yourself. One of the most important figures aboard ship is lying in there.

Chips was always chary of speaking directly with officers. They were godlike beings who had only to speak and hundreds of craven fellows like himself leaped to make their words into act. Still, he clutched his hat with both hands and entered bowing and scraping into the midshipmen's quarters. There he saw a pale youth stretched out on a bunk, with only his face and arms showing, the rest of his body littered with ink-spattered paper and lines of words. Chips gaped and spake haltingly to this strange word-covered creature, trying to explain that the ship was leaking. The youth rose up, chill as carven marble, the only sign of life a drip of bile at the corner of his mouth, and spoke in a voice louder than seemed possible from such a wasted figure.

— There are no leaks in an epic.

Cowed, Chips backed out, still bowing and clutching his knit cap between his two hands. On deck, seamen danced jigs and hornpipes, and voices spoke of liberty, a glorious day of sailors' liberty, upon the conquered land. Chips moaned, caring nothing for liberty but only for the act of conquest, all too easily achieved on this green shore, which still floated lovely and untouched above the bright bay. When he saw the pueblo of Monterey, still and whole, he groaned for the cannon's roar to repeat again and again a cry of revenge on that vision. Then he returned belowdecks, out of sight of the land, and continued down ladder after ladder to where sea water tinged with blood seeped between the planks. He stopped where the ship's yeoman, Keyes, sat in a gloomy compartment lit by a single lantern, surrounded by shelves and bins and heaps of ratline stuff, and seizing stuff, and marline, and serving mallets and fids and marlinespikes, near the tin-lined room where the ship's biscuit was stored to keep out rats. Keyes looked up from his ink-and-gunpowder-stained desk, his face red with satisfaction at a column of numbers he was adding up, and he asked the Carpenter what was needed.

— Oakum, Chips said.

— None left, Keyes said. You've used it all up. Don't you know there's a limit to things?

Chips held his head and turned away.

— The only thing we don't run out of on this voyage is

paper and ink, Keyes called, while Chips descended slow and moaning to the bilges.

Keyes returned to his column of figures, chuckling fatly. In fact, the last of the oakum had been offloaded late the night before into the muffle-oared boats of smugglers. A strange man had appeared in Keyes's storeroom during that night, wearing a broad hat lowered over his eyes and a heavy gold ring on his right hand. Keyes couldn't have said how the man arrived, but the man spoke instantly, cutting through Keyes's surprise, speaking as though he understood every one of Keyes's venal thoughts and desires.

— I've heard, the man said.

— Yes? Keyes leaned forward.

— Stories that one of the aims of the voyage is not to spread freedom and democracy, but to open California up to commerce.

— Yes, Keyes said.

— But it amounts to the same thing, don't you think? Shouldn't a pair of shoes in California be as free to be bought and sold as a pair of shoes in Boston? Or a belt buckle? Or, say, powder and shot? Free circulation of belt buckles. Every lead ball . . . *equal* . . . to every other lead ball.

— Everybody benefits, Keyes said.

The man seemed to smile under the shadow of his hat. — It's said that ruinous tariffs are keeping the land backwards, wasting its potential, stifling its progress.

— Is it true?

— All stories can become history, if only men of will choose to make them so.

Keyes felt that he was the man being spoken of, he was the man of courage and industry. — So any action to thwart tariffs . . .

— Furthers the aims of the voyage. Any profit you make . . .

— Purely incidental.

— No, the man corrected. A reward for taking risks.

— A reward for taking risks, Keyes repeated in wonder.

— To further the aims of the voyage.

Keyes was astonished at his own courage, selflessness, nobility.

That night, he made arrangements to ship off not only oakum but also iron tools and nails, which weren't manufactured in California, loaves of sugar, barrels of grog and white flour, tins of butter, and a certain number of rifles, together with powder and shot, which would later be carried into the San Gabriel Mountains by Bragas de León. However, Keyes could not interest the man in paper and ink, because few among the six thousand Spanish-speaking inhabitants of California could read, and even fewer could write.

At the chill hour before dawn, when the sun was still just a glowing red hint over the coastal range, and the *National Intention* swung quietly to anchor in the bay at the center of large circular ripples expanding across the deep green water, while the smaller vessels the *Don Quijote* and the *Paz y Religión* rested at the center of their own circular ripples, and the pueblo of Monterey was about to awake for the first time under a new flag, Jimmy F. Bush sat on a crosstree high on the mainmast with his lambskin about his shoulders, looking to the east, whence his parents would come.

As he kept vigil, handsome Jack Chase climbed lightly up the rigging and stood out on the yardarm next to the boy. He looked to the east as well and shook his head.

— Where do you think they are? Jimmy asked.

— No telling, Jack Chase said. Rootless folk, wandering west with the mob. They'll fetch up against the coast sooner or later.

— Do you think they'll beat me when they see me? Or be happy?

— Or both? Jack laughed. Like as not they *will* beat you, unless they've found a kind of home I know naught of. Look here, look at Monterey lying like a Georgic that needs no Virgil to write of it. You think we're going to be at home here? Look down at that boat sneaking off underneath the chains.

Jimmy looked down and saw a smuggler's boat begin to quietly part the water away from the ship's bows, drawing diverging lines through the still, verdigris surface between the two Mexican vessels.

— That's commerce, Jack said. What a marvelous thing we are. I wonder whether your folks will be any happier where they end up than they were in the place they left.

Jimmy leaned against the crosstree and looked again to the lustering east.

— But I don't think I'll ever be happy unless I find them again.

— Then you may search and be searched for, be punished and be yourself the one who metes out punishment. And you may never be any happier than your mother and father.

The upper limb of the sun cracked over the hills, a cold

crimson arc, and it brushed the circular ripples about the ships and the diverging lines traced by the smugglers with a dim liquid red above the blackish-green ocean. In that moment, the repaired and renamed cannon began to bray from the Presidio at the orders of Major McCormick. One after another, in regular succession, the cannon heaved leaden balls into the shaggy forest that crept to within two hundred yards of the Presidio walls. Finally, McCormick himself lit the torch hole of the eighteen-pounder dubbed The Blessings of Freedom. The cannon boosted a ball into the forest with a mighty poot, and it landed on the future site of the eighth green of a famous golf course, scaring out two coveys of quail, three elk, and a grizzly bear afflicted with mange.

Capítulo IV

In the aftermath of the invasion, Arcadia had retired to her room with thin barred windows and declared her decision never to marry. The invasion, she claimed, had been a sign from Santa Teresa that she should not marry Don Ignacio, but rather become a *beata* and devote her life to good works. She began by taking up her embroidery as soon as she returned home. Her aunt and uncle, outraged at her refusal to help Don Ignacio bring more Castros into the world and despairing over the lack of heirs their family had produced and fearful that her eleven leagues would remain without a possessor and therefore return to the control of the devil, locked the door to her room from the outside, which suited Arcadia just fine, as she had already thrown the bolt inside.

Duenna Recta felt herself blamed for Arcadia's change of heart, as though she had been too successful in teaching her virtue. When both sides agreed, she was installed in the room to try to convince Arcadia to change her mind. However, it was impossible for the Duenna to speak in positive terms about anything, much less the state of marriage, which she had so steadfastly avoided. Instead, she only spoke of cautions and prohibitions, and she succeeded in making marriage sound like a minefield to be avoided completely, while the two of them finished a black lace curtain that would hang over the barred window and cut off most of the little light that could enter.

Only Magda knew that Arcadia had decided to take advantage of the invasion to find a way to avoid marriage with a man old enough to be her grandfather. Magda was allowed into the room three times a day to bring food and remove the speckled *bacinilla* in which Arcadia did her necessities. During one of these brief meetings, while the Duenna was absent, Magda told Arcadia that she would have to go to Monterey from time to time to have any chance of success. She could baffle Don Ignacio by staying within her room, but she would never find love. Arcadia asked her how, when she had employed all the tricks she knew just to be able to stay in the room. Surely she would never be allowed to dance again without being forced to marry Don Ignacio. Magda thought for a moment, then smiled knowingly.

— You must go to church once a day, no? To hear mass. I don't know how it will occur. But surely, as many secret looks have been exchanged at church as have ever been exchanged at a fandango.

Arcadia soon had a chance to plead her case, as her aunt and uncle had sent for Fray Echevarría to convince her to marry. The Friar was a faithful follower of the old Franciscan ways, and so he eschewed riding a horse, instead walking out on his bare, leathery feet, rejoicing especially when the sharp stones cut his flesh. He was thin as a wraith, his shaven head barely more than a skin-covered skull poking out of his robes, and his hands and fingers were long and bony. The only parts of him that seemed alive were his eyes, which flashed like bloody black marbles when the spirit took him, and his nose, which despite his ascetic diet of atole for breakfast, piñole at noon, and pozole for dinner, hung huge and fleshy from the center of his face.

Don Ignacio had visited the Friar as soon as Arcadia announced her decision to relinquish man and devote herself to a state of blessedness. He told the Friar that an invasion by heretics should not be taken as a sign that a marriage should be called off. In fact, that invasion called for more weddings, more children, more Castros to hold the land for the santa fe católica.

— What would happen, he asked, if we let our women interpret signs for themselves?

Fray Echevarría's nose quivered at the thought. He had already prayed that the fruit of Arcadia's womb be blessed with glory and power, be the defender and preserver of California's faith, be someday Master of Monterey. He set out on foot, accompanied by Don Ignacio's eldest son, Ignacio Jovencito, on horseback.

When he arrived, he was conducted into the black-draped room after both Arcadia and her aunt and uncle unfastened the door. He immediately launched into a long harangue in which he pointed out that California had fallen into iniquity since the Franciscans had lost control, and now as penance they all must endure an invasion by heretics, but that she, Arcadia, could be part of the restoration of the one true church, she had been chosen by the Holy Spirit to bring forth a renewal of the primitive virtue of Junípero Serra, the fruit of Arcadia would hold

California pure and motionless until the Lord should finally return to end the degraded history into which we are born to suffer. Mary had said yes, and called herself a handmaiden of the Lord, and what would have happened if Mary had said no? It's unthinkable. And a sí has as many letters as a no, and is as easy to say, is it not? So she should stop thinking and say yes and put an end to history, and blessed be the fruit of Arcadia.

To herself, Arcadia thought the Holy Spirit would look nothing like Don Ignacio. However, she remembered Magda's advice, and asked only that she be allowed to go to church and pray beneath the painting of the Virgin Mary, asking for wisdom and guidance until she understood what to do. Fray Echevarría took this news out to Uncle José and Aunt Josefina, claiming that he was certain she had taken his words to heart. Duenna Recta rejoiced along with Uncle José and Aunt Josefina, but Don Ignacio's son immediately rode off to his own land, fearing his father's gloom and displeasure at being told he would have to wait further.

Don Ignacio sat his stallion on the small square of beaten earth in front of the family adobe, brooding on the postponement of his marriage, his two shoulders curving in like bat wings over his sunken chest, and his head lowered, weighed down by the fine high hat of yellow wool that perched forlornly atop it. His eleven daughters waited quietly in the shadows of the sala, afraid to make much noise or chatter while their father waited, morose and expectant. From time to time, one daughter would take him a hand-rolled cigarette and light it for him between his lips. Between puffs, he would study the paper twinkling and dwindling around the tobacco.

Ignacio Jovencito rode into the square at a full gallop, rounding toward the house and sharply reining in his lathered mustang to a sliding stop. He leaped from the saddle before the horse had completely come to a halt, threw the reins to a sister, and swept off his hat to approach his father. Don Ignacio looked at him through hooded eyes, already knowing that ill news was coming. His son told him that after talking with Fray Echevarría, Arcadia had decided to pray before the Virgin Mary.

— Pray? Don Ignacio demanded. Pray for what?

— Wisdom and guidance, his son answered.

— What do wisdom and guidance have to do with weddings? Don Ignacio asked. What do they have to do with having children? Nothing, nada, that's all. For a moment, his head lifted, and his stallion pranced around from left to right.

— When will she go to church? he asked.

— Tomorrow morning, for the earliest mass, his son said.

— And what will the Virgin tell her? What does the Virgin have to do with weddings? Nothing, nada, that's all.

As the grim horseman spurred his stallion, making it walk forward and backward, Pablo Assis, the Ohlone musician, rode into the square on one jenny, leading another. He wore an unbleached muslin smock, not tucked in, and muslin trousers rolled up above his ankles, and a red sash of coarse cotton, and he had his violin tucked under his chin, playing a slow, sad tune. Pablo and several other Ohlone had been hired by Don Ignacio to provide music for his wedding and the fiesta that was to follow it, and he reasoned that, although the wedding and fiesta had never come to pass, he would still ask for the bags of seed corn he had been promised for his people's services. He approached the angry Don, scratching out an old tune the Moors had left behind them in northern Spain, while all eleven daughters held their breath.

Pablo Assis had been given his name by an old Franciscan, Padre Salvierderra, in honor of his musical ability, which decades earlier had attracted gentile Indians to the mission, just as San Pablo had attracted Greeks and San Francisco de Assisi had attracted the wild and savage beasts and birds. Since the missions had been secularized and the native peoples found out that the promised land had not been promised to them after all, Pablo and a number of ex-converts had returned to their ranchería of Temecula, which fell between the ill-defined edges of two land grants, and worked as seasonal vaqueros, sheep shearers, and musicians. He dismounted before Don Ignacio, holding his violin and bow in his left hand, and he took off his palm leaf hat with his right.

— Don Ignacio, he said in passable Spanish. Muy señor mío, Illustrious sir. I come to beg of you the bags of seed corn, which my people will need for their spring planting, as I learned at the hand of the holy mission fathers, while a neophyte in the Catholic faith.

Don Ignacio, in recompense for hearing the song that was to have been played at his wedding of Arcadia, saluted Pablo with three blows of the *reata* about his head and shoulders. Pablo continued on, speaking in most reasonable terms about why he and his people needed the corn. Don Ignacio was astounded. He called his eldest son over to hear Pablo's petition, and asked him what answer they should make. Pablo repeated with sweet reason his people's need for corn, their desire to grow food and feed themselves, as they had done in the days when the missions controlled all the land that had been christianized, and he expressed his own willingness to come and play music again when Don Ignacio's wedding should be celebrated. Ignacio Jovencito immediately took Pablo by the shoulders, turned him around, and kicked him in the backside, sending him sprawling.

Don Ignacio, with gladness in his heart, allowed his son to kiss his hand.

— Mount your horse, he said. We'll gather all the boys and kill an elk.

His son took the reins from his sister, struck his horse sharply, and sprang into the saddle as the animal started forward. He and his father rode several times in a circle around Pablo Assis, and then Don Ignacio shouted to his daughters.

— Ea. Give this man the seed corn he wants.

Pablo dusted off his hands and knees as he rose to his feet, and he followed one of Don Ignacio's daughters to where he could pick up the seed corn and load it on his jennies. Most of the boons brought by white people were accompanied by beatings brought by white people. This also he had learned at the hands of the holy mission fathers. He rode off, with his palm leaf hat back on his head and his violin tucked under his chin, playing a slow, sad tune and leading his jenny packed with what was needed for spring planting.

Don Ignacio rode out onto the highlands near the sea, moving through the wild green grasses quickened by the early October rains, alfileria, bunchgrass, burr clover, wild oat. He was accompanied by eleven of his sons, picking them up one by one as he moved across his eleven leagues of land, leaving behind Fidel Segundón to watch over the cattle, and they fanned out as they rode, a rough skirmish line breasting through the ballock-tickling grass, unarmed except for *la reata*, the lariat of woven rawhide draped over their saddle horns, and a long, crescent knife known as *la luna*. When they passed a stand of young trees, one son cut a small stout branch, tied the knife to it, and handed it to Don Ignacio.

They rode beyond the range of cattle, onto land unnamed and unmanned, the words and worlds once attached to the seed-bearing bushes now buried beneath the roots, beneath the bright green stalk and branch. Don Ignacio held his reins in one hand and the improvised lance in the other, and they advanced easily over hills rounded and smoothed by ocean storms, toward the innocent shore. The grasses opened before them and closed behind them like water.

They found the headland trembling with slow, untamed life. There were more than four hundred elk, shoulders and haunches seeming to float above a sea of grasses, legs and hooves hidden by the startling green. The males were husky and musty brown, thick in the shoulders and neck, racks of antlers held easily aloft on their high heads. The females were more finely shaped but stood equally tall, their eyes large and wise and endless. The heads of the vast herd dipped and rose in uneven ripples, dipped down with soft muzzles to the tender seedpods, then rose again, chewing and cautious and walking slowly forward. They moved gravely through the grass, bowing forward with muscled necks, then lifting their heads in calm watchfulness.

Don Ignacio and his boys advanced toward the herd at a

measured pace, allowing the elk to retreat easily before them, but gradually defining an inside and an outside with their evenly spaced line of horses. Don Ignacio rode at the center, with five sons to his right and six to his left. As they drew nearer to the cliffs near the ocean, elk began to leak out around either end of the line, suddenly sensing danger and leaping free with a push from their powerful hindquarters. The elk remaining within the line grew restless, the bulls no longer grazing, but standing their ground, watching, then finally retreating before the inexorable horsemen.

Don Ignacio saw, in the midst of the trapped herd, a bull elk that was, if possible, as old as himself. He saw the old bull as the *semental*, the *padre arce*, the fountain of life populating the native and unbordered land, the land he wanted to cover with the name of Castro. The elk stopped and watched as the space around the herd grew smaller, retreated and stopped again as the line of eleven horsemen now cut off completely any escape route. Its rack of antlers spread across five feet of space, and its long shaggy neck was flecked with white, its blunt muzzle also whitened with age. It stood still in the space suddenly delimited about it as the herd quaked in incomprehension, and it snorted and pawed the ground and lowered its rack toward Don Ignacio, in the ancient gesture that had won it glory during rutting season.

Don Ignacio stood up in his stirrups and shook his lance at the old bull, while the two sons who flanked him took their *reatas* from their saddles and built loops.

— Ea, hermano, Don Ignacio shouted at the elk. I'm in want of your help to win Arcadia.

— And a little of your fat to cook tortillas, the son at the right added. Don Ignacio pointed with his lance.

— ¡Adelante! he shouted.

The two sons flanking him spurred their horses forward, *reatas* in their hands, and they plunged into the middle of the herd. The elk panicked, boiled up into a ball of thrashing hooves and antlers, then exploded outward, fighting toward the undefined land. One of the sons flipped a large loop through the air over the spreading antlers of the old bull, then took a dally around his saddle horn and reined in his horse. The horse braced, stiff-legged, as the elk leaped toward the sun, then jerked back to earth, strangled with its own strength as the loop closed and the rawhide rope stretched tight. Restrained for the first time in its long memory, and not under-standing the meaning of restraint, the old elk danced at the end of the line, seeking again and again a certain arc through the air, a certain lurch, a certain spring against gravity and the mystery clutching its neck that would leave it free to join the herd scattering around it. The son with his rope dallied sat coolly in the saddle, maneuvering his horse right and left against the sudden shocks of the beast.

The other son flipped a backhander over the elk from the opposite side and drew it tight. Now the old bull was bound to the earth and could only plunge forward and backward, tram-pling down the grass of its death space, the rude altar of its sacrifice. It shook its rack of antlers up and down at the antag-onist it could neither reach nor understand, alien from the few native foes it had either eluded or vanquished, the big cats or the men on foot wearing hides as camouflage. The two horsemen kept it in play between them, the horses stepping and then bracing with bulging eyeballs as the elk struggled. It threw its heavy shoulders and thick neck muscles against the two *reatas*, but it was able only to dig its hooves deeper into the earth from which, so it was told, it had emerged long ago.

Then Don Ignacio spurred his stallion forward. The elk thrashed left and right and lowered its antlers at his approach, an animal that dimly appeared like another bull at mating season, but the two sons held it back from charging. Don Ignacio lowered *la luna* on the end of his young tree shaft, and when the old bull heaved up its head, he thrust the sickle-shaped knife deep into the long shaggy neck, through the wrapped layers of muscle, and into the elk's neck veins. The elk screamed and then gurgled as the bright-colored blood spilled from its neck and watered the ground, and great tears began to spill from its eyes and mix with the blood and soak into the earth it had marked in its agony. It found within its heart one last leap to the sun, a leap that would surely take it past the incomprehensible nooses and the single long ridiculous spear. And then it was still.

Don Ignacio lifted *la luna* to his wrinkled lips and let the hot blood drip onto his tongue, and he watched gladly the blood he had loosed from the wild beast stain the green grasses and settle down through their roots. In his sixty years in California, he had killed three thousand and sixty-four deer, seven hundred and thirteen elk, three hundred and seven grizzly bear, some for bull and bear fights, and an even three-score of cougar. Most he had killed in the old way, with sharpened metal, knife or lance or sword. He had stained three wedding beds with the blood of women. And every drop of blood he spilled or touched or saw pour onto the soil made him feel more at home, eased his loneliness in the silent, empty land.

He pointed the *luna* at the fallen elk. — Ea, hermano. Arcadia will bear the name of Castro!

While the sons of Castro dragged the elk behind them on its hind legs like the corpse of Hector, and the elk's blood marked a trail behind them where no trail existed before, Arcadia laid out the clothing in which she would visit church the next day. It was foreseen that she would be accompanied by both Magda and Duenna Recta, but she had schemed with Magda to evade the Duenna's vigilance. Later that night, once the Duenna was asleep, Arcadia carefully took the black lace curtains and embroidered mantillas and black lace undergarments from the trousseau she had been putting together in imitation of her governess, and draped them around the Duenna's alcove, so that little light and sound could penetrate, which didn't disturb the Duenna's sleep as she was long accustomed to little light and sound and air.

Arcadia scarcely slept that night, tossing with thoughts of suffering misery and woe in order to find love, wondering whether the Virgin would lead her to the snake man, or whether it was all futile, and she would live out her life as a fruitless bride and a bitter widow.

Then Magda hissed through the door, and Arcadia dressed quietly in her everyday church wear, a plain dress and a simple black fan, and a rebozo to cover her head, as a woman could not enter church with an uncovered head. She held her wooden-soled shoes in her hand, and at the sound of a bolt slipped from outside, she slipped the bolt from inside and tiptoed out the door. Magda led her to where an Ohlone vaquero held two mares with shortened saddles, and they rode off to seek wisdom and guidance and misery and woe at the foot of the painting of the Virgin.

It was after dark when Don Ignacio and his sons arrived back at the Castro adobe, dragging the dead body in triumph. Some of the Ohlone servants had laid a fire in a pit, and they lit it as the hunters returned from the unbordered land, greeting them with high yellow flames, while the eleven daughters all came out in front of the adobe to prettily watch the elk dragged in a circle on the square of beaten earth and left next to the pit fire. Then some Ohlone butchers set to work, peeling the skin back and crooning with delight at the layers of glistening fat. They set the haunches, saddle, and ribs on to barbecue, and carefully fried the elk's testicles with cornmeal and lard in a cast-iron pan. A Castro daughter wrapped them in a tortilla and brought them over to where Don Ignacio still sat his horse, and he snapped through them with his strong teeth and worked them down his skinny neck.

They feasted through the night with brandy and roasted meat until the full moon rose to its zenith. One son played guitar while brother danced with sister under the watchful eye of their father. Then Don Ignacio had his sons take the elk's rack of antlers and break off the two outermost forks, the newest and most vital growth, and he placed them in the band of his hat as though they grew from his own head. He spurred his stallion in a circle around the plaza several times, and two other sons mounted up, one carrying the guitar, and they rode at a gallop for the ranch of Arcadia Serrano.

Don Ignacio and his two sons approached the Serrano adobe after Arcadia had already gone to seek the Virgin. They found Arcadia's window, narrow and barred with iron and hung with black lace curtains, and they formed a small semi-circle around it. Don Ignacio, wearing his horns, sat his horse at the center, while one son took the guitar in his lap, and the other son cleared his throat. Don Ignacio nodded, and they began to play a jota.

Palomita, vete al campo
y diles a los tiradores
que no te tiren, porqu'eres
la dueña de mis amores

If stone is hard
You are a diamond
Because all my love
Has not softened you

If I offer you affection
You despise me
And you call me a fool
As if to love you were folly

But I know, ungrateful one
Someday in your dreams
You will remember
That I was always your master

As they played the song outside the window, Duenna Recta

awoke amid thick swaths of the black lace she had twisted together with her own hands and seemed to be awakening from a dream in which she was in a strange land where she was not blessed or respected, strange because she was happy in spite of it all. She awoke slowly and softly, parting the layers of lace and embroidery, and the dream continued into her waking life, as the music of love filtered into the veiled room. She rose from her bed, trailing scarves and fronds of black from her neck and limbs, and found her way to the barred window where the music rose and fell. She peeled back layer after gauzy layer from the window, until only a delicate scrim of black separated her from the music, and she saw a colossal horse standing before her, and a caped horseman with forked horns growing from his head leaning toward her from the saddle.

— ¿Quién es? she whispered through the scrim.

— Your lover and your husband, tu señor natural, as you are my lady.

She heard the horseman speak, but she felt the dream begin to break apart, the pieces of her dream scatter and scurry away.

— Why have you come now, sweet devil. To torment me?

— To torment you, no. Only to make you fruitful and content, as it is in your nature to be.

The Duenna tried to hold on to her state of unconsciousness, but the more she tried to keep it close, the more separate she felt from it, until it was gone and she found herself screeching in an aged voice.

— It is too late, too late, too late. Could you not let me live out my life in peace?

Don Ignacio stood up in his stirrups, straight up in shock

and anger at the old voice, and then he wheeled his stallion around. He rode around the adobe until he came across the Ohlone vaquero who had saddled the mares.

— Where is Arcadia? he shouted.

The Ohlone pointed toward Monterey. — Praying, he said.

Don Ignacio spurred his stallion around to where his two boys waited.

— Vámonos, muchachos, he shouted.

They rode off, in pursuit of Arcadia, the horned Don Ignacio in the lead. They rode off, following the two women dressed in black with heads wrapped in rebozos, who were entering the church to pray. They rode, unaware that the pueblo of Monterey was preparing a huge fiesta to welcome on shore the triumphant conqueror, a celebration to mark the advent of the curve-backed, questioning Commodore Jones. They rode, still followed by the voice of Duenna Recta, charging them with unspeakable injuries of pain and regret.

Capítulo V

While the officers and midshipmen began to brush off their fancy dress blue uniforms which they had not worn since leaving Hampton Roads, preparing to celebrate a victory that would no doubt advance their careers, and that had the added good quality of not having caused them to risk their lives, William Waxdeck lay belowdecks and struggled to compose the proclamations that the Commodore was to read. The first steps of the conqueror upon the land were to be celebrated with music and dancing and games and feasting, and Waxdeck had to prepare a speech in which the Commodore both proclaimed himself conqueror over the land and established that the land had always expected him, that his presence merely fulfilled a potential already inherent in the land.

Waxdeck was still sick, even with the gentle rocking of the *National Intention* at anchor, and had not even been topside to see California. Yet he knew, according to the epic tradition, that what he needed was a sign that the gods favored and recognized the American possession of California. Best of all, of course, would be theophany, in which God Himself, or perhaps Louisa Darling, would actually show up and speak, but Waxdeck didn't think he should anticipate that occurring when he crafted his speech. More common was some event that would be recognized as a sign of divine sanction, as when Aeneas and his son ate lunch in Italy and thus founded the Roman Empire. But Waxdeck thought that Virgil had it easy, since he was writing eight hundred years after the fact, whereas Waxdeck had to write a speech in which the sign was recognized, before the sign had even manifested itself. He finally decided to leave it to the discretion of the Commodore to recognize the sign, and merely wrote in parentheses

(refer to the manifest sign that indicates superiority
of American ideals and rightness of American possession).

Waxdeck called for more paper, and yeoman Keyes brought it up gladly. Although he was involved in selling off as much of the ship's store as possible to Míster Lurkin's smugglers, paper and ink were two items of which he still had a nearly limitless supply. Keyes, his face round and red, looked with interest over the speech that the young midshipman was penning. Although he was convinced he was contributing to the ship's mission by despoiling the ship of its stores, he thought it might not be bad to have some warrant for his activity immortalized in word from the Commodore's own lips.

— Have you put anything in the speech about commerce? he asked insinuatingly. The land is a ripe field for the American merchant.

— It's true, Waxdeck said. Nihil tam munitum quod non expugnari pecunia possit.

Keyes didn't have the least idea what Waxdeck was talking about, and in fact had harbored a grudge against him ever since he had been forced to offload barrels of salt pork in favor of paper and ink — a grudge well justified, he now thought, due to his inability to market paper and ink. Salt pork, on the other hand, could always find a buyer. But as rancor was not marketable either, and the young midshipman had the Commodore's ear, Keyes simply backed out humbly.

— Just a suggestion, Mr. Waxdeck.

— Pecunia regimen est rerum omnium, Waxdeck said.

— Aye, Mr. Waxdeck.

Waxdeck let a string of green bile spill from the corner of his mouth into the bile bucket, and he gnawed on his pen. He wondered whether Keyes was right, whether commerce would provide the sign that indicated superiority of American ideals and rightness of American possession. If every product of the land could be bought and sold freely, if the land itself was constantly exchanged for more and more money, wouldn't that show that the Commodore's advent fulfilled a potential already inherent in the land?

Waxdeck scratched out a few lines in the speech and was writing something about free land and the market when the door opened and Captain Rafael Rafael entered. Rafael Rafael was already dressed to go ashore, in blue with gold epaulettes and a sword at his side, and he gravely entered the midshipmen's noisome quarters, looking for Waxdeck through the thick air flavored by the smell of bile. Waxdeck was too weak to rise to his feet, but he tried to salute and stabbed himself in the forehead with his pen. The Captain motioned him to be at ease and sat down beside his bunk. They remained in silence for a short time, Waxdeck waiting and wondering what could have brought the Captain down to see him. Finally, Rafael Rafael breathed out a long sigh.

— You said, through the Commodore's steward, that marriage with a native of the place is sometimes important? Rafael Rafael began.

— Aye, sir. Waxdeck gave a brief lecture on why Aeneas had to leave Dido, in order to bring his people and his line to the place foretold and wed Lavinia, the daughter of Latinus.

— And what of Dido? Rafael Rafael asked.

— She fell on a sword. And the smoke from her funeral pyre was seen by Aeneas out at sea.

— And was Aeneas happy when he reached the right place? he asked. Did he love Lavinia?

— Aeneas was pious, Waxdeck said. I don't think he was ever happy, sir.

Rafael Rafael nodded again. — He would have been happier if he had remained with Dido and never sailed to Italy at all.

— Then the Roman Empire would never have been founded, sir.

— Exactly, Rafael Rafael said. Exactly. You must put something in your proclamation about love.

— Love, sir?

— Yes. Love.

— Aye, sir. Something about love.

While the Captain left with measured steps, Waxdeck wondered if love could somehow provoke the sign of the rightness of American possession. Or if the American presence fulfilled a potential for love already inherent in the land. Confused, he scribbled out a line or two of what he had written about commerce, and began to compose something about love. Waxdeck understood very little about love, since he had only come across it in the works of poets, but it seemed to him that in the tradition of love poetry, you could only truly love a woman whom you could never possess, and so love mainly had to do with suffering for what you couldn't achieve. Nitimur in vetitum semper cupimusque negata. Looked at abstractly, it seemed to Waxdeck to have much in common with constipation. But in accordance with the Captain's orders, he tried to include something about love in the proclamation.

Then, as he wrote, two horny hands smelling of gunpowder covered his eyes from behind.

— Guess who, dear boy?

Major McCormick had come aboard to oversee bringing ammunition ashore, and he couldn't resist stopping in to see the pale and lovely scribe. He sat beside him and stroked his forehead while Waxdeck told him he was at work on the Commodore's proclamation.

— Though I can neither read nor write, the Major declared, pulling on his crotch, I'd admire hearing somewhat of American arms. For there's rumors that this Micheltorena is on the march with five hundred men, and it would do the people here good to know that Micheltorena will have no chance against the strength of American arms.

Then the Major kissed Waxdeck's pale green brow, stood upright, and told him he had to return to the ammunition. Waxdeck, who already knew firsthand the strength of McCormick's American arm, began crossing out and adding lines about American military might, and the noble virility of

American soldiers. Hostis si quis erit nobis, amet ille puellas. Gaudeat in pueros, si quis amicus erit.

In an hour, his sheaves of paper were a confusing map of arrows, blotches, and conflicting sentiments, and Waxdeck himself had trouble separating his partitio from his peroratio. Then Hannibal Memory entered to pick up the speech for the Commodore, and he told Waxdeck that the Commodore wanted to make sure that freedom, democracy, and Louisa Darling all had prominent places in it. Waxdeck desperately gathered papers up into order and assured Hannibal that freedom, democracy, and Louisa Darling were the first things he had written about. However, he asked Hannibal to make a clean copy for the Commodore, as he had made many corrections along the way.

Over Hannibal's shoulder, peering in at the mass of papers, Waxdeck saw the mottled face of Chips looking at him beseechingly.

— No, Waxdeck said. Nothing in the proclamation about leaks.

Chips turned away, disappointed. Hannibal took the speech in one hand, and in the other he carried out Waxdeck's bile bucket, which was full to overflowing.

When Hannibal set to copy out Waxdeck's written speech, he was certain he would have to change it in some way. His own narrative of the voyage in prose had brought the *National Intention* to Monterey Bay, and only his narrative thus far had seen the leak in the hull, but he knew that Waxdeck was already writing heroic couplets about the takeover. The couplets, Hannibal was afraid, were already infiltrating the land, killing memory and fixing the way people would be able to think about what was happening. If the Commodore proclaimed Louisa Darling in this new land, Hannibal thought he would once again have fallen into someone else's history, the history in which he and his people were slaves, and he would never have the chance to write his own line and author his own descendants. Yet he knew he could not stop the Commodore from speaking Louisa Darling's name in California.

He spread Waxdeck's confused speech in front of him, along with a stack of pilot crackers and jerky, and he made one clean copy to return to Waxdeck, and another for the Commodore to read in which, amid the commerce and love and war, he tried to signify for himself a possibility of living free from Louisa Darling and the *National Intention*.

While the ship's officers brushed their blue uniforms, and the men of Monterey wound scarlet sashes around their waists and put on their brilliant silk and velveteen jackets with buttons made from gold and silver coins, and the women of Monterey put up their hair in high tortoiseshell combs and draped lace mantillas over their shoulders and hung Gulf pearls round their necks, and the pueblo made ready for the fiesta, Arcadia was kneeling in front of the painting of the Virgin Mary. She was dressed in black, and her head was wrapped in a black rebozo, and the sleeves of her dress were long and wide, so that her folded hands rose like pale flowers out of the folds of black cloth.

Arcadia felt that she had at best achieved a standoff with her aunt and uncle and Don Ignacio. As long as she declared herself a *beata*, dedicated to a pure life, they would let her stay locked in a room. After all, her aunt declared, one could be as pure as one wanted inside a room as well as outside, but one could be more wicked outside a room than in. But if she wanted to go forth into the hills, she could only do so under the protection of a husband. For tales were told of women who risked the golden hills alone while of marriageable age, and who then found that they had caught fecundity like a disease, like vapors, to the eternal disgrace of their families.

The mysterious words still twisted into the Virgin's ear. Fray Echevarría had told her simply that the dove was telling the Virgin to say yes and then be quiet. But Arcadia was certain that the Virgin would never have been called blessed among women if the words had led her to someone like Don Ignacio. She thought that if Magda was right, and the words led the Virgin to the snake man, it was because the snake man was also a part of God, a part that dwelled in the golden hills, and the Virgin was blessed because she had been able to be with him there.

But Arcadia wasn't sure if Magda was right, or if the Friar was right, or if both or neither was right. The words twisted, unreadable and mysterious, as Arcadia prayed. And she felt far away from the Virgin, far from God, alone despite Magda kneeling beside her. Before she had reached marriageable age, she had been able to live without making choices, and now she was given a choice between a locked room and an old man, which was no choice at all. She suddenly felt alone as she prayed, abandoned as though being abandoned were the punishment for having grown older, and that the choices she now had before her would leave her more alone than ever. She prayed that the Virgin, who now seemed so far away, speak to her. She prayed that Mary no longer just listen and say yes and be quiet, but speak and tell her how to return to the time when she didn't have to make choices, or tell her how to pass through misery and woe and find love.

But the Virgin didn't speak. Arcadia turned to Magda and said, — She doesn't answer.

— She waits, Magda said.

— Why does she wait? Arcadia asked.

— I don't know, Magda said.

Arcadia lifted her hands again to the Virgin and closed her eyes. From far away, she heard a voice, many voices, a multitude.

— ¡Abre la puerta!

She opened her eyes. The words were repeated many times in many voices, shouted and roared and bellowed and laughed.

— ¡Abre la puerta! Open the door!

The fiesta had answered her. The doors to the church opened and a crowd of *desterrados*, landless sons and daughters of Spanish men and Ohlone women, rushed into the church beating drums and tambourines. They wore white muslin with red sashes, and they were led by a clown who wore a wooden mask over his face, a mask of anguish, painted white with large red teardrops around each eye, and a mouth stretching down at both corners with sharp jagged teeth like a beaten dog. The crowd danced across the beaten-earth floor and flooded around Arcadia and Magda kneeling before the painting of the Virgin. Then Fray Echevarría appeared at the altar and addressed the crowd with the words always used on such occasions.

— Quem quaeritis?

The clown answered. — We seek the Virgin.

— Why do you seek her?

— To carry her in triumph. To celebrate her coming into the world.

Fray Echevarría sighed deeply. — My children, this is not like other fiestas. A stranger to the Virgin is coming into the land. Yet take her in procession, and may she intercede for us all.

The crowd shouted and beat on their drums and shook their tambourines, and they surrounded Arcadia. — She must come too, they shouted. As the Virgin comes, she must come too.

Arcadia rose to her feet, suddenly exalted. To go with the Virgin through the open doors, outside the church, was what she most wanted to do in the whole world. — Yes, as the Virgin goes, I too will go.

The crowd shouted in triumph, and two large men took the painting by its frame and lifted it from the wall. They ushered Arcadia to the head of the procession, while Magda stayed among the others, and then they marched and danced toward the door, beating drums and clappersticks, following the image of the Virgin. Fray Echevarría made the sign of the cross over them as they paraded the Virgin first toward the altar, then toward the door. But as they approached the door, a horned figure on horseback suddenly blocked their way. Arcadia stopped, but she stood firm before him, and the *desterrados* swelled around her, grouping protectively around the Virgin.

— It is the Evil One, a man said.

— It is her father, a woman said.

Don Ignacio sat his stallion in the door of the church, two of his sons behind him. He saw Arcadia, dressed all in black, before the image of the Virgin, not hiding from him in a room now, but standing with her face pale and firm, seeming more uncovered and open to him now wrapped in a black rebozo than she had at the fiesta, and he suddenly felt that no other sight would ever content him, that instead of pursuing Arcadia, he would be pursued by this face, open and uncovered and forever inaccessible to him.

— It is her father, the woman said again.

— It is an elk, the clown said. An elk, a stag!

The clown threw himself to all fours and scrambled toward the church door, barking like a dog. Others followed, barking and growling, and the clown lunged at the flank of Don Ignacio's stallion and raked its flesh with his sharp wooden teeth. One of Don Ignacio's sons raised his *reata* and beat the clown about the shoulders, but it was too late. The stallion reared away from the crowd of barking men and women and plunged crazily down the way, carrying along the horned Don Ignacio. The two sons wheeled their horses around to ride down their father's stallion, while Don Ignacio barely kept his saddle, trying to regain control over the rampant beast.

The clown leaped to his feet, then turned somersaults in front of the church, while Arcadia and the Virgin proceeded through the open doors out into the world outside the church, along with the joyous *desterrados*.

While the procession began, the Commodore's barge waited below the quarterdeck of the *National Intention*, the barge men dressed in frocks of white duck with their oars in their hands. Commodore Jones was stalking back and forth in his cabin, holding the copy of the proclamation that Hannibal Memory had made from Waxdeck's confused notes. He moved back and forth, moving his lips as he went over the speech, sometimes waving his left hand in the air to punctuate a particularly salient point, while Hannibal stood quietly, round and firm, waiting. Then the Commodore stopped and looked at the speech, puzzled. Hannibal watched him with interest and anxiety, hoping the Commodore hadn't found his special addition. The Commodore laid a finger to his thin lips and looked over at Hannibal.

— What on earth could be a manifest sign that indicates superiority of American ideals and rightness of American possession? he asked.

— Something from the epic tradition, sir, Hannibal answered. Midshipman Waxdeck explained that a sign, as in hierophany, would reveal that our journeys were at an end, that we had come to the right place, that we were meant to be here.

Commodore Jones was troubled, nagged by the knowledge that he had conquered Monterey on the mere rumor of war. If a sign did not appear, would that mean that he had taken over the pueblo in error? What would a sign look like? Would he be able to recognize it if it came? What would he say in his proclamation if no sign appeared? He thought of Louisa Darling, pure, white, undefiled, gazing down upon him. He wished she could be present today, to see him in triumph. He wished she could hear him dedicate the victory to her, hear herself proclaimed the spirit of freedom and democracy. If she were here, Jones was certain that a sign would be blindingly clear; if she were here, he could feel truly at the end of the continent that his journeys were at an end, that he was meant to be here.

On deck, the bugler was beginning to play "Yankee Doodle." Hannibal cleared his throat.

— The Commodore's barge is ready, sir, he said.

Commodore Jones folded the sheaf of papers of the proclamation and placed them inside his uniform coat, next to his heart. Then he walked up the ladder and out onto the quarterdeck. In the ship's waist, the marine guard made up a lane of side-boys, while the ship's boatswain blew a shrill trilling salute on his silver pipe. Captain Rafael Rafael and all the ship's lieutenants, dressed in their fancy blues, took off their hats. The Commodore approached, long and sinuous, and as the side-boys presented arms, he walked down the lane they formed, like a walking question mark, unable to gaze above the horizontal, looking down the lane of marines toward the green shore, seeking the sign that had been promised him. The bugler played in his honor, and the boatswain blew with his cheeks puffed out like plum puddings. The Commodore, in dignity, turned and acknowledged his Captain with the slightest of nods and a touch of his fingers to his hat. Then he descended a ladder to the Commodore's barge.

Hannibal, who had already swung hand by hand down a line made fast to the bitts, was there to help the Commodore gain his seat in the stern of the barge. At an order from the coxswain, the barge men shipped oars and pulled away, carrying the Commodore seated toward Monterey, with Hannibal standing at his right shoulder.

The Commodore was followed by Captain Rafael Rafael in the Captain's gig, and several of the lieutenants in the ship's first and second cutters. They rowed as a small flotilla after the Commodore's barge, through waters that were blood-tinted by the slaughtering of steers for the fiesta, which had begun at dawn.

At the boat landing of the Custom House, the leading men of Monterey waited to greet the Commodore, while Major McCormick readied an escort of marines. Míster Lurkin, dressed in a swallowtail coat and wearing a beaverskin hat that shadowed his eyes, arranged the ranks of worthies so that the Commodore would meet first the ex-Governor, then Comandante Silva, then other large landowners, and finally himself. As the barge approached, the coxswain shouted *Oars!* and the rowers lifted their oars dripping upright as the barge floated in to the landing and the marine band struck up "Yankee Doodle." Hannibal jumped ashore first to help Commodore Jones up the ladder, and as the marine escort presented arms, Commodore Jones set foot on the soil of California.

He stood where he was and gazed all about him, not really fixing his attention on the line of dignitaries. They began shifting uneasily, waiting for the Commodore to move toward them, but he continued to peer all about, squinting his eyes and gazing into the distance, turning left and right but unable to raise his vision from the horizontal.

The ex-Governor was agog at his first sight of the new Master of Monterey, sinuous, seven feet long, shaped like a question mark, shifting his eyes all about.

— Thank God I am ex-Governor, he muttered as the band played "Yankee Doodle" relentlessly.

While everybody wondered why the Commodore had stopped to look around, the Commodore himself was worried about finding a sign that would tell him that he was in the right place, a manifest sign that indicated superiority of American ideals and rightness of American possession. He had hoped that the very act of setting his foot on the ground would somehow reveal the sign, but nothing had happened. The land about him still seemed foreign, amorphous, not yet recognizable as the place where his journeys would be at an end.

Mister Lurkin took matters into his own hands, as though he knew what the Commodore was seeking and also knew that it would not be manifest at the loading dock, even with an American flag flying over the Custom House and a band playing "Yankee Doodle." He took the Commodore by the arm, welcomed him as a fellow countryman to land that now, it appeared, was part of their country through the Commodore's magnificent efforts, and introduced him to the other men waiting. Meanwhile, the Captain's gig had landed Rafael Rafael, and the cutters had dropped off the lieutenants. When all had been introduced, Lurkin pointed to a magnificent silver-maned palomino with a richly embroidered saddle and silver cheek plates in the form of conchas on the harness.

— The people are waiting for you at the Presidio, Lurkin said.

The Commodore stepped up to the horse, and with Hannibal giving him a boost, mounted into the saddle. As others mounted their steeds behind him, he began to ride up the rutted oxcart path toward the decrepit fort, passing between the Appian Way crowds of people who had lined the path to see the curve-backed conqueror. Ahead, the Commodore heard the music of flute and guitar, while behind him came the endless rendition of "Yankee Doodle."

As per instructions received from Waxdeck and confirmed by the Commodore, Hannibal trotted alongside the Commodore's horse and shouted up from time to time, in the manner of Roman processions.

— Glory is fleeting. Glory is fleeting.

Lurkin rode beside the Commodore at the head of the procession, speaking quietly but steadily into his ear as the Commodore continued to search for a sign. He pointed out the beauties of the land surrounding them, the wealth of cattle, the unharvested timber, the mineral riches that no doubt awaited discovery, and he asked how it felt to be their master, to have brought them into the possession of the United States. — *If,* Lurkin added in his low, whispering yet penetrating voice, if indeed a state of war has broken out between Mexico and the United States on the southern borders, as you have claimed. We've also heard stories of war, but one wonders about stories, and how desire makes them appear to be facts of history. When you gaze on all these things, glorious as they are, you must ask, is it to be given to you, the glory of conquering them all?

Commodore Jones heard Lurkin's voice like a worm boring into an apple. He heard it, but he still looked horizontally about for a sign, or something he could name a sign. Lurkin continued in his quiet, buzzing voice, — We've also heard stories of peace in Mexico. It might not yet be the time. What would you do then? Would you, the bloodless conqueror, shed blood upon the land? For there's also a story that Micheltorena is marching from El Pueblo de la Reina de Los Angeles, with six hundred men under arms. And stories are only proven to be history by shedding blood.

While the Commodore and Lurkin continued at the head of the procession, Captain Rafael Rafael also searched for a sign that he had come to the right place, a place unmapped and only dreamed about, although he felt the sign would be the face of a woman. There were many women lining the route, dressed in pale greens and blues with brilliant sashes of purple and scarlet, waving handkerchiefs at him. When the procession entered through the splintered wooden doors smashed by the *National Intention* on the previous day, more women wearing high combs and lace shawls draped over their shoulders signaled him with their bright fans folding and unfolding, tried to capture his eyes the color of fragile blue china.

Rafael Rafael saw them all, possessed them all easily with his eyes, and in each splendid and shining woman he looked at, he saw utter misery, a continuation of loneliness and discontent.

Inside the Presidio, the fandango had already begun. A rude wooden corral had been erected for the bull and bear fight in the center of the plaza, and huge cauldrons of beans and chile were simmering over low wood fires next to the sides of beef spitting and smoking as juice dripped into the open flames. Ohlone women had been at work all night grinding corn by hand and making tortillas, and yellow stacks rich with lard stood by the cauldrons. There were only two hundred and twelve spoons in all of California, and so most of the revelers dipped out beans with a tortilla, then ate it with a rib of beef from the meaty sides. The procession circled the plaza slowly, and Rafael Rafael continued to look deeply into the face of every woman he passed as the flute and guitar music continued and Major McCormick mercifully had the marine band stop playing "Yankee Doodle."

Then from a side entrance into the plaza, the painting of the Virgin Mary entered, carried high by the *desterrados* dressed in white, led by Arcadia dressed in black, her head covered by her black rebozo, looking down toward the ground. The music played on in praise of the Virgin, but the dancing stopped as dancers crossed themselves or fell to their knees. The *desterrados* went to the food and drink, and were allowed to eat their fill and drink deeply from the barrels of wine and brandy, to sustain themselves for the burden of carrying the Virgin, which would continue all day. All others fell back, for the *desterrados* were sacred and untouchable on this day, although tomorrow they would again be the lowliest of dung slingers. The Commodore asked Míster Lurkin about the group, and the Trader replied with understanding and amused tolerance.

— Landless ones. Who own nothing, not even debts.

Captain Rafael Rafael overheard Míster Lurkin, and he almost thought he recognized the voice. But he was too preoccupied with what he had just seen to consider it at that moment. He yearned with his eyes after Arcadia, leading the procession with her head bowed. There was something unreadable about her, something mysterious, which couldn't be captured by his gaze. The blackness of her dress, like an empty shape, never filled with the finery he knew too well, drew him after her, as though she herself enigmatically was a place he remembered from the past to which he could not return, or a place he dreamed about, where he could never arrive.

Then Arcadia opened her fan as Magda had taught her, and she found Rafael Rafael's eyes with her own, and shared a look with him that nobody else in the square was aware of. She had felt him seeking her out with his china-blue eyes, understood that he was the last person her aunt and uncle would wish her to marry. He would be denounced by Fray Echevarría, would inspire horror in the breast of Duenna Recta. He was perfect. And since she felt the Virgin had led her here, and not back to a time when she didn't have to make choices, she chose to share a look with him. And in that moment, as though her free choice were no longer free but doomed and inevitable, she chose him as the end of all her misery and woe.

She closed her fan again and bowed her head, but she had chosen him and she knew that he knew it. The sad clown turned somersaults near the Virgin, and they paraded through the splintered door and back into the country. Captain Rafael Rafael, still on horseback, was prepared to ride after them when a boy took his horse by the reins. The Commodore and Lurkin had already dismounted and were taking seats on a kind of dais, and the Captain was forced to take his seat beside them, alongside the leading men of Monterey, overlooking the arena.

Commodore Jones watched all the proceedings carefully

and nervously, fingering the proclamation he held close to his heart. He still had not seen anything he could construe as a sign, and he wasn't sure what he was going to do if nothing became manifest. He thought vaguely of the young boy, Jimmy F. Bush, and wondered if flogging him might provoke a sign, as flogging him had gotten them out of Hampton Roads. He looked around for Hannibal, and saw him coming back from the cauldrons loaded with steaming tortillas and a rib of beef.

— How can you eat when we're making history? he asked in a whisper.

— You can't make history without eating, sir, Hannibal whispered back.

The ex-Governor Alvarado glanced covertly over to Míster Lurkin, who lowered his hat over his eyes. The ex-Governor had been following Lurkin's advice in everything, deciding he would know more about how to negotiate with his countrymen. Whichever flag flew over the territory, Alvarado wanted it recognized that he and the other Dons owned their land, and cattle and horses. And he knew Lurkin wanted to make sure that nobody would think that a change in governments meant that debts would be canceled. Lurkin would want it clear that a debt owed to a merchant was much more enduring than a government, and he would want the Dons to keep their land so that they could continue to pay him with next year's hides and tallow.

At a flash from the gold ring with the curious symbol on Lurkin's hand, the ex-Governor rose to his feet.

— ¡A los osos! he shouted.

A bull and bear were brought into the corral and held by lariats until a rawhide rope was attached to the hind foot of the bear and the front hoof of the bull. The bull's eyes were white with terror as it pawed the beaten earth, separated from the herd for the first time in its life, and the grizzly reared up on its hind legs and roared. The band played a jota from northern Spain to goad the animals to violence, while caballeros wagered money they didn't have on one of the beasts and the señoritas prettily called for blood in their musical voices. Then the bull charged, tossing its horns at anything that moved, and the bear took the charge in its right side with a rage that was admirable, and broke the bull's neck with its left paw while they tumbled over into a ragged ball.

The dead bull was dragged away, and another bull was brought into the ring and tethered to the bear. Again the crowd shouted and the music played until the bear stood and the bull charged, and the grizzly once more rose up from the blood and sand, wounded but alive with rage. Míster Lurkin leaned over to the Commodore and confided in him that the bulls always won, sooner or later.

— Why? asked the Commodore. When the bear is a superior beast?

— Fecundity, Míster Lurkin said. There will always be more bulls than bears.

Four more bulls were brought into the ring, and each drew blood before tumbling lifeless to the ground with its spinal cord snapped. When the seventh bull was ushered in, snorting and terrified, the bear rose on its hind legs and roared at the men with silver fringed coats and the women in lace and pearls.

Weak and trembling, he roared at them in rage and shame at paying their blood price, at watering the ground with blood that should be theirs, to make the land sacred to their God and wash clean the sin of taking the land from the gods who lived in every seedpod. Then the bull rushed at the bear and buried its horns deep into the grizzly's viscera, avoided the death blow of the raking left paw and threw the bear high into the air, where it seemed to fly, weightless for a moment, before settling lifeless onto the dark caked ground. The bull whirled and dug its horns again into the side of the grizzly, shoving it five feet along the ground before leaving it to be still.

The bull trotted around the ring, bellowing to be allowed out, back to its *manada*, its *querencia* in the hills. Instead, a man with a sword in his right hand and a small red flag on a three-foot-long staff in his left hand entered the ring. It was the second son of Don Ignacio, Fidel Segundón, dressed for the fiesta in his cutaway coat of brocaded silk, linen shirt, purple sash around his waist. He whistled at the bull, waved the flag to catch the nearsighted animal's attention. The bull turned, caught sight of an object to which it could attach all its fears. It pawed the ground, blood streaming from its hump where the bear had raked it, and made at the bobbing red flag. As it passed its horns through the insubstantial air, Fidel gave a shrewd thrust of his sword from the side, and the bull fell dead, blood gushing from its mouth and nostrils.

The crowd of onlookers cheered, and the music played celebrating the victory of the domestic beast over the wild beast, and the victory of man over both. The last bull was dragged out, to be flayed with the others and diced up into a savory stew to be eaten by all who had witnessed the spectacle. The bear would be skinned and left to the vultures, as the Californios would not eat its flesh because the taste was not pleasing, and the Ohlone would not eat of it because the entrails of a bear are exactly like those of a human being.

As the bull and bear were dragged out, Fidel Segundón bowed to the crowd, swept his Peruvian wool hat from his head, and acknowledged the shouts of approval that came from all four directions. Then he put his hat back on and slipped his sword under his sash.

— De parte de mi padre, ¿Qué americano puede hacer igual?

The crowd murmured, uncertain of how the new regime would take such a challenge on its second day of power, wondering perhaps what new rituals would arrive with the Americans. Captain Rafael Rafael asked what had been said, and Lurkin tilted his head and spoke quietly, so that Rafael Rafael had to lean toward him to hear.

— He asks, can any American do the same? Captain? Could you do the same?

Even though Míster Lurkin's eyes were shadowed by the brim of his hat, Captain Rafael Rafael felt he was watching him shrewdly.

— You could win the people over to you, Captain. You could win the love of those native to this place.

Rafael Rafael tried to force his vision through the shadow, to see clearly the almost recognizable face, as the voice buzzed on, describing for him exactly what he desired, painting for him in the most vivid colors the affection he could win for himself, the place in people's hearts, and in one person's heart, which could be as dear as a place in the past that he remembered, to which he could not return, or a place he dreamed about, where he could never arrive. Rafael heard all this in the low, insectlike buzzing of Lurkin's voice, uncertain whether what he heard was being spoken aloud or was just sounding inside his head, incited by the shadowed eyes of Míster Lurkin.

— ¿Qué americano puede hacer igual? shouted Don Ignacio's son.

Captain Rafael Rafael stood up, straight in his blue uniform with heavy gold epaulettes, and drew his sword from its scabbard. As he marched down to the corral, his fragile china-blue eyes seemed to look at every person in the crowd equally and individually, and the women spontaneously brought out handkerchiefs and waved them at him while he passed. Commodore Jones stood up, huge and curved, seeing in front of him what he was certain now would become the sign he sought, just before his proclamation.

Rafael Rafael entered the corral and took the small red flag from the son of Don Ignacio. Then he took off his highplumed fore-and-aft hat, bowed to the crowd in all four directions, and waited facing the gate.

A bull entered the ring, frightened and bleeding from a row of small paper flowers that ran along its spine, attached to its flesh by iron hooks, and a garland of beautifully cut and painted flowers nailed to its forehead. The Captain waved the red flag as he had seen Don Ignacio's son do. The bull, scared out of its wits, hurled itself at the flag, and passed the Captain too fast for him to slip more than an inch of blade into its side before butting its head against a post of the corral and making the entire rude structure shake.

The Captain backed to the other end of the corral and shook the red flag. The bull charged at the flag, tossing its horns at the insubstantial enemy it had been decorated to be slaughtered by. Captain Rafael Rafael again sought a vital spot, but hit bone instead, and as the bull tossed in torment, the sword was ripped from his hands and flung outside the corral.

The Captain backed again to the other end of the corral, defenseless now save for the red flag. He heard Míster Lurkin's voice still burring inside his head, promising so much of his desire, and leaving the corral did not seem possible without despair, and perhaps he would arrive at a place he dreamed about only with this bull, dressed for sacrifice, bleeding from several places and pawing the earth, fixing its nearsighted eyes on its would-be executioner.

Then the *desterrados* danced up to the edge of the corral, still holding the portrait of the Virgin, and Arcadia stepped between the fence posts. She saw Rafael Rafael facing the bull, and it was as though she were seeing replayed the scene of her father's death, a scene that she seemed to remember although she had not been there. Rafael Rafael stood unarmed before the bull, and she stepped between them, trusting in her charm and her sacredness of that day, as she would have done for her father had she been able. She held out her hand toward the bull.

— Stay, toro, and don't charge. Stay, and live.

Arcadia had chosen Rafael Rafael, and though it be blasphemous, she wouldn't allow God now to choose between him and the bull.

— In the name of Saint Francis and Santa Teresa.

The bull pawed the ground in uneasy fear.

—In the name of the Virgin, don't charge.

The bull lowered its head, but a pistol shot split the air and the bull dropped to its knees. Major McCormick stepped into the corral, stuffed one pistol back in his belt and drew another. He took aim and blew a lead ball behind the bull's right ear.

— I may not know why a bull has to be killed. But if one must, I can kill it well enough with my gun, he said, pulling on his crotch.

Arcadia looked first at the fallen bull, certain that God had chosen despite her hope that all might live. Then she looked back at Rafael Rafael, who stood oblivious of all else in the world besides her presence.

The Commodore stared before him. The virgin in the center of the circle. The beast, the dragon, slain by American arms. The blue-eyed man, now free to possess the arena. He had to find a manifest sign somehow, and this might be as close as he could get.

He fumbled with the papers that contained the proclamation, dropping them once and mixing them up. Míster Lurkin touched the brim of his hat, an ambiguous gesture that made the ex-Governor Alvarado leap to his feet and call the people's attention to the dais, shouting that the American leader was about to make a historic proclamation. Hannibal Memory stood by, waiting to see if the Commodore would read the lines he had prepared. The crowd gathered around the corral now turned toward the dais, eager, fearful, wondering how they would be brought into American history.

The Commodore stood up, attempting to put the papers on which the speech was written in a kind of order. He loomed over the interior of the Presidio, a human question mark, cleared his throat, and began to speak.

— To the inhabitants of California.

— Although I come in arms, as the representative of a powerful nation upon whom, (it is believed), the Central Government of Mexico has waged war, I come not to spread desolation, the dread consequences of the unjust war into which (so the story goes) Mexico has suddenly plunged you.

— Instead, I come to bring you into the realm of freedom and democracy, in the name of our pure guiding spirit, Louisa Darling. The Stars and Stripes, infallible emblems of freedom and democracy, now float triumphantly before you, and henceforth and forever (it is hoped) this flag will offer you protection and security.

— The manifest sign of the rightness of American possession, the superiority of American ideals is . . . he cleared his throat . . . the slaying of the bull, the safety of the virgin, the virile courage of American men devoted to those ideals.

He shuffled through the papers once more.

— Love, he said. We come to bring love into the land. We love to exchange the land for ever more money. Freedom to buy and sell the land, ripe fields for American Commerce. Love for the land shouldn't be like constipation; don't hold on to it until it hurts. Land isn't free until it can be bought and sold. Now you will be free to be bought and sold.

The Commodore grew confused, unsure of what he was

saying. Waxdeck's words didn't seem to make any sense. He snatched another leaf of paper out of the jumble.

— We love American arms. The superior strength of American arms, and the oral tradition we bring to California. American arms are now overwhelming, ravishing. You, the peaceful citizens of California, will feel forever embraced by American arms.

Commodore Jones blushed, plucked out another piece of paper, and read quickly.

— Warrior's genius rhymes with horse's penis.

He dropped the pile of papers, utterly distraught at the botch he was making of the proclamation. Hannibal picked up the pile and handed him one paper, whispering, — Here is the peroration.

— Thank the Lord, Commodore Jones replied.

He read off the single leaf of paper in rounded tones.

— As Louisa Darling is the true spirit of freedom and democracy, all I have said is so. As she is the living embodiment of American ideals, California will enter into the great history of America, the inevitable progress of those ideals across the continent.

Hannibal silently thanked Jack Chase for his refresher course in logical fallacies, particularly reasoning from false premises.

— All the rights and privileges you now enjoy will be secured to all who remain peaceably at home and offer no resistance to the forces of the United States. All provisions and supplies for the use of the United States, their ships, and their soldiers, will be paid for at fair rates. No private property will be taken for public use without just compensation.

signed Commander in Chief, U.S. Naval Forces of the Pacific, Thomas ap Catesby Jones.

The end of the pronouncement brought a prolonged silence, as nobody had prepared a translation and none of the Californios spoke English. Still in the corral, Rafael Rafael and Arcadia looked at each other in silence, as though they were going to fall into each other's eyes. Major McCormick pulled on his crotch, and Hannibal thought he was on the verge of escaping the history in which he and his people were slaves. Then Míster Lurkin shouted an impromptu translation in Spanish, emphasizing that the Stars and Stripes protected the rights of merchants to charge whatever the market would bear, but that the Dons still owned all their infinite leagues of land encumbered with debt and would for all eternity. This inspired the musicians again to play a jota, and men and women crowded onto the blood-soaked soil to dance.

As the women raised clotted dust with the wooden heels of their satin shoes, and the men shouted verses of tribute to ethereal beauty and undying desire, Arcadia's uncle and aunt appeared and had servants lift her onto a horse. Don Ignacio was also there, sadly sitting on his stallion, no longer wearing the elk horns. Captain Rafael Rafael would have tried to stop them from carrying her off but for the sudden eruption of a raiding party into the Presidio, led by Don Bragas de León, the lionhearted one. Inflamed by the latest rumors that Micheltorena was on the march with seven hundred men, Don León led five horsemen on a daring daylight raid into the midst of the celebration, where they wheeled around the plaza and lassoed a barbecued side of beef and a sack of flour, and Sergeant Vargas, his face masked in imitation of Ivanhoe, rescued an entire tub of lard, carrying it in his arms and holding his reins in his teeth, for the guerrillas had forgotten to take any food with them on their valiant march into the mountains to oppose the new Master of Monterey, and they were on the brink of starvation.

PART THREE

Chapter One

Although at the apogee of his power, the Commodore could not sleep that night, as all seemed fleeting and tenuous. He spent the night gliding back and forth across the beaten-earth floor of the quarters he had taken in the Presidio, pondering the possibility that Mexico and the United States were not at war on the Southern Marches, and the rumors that Micheltorena had seven hundred and fifty men under arms. He wondered whether he had gotten the sign wrong, whether freedom and democracy were truly established in California. And he grew most pensive when he thought about Louisa Darling. No matter what lands he possessed in her name, no matter how far he spread the realm of freedom and democracy, he was uncertain that the end of his journeys would come until all his intentions had ended in her love.

Just outside his door, Hannibal Memory slept soundly, snoring now and then, content that the Commodore's proclamation had opened a way for him to author his own line. But two doors down, Captain Rafael Rafael was also pacing, thinking about the woman in black who walked with the Virgin, who had looked at him in a way that made him forget death. Míster Lurkin had told him her name, Arcadia Serrano, although she was promised, it was understood, to Don Ignacio Castro, one of the most powerful landowners in California.

When the sun dawned the next day, the boatswain blew his pipes to the rising sun in a way that quickened the heart of every Jack Tar aboard ship. Liberty, liberty, sailor's liberty ashore on the newly conquered land. One quarter of the crew at a time, for twenty-four hours, sailor's liberty in Monterey. Lots were drawn, and the starboard-quarter watch, the watch of Jack Chase and Jimmy F. Bush, was chosen to be the first of the common sailors to go ashore.

As the starboard-quarter watch drew buckets of fresh water, which was allowed in port, and soaped and rinsed themselves naked on deck, and brought out their go-ashore white duck trousers and blue jackets and neckerchiefs and beribboned straw hats, Chips took advantage of the commotion to creep quietly into the midshipmen's quarters, where William Waxdeck lay. The butterfly-shaped plate of silver in Chips's skull glinted softly as he slipped into the compartment, deserted except for the pale youth lying on a bunk littered with papers. Chips scratched his bearded cheek. Waxdeck slept, as he had hoped, a carven marble visage with a drop of green at the corner of the mouth.

Chips was afraid of Waxdeck, as he was afraid of all those whose words had power, the ship's officers who could make men climb up flimsy rigging in a tempest to take in sail, the Captain who could with a word make a man a spread-eagle on the rigging to be marked with a dozen stripes from the colt, the Commodore who could turn a line of ships into battle with a simple utterance. He was afraid of them, and he had always worshiped them and served them, out of awe at their magnificence, and out of rancor and envy that he would never be like them. In his long seagoing career, which had begun further back than his own memory reached, he had sunk down in the ship's levels, from a maintopman, to a gunner's mate (where he had received the cavernous head wound stopped with silver), to the ship's carpenter concerned only with the keel and keelson deep in the bilges.

But now, as the bilges filled with seeping sea water that had a tang of blood, and the oakum had been used up or sold by Keyes, he felt compelled to sneak up on Waxdeck. Chips's mouth was a ragged circle, and he stifled a moan of fear as he approached on his hands and knees, in a position of obeisance should the poet awake. At the foot of the bed, he lifted carefully from the blanket a number of sheets of paper, marked with even hexameters in India ink, though to Chips they were merely terrifying symbols that he clutched away from his sight, as though they were the head of a Gorgon. Then he backed up slowly, still bowed down, until, two steps from the door, he turned and scrambled out in a panic. Waxdeck stirred on the bed, but did not wake.

Chips scuttled down to the bilges, where the water continued to creep higher, and wondered at the papers in his hands. He wished he knew something about words, and how to give them power. He wished he knew how to use these words in his hands, change them to make the pumps be manned and the leaks be fixed. One family of rats hovered near him, crouched in the shadow of the ship's ribs, questioning him about the leak with their sensitive quivering noses. But another family of rats, companions of his for many voyages to fight and conquer, had deserted ship, clutching to the stern of one of the stealthy boats that ghosted in with muffled oars under the chains at midnight. This family of rats too would soon be gone as well, recognizing no allegiance to the *National Intention*.

He wondered at the letters again, slim discrete marks on the page that frightened him even though he had them in his possession. *That Jones who brought to California's Breast / The blessings of our Destiny Man'fest*. He moaned as he took up the bucket of tar he had prepared, warm and gooey, as there was no more oakum to be had aboard ship. He took up the thick round brush, the sash tool, and gobbed tar onto both sides of one sheet of paper, melting the ink into one black smear. Then he took the tar-soaked paper and dove into the bilge, down where the ribs met the keel and water seeped in, and he shoved the paper between the timbers, holding his breath and tamping it in with a long-handled maul. He came up for air, soaked another leaf of paper in solid black, and dove again.

The yeoman, Keyes, sat in the ship's waist with a marine guard at his back and several buckskin bags of silver dollars before him. As the liberty-men filed by, he counted out six dollars and marked carefully beside their names on the pay list, anguished at having to hand out money and consoled only by the fact that some of it would go to the stores of the captivating Míster Lurkin, who might then use it to buy more of the ship's goods, which Keyes would arrange to smuggle off. The circulation of money and goods, he reminded himself, would lead to the prosperity of all, until the sailors were drunk and penniless.

Jimmy sat at Jack Chase's side in the stern sheets of the first liberty boat, being rowed ashore like pay passengers by members of the port-quarter watch. He had the lambskin draped over his left shoulder, and he wore his blue jacket loose so it wouldn't chafe his back, scourged and suppurating from his last flogging. To the east, beyond the pueblo, twisting, tree-lined creeks ran to the bay between smooth hills of grass studded with solitary oak trees. Higher in the hills, tall evergreens, fir and redwood. A low blanket of sea fog softened over the pueblo, frayed into separate mist clouds in the tall trees, weightless and floating in the green prickly branches.

When the liberty-men set foot ashore, every one of them breathed in deeply, feeling master of himself and his time for the first time in months. They walked past the Custom House onto the rutted oxcart path that led to the Presidio, digging their feet into the plush, unaccustomed ground, six men suddenly free from the *National Intention* and with wings on their feet. No bands greeted the liberty-men, no lines of dignitaries waited for them. But Míster Lurkin sat behind the counter of his trading house, ready with bottles and cups, where Jack Chase led them all for a round of pulque.

They drank to the new land, which they had won for freedom. They drank to the end of the continent, and an end to wandering at last. They drank to the paradise found, where generous abundance would reign and contentment only was man's lot. They drank to themselves, the liberty-men, who had won the victory. And as they drank, wet the swab, spliced the main brace, and pushed more dollars across the counter to Míster Lurkin, California grew ever more lovely in their minds, and their own joy in freedom more invincible. They drank royally and gloriously, drank until they believed that everything they desired would come to them with the speaking of the word and their word was always the same: drink. They drank until they believed it would always be thus.

Jimmy drank with the rest, paid for rounds with his store of dollars and downed the thick, warm liquor. From the rafters of the trading house hung a wedding dress, stiff and white, along with woven lariats and iron ploughshares. On the floor, barrels of seed corn and gunpowder crowded together, and the walls crawled with shelves, overflowing with calico and silk, cheap shoes and dried fruits and boxes of shot. Jimmy recognized some things from the *National Intention* — a kind of tinned biscuit, rolls of marline, and boxes of sewing needles — only now they didn't seem to belong to the *National Intention*, but rather to anyone — himself — who could rap the counter with a dollar. Someone called for another round, and Jimmy held up a fistful of coins.

— I'll pay, he said. I'll pay.

Jack Chase didn't seem drunk, no matter how many rounds of pulque were hoisted. Even when they had drunk enough to declare themselves sovereigns of all California, to proclaim that the land was their new homeland and that they would never leave, Jack drank as one who had many times declared his freedom to be invincible and as many times found himself back aboard one of the countless warships of the world. When Major McCormick and a squad of marines showed up at the door of the trading house, Jack didn't show surprise but only continued to sip his drink.

— Is everything in order, sir? asked the Major.

— Indeed, Míster Lurkin said, scraping a dollar into a drawer. Everything is in order.

— I wanted to remember the starboard-quarter watch, McCormick said, that their liberty ends tomorrow. We'll need them back aboard the *National Intention* then. Especially you, he said, fixing Jimmy with a piercing stare. To keep the ship on an even keel.

— Aye, Major, Jack Chase said. We are remembered.

When the Major left, nobody called for a drink. The liberty-men had plummeted from the heights of delirium to the pit of ashes, and they thought that their liberty would only last twenty-four hours, and their sovereignty only as long as they could push a dollar across the counter to the man with shadowed eyes. Jimmy felt in his pockets and found that he had spent every penny, and he staggered over to Jack's side. Jack put an arm around his shoulder and straightened him up.

— If you want to find your mother and father, you'd best go now. Perhaps you'll find them in a home I know naught of. You've paid with flesh enough, and more. Let the rest of us be damned to keeping the *National Intention* on an even keel.

He embraced Jimmy, then pushed him toward the door. Before he reached the threshold, Míster Lurkin called to him.

— Lad, he said. You might want some coin if you're leaving. I've admired that lambskin you're wearing, and just as a favor to you, I'll give you back what you've spent here in exchange for it.

Jimmy looked at Jack, but the older seaman gave no tells and left it his own decision. He looked back at the shadow over Lurkin's face. Then he turned and stumbled over the threshold.

Jack Chase spoke to Míster Lurkin as though he could see through to the Trader's eyes.

— He's going beyond your reach. Out of circulation, you might say.

— For the time being, Lurkin said. *Et in Arcadia Ego.*

Out the door, Jimmy F. Bush fell into a new world. The light of midmorning seemed thick and liquid, blurring the rounded hills and the dusky forest with a wash of gold. He staggered east, in the direction the light came from, certain that he was at last heading in the right direction, toward a rendezvous with his mother and father, who even now might be descending over the last foothills and into the great valley of California. He strayed off the ox-rutted path, following his own true compass, and barely pausing to vomit out a stew of eleven glasses of pulque, as well as that morning's lob-scouse, and the previous day's burgoo and dunderfunk.

On the edge of town, a group of Ohlone vaqueros were smoking hand-rolled cigarettes, while behind them a mare was grazing on the green, new-grown grass. The vaqueros didn't pay any attention to the mare, as none of them would ever ride anything but a stallion, and they had only the week before stampeded a herd of the overly plentiful mustangs into the sea to leave more pasturage for cattle. When they saw Jimmy walk unsteadily toward them, with a face pale as linen, they took off their hats to him. Jimmy took off his hat in turn, and he pointed at the mare.

— Can I use that horse? he asked.

The vaqueros didn't understand him, as they only spoke two languages, and if they had understood him, they would have laughed, as the mare belonged to nobody. One of them, thinking that the boy was perhaps scared of the mare, slapped it on the hindquarters, and it moved several steps away.

— Here, Jimmy said. Take my hat. And my neckerchief.

The vaqueros took the hat and scarf into their hands, turning them over, admiring the dark blue of the scarf without understanding at all what the boy was saying. Jimmy then took off his jacket and shoes, and handed them over. The vaqueros were confused, and asked each other if giving away clothing was some strange custom of the new people who had come. Jimmy explained in very clear and simple English that he wanted to give them something for the horse grazing behind them, but they only discussed low among themselves what it could mean, handing the clothing from person to person and giving no sign that Jimmy could interpret as meaning that they were willing to part with the mare, in which, after all, they had no interest whatsoever.

Then he took off his jersey and handed that over, and walked through the Ohlones to the mare, his lambskin draped across one naked shoulder. Jimmy's back crawled with luminous red flesh and hung with loose strings of skin, and it seemed to pulse as though one could see right through the punished body to the heart. He turned to face them, one hand on the mare's neck, his pale white skin barely stretching to fit over a pointy rack of bone.

The vaqueros felt a sudden awe at the boy. One of them wondered aloud whether all the people of the ship had raw wounds under their uniforms, and another asked if they all wore their hearts so close to the surface under mere rags of flesh. A third stated that although he had often seen *indígenas* beaten and had been beaten himself more than once, he had never seen a white man beaten. This boy, then, must be special in some way. Finally, one who was more pragmatic said that the boy obviously wanted the mare. They should put him on it, because whoever beat him before might come looking for him again, and beat them as well, as they would certainly beat an *indio* with less cause than a white man. This they all knew.

The last one to speak knotted a hackamore for the mare, pushed it over her nose and around her cheeks, and then cupped his hands for Jimmy to mount.

— Is it my horse now? Jimmy asked.

The vaquero, although he didn't understand the question, explained that the horse belonged to nobody, that it was nobody's horse. He explained it first in the tongue of his people, and then in Spanish, that it was nobody's horse.

Jimmy placed his foot in the cupped hands and pushed himself up onto the mare's saddleless back.

— My horse, he said.

Jimmy took the mare around in a circle, testing the hackamore against the mare's understandable desire to stay right where she was and continue grazing. Then he kicked the mare in the ribs, and the pragmatic vaquero slapped it on the flank with his hat, and Jimmy rode off to the east.

He kept the mare mostly at a walk, as he was afraid he would fall off at a gallop, and when he tried to go at a trot, he felt so shaken that he vomited out whatever vestiges of shipboard food that had remained. As he rode, he began to feel light and empty. His stomach was beginning to shrivel and his skin stretched tight upon his face. The world still seemed new and blurry, and as he rode, he sometimes had the feeling that his body was about to burst into feather.

Jimmy rode easterly for three days. The mare walked willingly where he directed her, because there were fresh grasses everywhere, and she ate as she went, growing fatter and rounder as her rider grew thinner and lighter. At the end of the first day, Jimmy's pants split and he rode with his back leaking and only the fleece for covering. He spent that night in a tree with the mare tied to the trunk, wakeful throughout the night while the horse below grazed and dozed. On the second day, he passed through the village of Temecula, home of Pablo Assis and his young son, Alessandro, who was destined to be Ramona's unhappy husband and end in madness. As he rode through the village, people turned from him in fright and horror, although some women thought he looked like the Savior and ran out to kiss his feet and weep over his whipped and sun-beaten shoulders.

On the third day, Jimmy struck the San Benito River and rode through the deep earthquake fault below the crumbling Mission San Juan Bautista. His head was light now, after three days without food, and everything seemed to waver brightly and unsteadily in his vision. Oak trees seemed to shimmer, as though illuminated by an inner fire that was always on the verge of breaking through, and each turning oak leaf was a quaking flame. The large stones that stood out in the fields shifted position, animate and unpredictable. He knew, somewhere in his floating mind, that he was looking for his mother and father. But his mother and father had become unstuck from his image of them. He no longer could remember what they looked like. Perhaps they were that deer there, that black bird with flashes of white on its wings that looked at him curiously as he walked, that large-eared coyote.

At the end of the day, he entered a ranchería of tule huts scattered around a grassless open space. People walked out and surrounded him, and one man took the rope hackamore from him. When Jimmy felt the rope slide from his hand, he thought for a moment he would rise into the air. But instead he fell down from the horse, into the arms of the village men and women around him.

The ranchería was called by its people Pagsin. It was a hybrid village, made up mostly of former neophytes from the missions who, when the mission system decayed and fell after secularization, had sought out again a way of life they only had notions of in remembered old songs and dances, and in the minds of a few old ones. They had settled just beyond the boundaries of the land grants, joining with a few gentile natives from tribes that, although they had not been blessed with Christian Instruction, had still been instructed in the ways of smallpox and syphilis, and they spoke a fractured and pieced-together language, made up of Yokuts, Plains Miwok, Patwin, Ohlone, Spanish, and the Latin they had recited ignorantly on Holy Days.

They laid Jimmy down gently, but when he felt the ground bite into his back, he rolled over. One old woman peeled off part of the lambskin, and saw his back glowing and pulsing, crawling with naked ropes of muscle.

Vade retro, Satana! she said as she had been taught, and they all drew back, leaving Jimmy prone and moaning in the middle of the ring.

— What does this mean? they asked each other, and they looked to their Chief Man to speak.

The Chief Man was one of the only survivors from a small tribe, a man who had never been to the missions, and he had been chosen chief because he still knew when to tell the people to go out and gather acorns, when to tell them to collect duck eggs and, later, fledglings. He knew how to wear a deer's head on his brow and paw in the grass, to draw the deer close enough for the kill, and he had been taught to close up a dead deer's eyeholes when its flesh was being dressed, so that its spirit would not be shocked and it would come again next year and bring its brothers.

But as he looked at Jimmy, he didn't know what to do, because he didn't know what the boy meant. Nothing seemed to mean in the same way it used to, in the way it did in songs. The world was more confounding now than it had been for his grandfather. Even his language seemed to be decaying, as he could not speak it with the people, and he found himself speaking words of Spanish as the world ripped around him. He had a dream he could not control, a dream in which he had lost a word. The word was not a physical object, but in his dream he looked for it as though it were a physical object, under rocks and along the banks of the slough. The word was lost, and when he tried to speak it, foreign words came from his mouth, which were sometimes close, but never just the right word, and the word he was seeking was the central word, and no other words meant what they were supposed to without the word as a roof pole. All other words meant what they meant in relation to that word he had lost. When the sun came up in the morning, he was still looking in his dream. He had dreamed this many times.

Jimmy raised up his head and saw the Chief Man deliberating. He said in pained syllables that he was looking for his mother and father, but he had discovered while riding that he no longer knew exactly who or what they were, they were changing, shedding their skin, and he didn't know if they were only going to turn out the same on the inside as on the outside. — I only lost them because they were always moving, and I'm moving because I want to find them. But if I go to where they were, I'll never be where they are.

Exhausted, Jimmy let his head go limp.

The boy's words troubled the Chief Man further, although he kept his face impassive. If the boy had come with a bundle of arrows clutched in his hand, the Chief would have known what that meant. Or if he had come with white feathers threaded on top of a wand, or a cord with seven knots, he would have known what that meant. But he had come on a horse with his back flayed, and he spoke a rude and uncouth tongue, and the Chief suddenly feared that some of the boy's words were the words he himself had spoken in his dream, in search of the lost word.

The people were still looking at him, waiting for him to speak. The last thing he wanted to do was to make a hasty decision that would lead the ranchería into bad luck, war from the boy's people, or haunting from the boy's ghost.

At last he said, — Where is the Doctor?

— Away from the village, one answered. Since morning.

That pleased the Chief Man. He didn't like the Doctor, but he was afraid of her. Nobody knew where she went when she left. She might be out gathering herbs, or she might be singing in a secret place. But she had not been there to keep this sickness and disorder from entering the world. The best solution was perhaps to let the Doctor decide what to do, and then blame her if the decision proved ill.

— The Doctor will return soon, the Chief Man said. Perhaps the boy is to be cured, and she will do so.

Then Sigelizu Joseph stepped forward, a man who had been a neophyte at Carmel Mission. He had refused to work for the great landowners once the mission lands had passed into their hands, and he had been one of the leaders of those who had chosen to seek out a place beyond the land grants. He had always been a rival of the Chief Man because he knew more about the white men who now lived near the shore, and he had powerful dreams that the tribe would once again live by the ocean.

— No, he said. This boy cannot be cured. None of them can be cured. They are all wounded, and they will kill us to cure themselves, but they cannot be cured. I know who this boy is. He is the rolling head.

A shudder ran through the crowd, and the Chief Man stepped back from Jimmy. They all knew the story. It belonged to Sigelizu Joseph, and he had told it before. But now he told it

again, to put the boy into it, so that the boy would no longer be
unknowable, so that he would exist in their language.

A group of four brothers was living together
The youngest brother had not yet been marked by Kuksu
He could not stay in the sweat lodge for long
And he had not yet dreamed of killing a deer.
    All this, his brothers knew
    And they said to him:
        Stay home while we hunt
        Stay home and gather acorns
        Stay home and help our mother
        Stay home!
But the boy had a dream that he tasted blood
    with his brothers.
A dangerous dream!
                    (but the boy didn't know it)
A bloody dream.
A dream of blood.
And when the brothers went out to hunt
With their talking bows and favorite arrows
    (you see, they knew how)
The boy followed them.
The boy followed them even though he was forbidden.
The boy followed them to the edge of a meadow
Where one brother waved a piece of deerskin
To attract the curious antelope.
    The brothers knew he was there
    But they did not speak to him.

But they did not take notice of him.

The brothers wanted him not there.

The boy took out his bow and one arrow.

(It was like his dream)

And he said, "I'll shoot the antelope, and we'll dry the meat."

And he said, "Antelope meat is better than acorns."

And he said, "We'll store antelope meat for the winter."

But he cut his finger on the arrowhead

And he began to bleed.

He began to bleed red blood.

At first he wiped it away.

But then he licked it.

(It was like his dream, you see)

And it tasted good.

He sucked the sweet fat out of his finger,

And then he ate the finger and he ate his hand.

The curious antelope turned and ran away,

Turned and ran away before any arrows were shot,

And the brothers knew that something was wrong.

"Where is the boy?" they asked.

"The boy who should have stayed home?"

The boy was tearing off pieces of his own flesh.

The boy was tearing off and eating pieces of

his own flesh

Until there was nothing left but his head.

The brothers asked, "Where is the boy?"

Until the boy's head bounced and rolled toward them.

(There was no more body, you see)

The brothers began to run for their sweat lodge.

But the rolling head caught one of them.

    Caught him,

    Killed him,

    Ate him.

The other two went into the sweat lodge and put logs
    over the entry.

They placed a sandstone over the smoke hole.

    The rolling head said:

        "Let me in, my brothers."

The brothers whispered to each other, "Don't let him in."

    The rolling head said again:

        "Let me in, my brothers."

The brothers whispered to each other, "Don't let him in."

    When he saw they would not let him in, he reared back

    And came at the sweat lodge with a great rush.

        (He was strong, you see)

    The sweat lodge shook, but did not burst.

    He came at the sweat lodge many times.

    Each time, it shook, but did not burst.

        (The sweat lodge was strong, you see)

The rolling head stopped and lay on the ground.

    "I dreamt I was with my brothers and I tasted blood,"
        it said.

    "Where will I go now?"

It bounded west and met some people,

Threw them in its mouth,

Ate them.

It went around the world, searching for people.

Each evening, it comes home to the closed sweat lodge.

Each morning, it goes around the world, searching
   for people.
Always, it goes searching
That is all.

— That's who this boy is, Sigelizu Joseph said. He has not yet become a monster, but he will. The best place for his head is on a pike outside the village, to warn off other rolling heads. Those who have been among them know I am right.

The Chief Man knew that if he let the boy be killed now, Sigelizu Joseph would gain power. But he thought, looking around the faces of the people, that most of them wanted the boy killed, either for revenge on the whites, or to rid the world of a monster, or just because they were afraid. The Chief Man knew he had remained Chief because he had done what the people wanted to do anyway. But now he didn't know what to do. Even if they followed the counsel of Sigelizu Joseph, any bad luck that followed would be blamed on him. He thought now that if he knew the word that he had lost, if he could speak the word he searched for in his dream, he would know exactly what should be done.

Then he heard the moth cocoon rattles of the Doctor, and he felt relieved that he would not have to decide. Sigelizu Joseph was as afraid of her as he was, and nobody would go against her word.

The Doctor walked into the circle, wearing a skirt of over-lapping raven feathers and a headdress of red flicker feathers woven into basketry, and she carried her otterskin medicine bundle. Everyone knew then that she had been singing, not just gathering herbs, singing in her secret place. Three blue bars were tattooed down her chin, and her ears and nose were pierced and held ornaments of abalone, like the women who knew. She walked all around Jimmy, who lay quiet with his back raw and crawling, and then she looked at the Chief Man.

— What has he brought as a gift? she asked.

— The mare, there, the Chief Man said after a moment's hesitation. And the skin.

— Good, good.

She lifted the fleece gently from Jimmy's back and understood exactly what his problem was. The Doctor was an old woman, old enough to have seen the last years of Junípero Serra's life. She had been stolen by Spanish soldiers on a recruiting mission for Carmel Mission when she was three years old, and her parents, out of love for her, had left the mountains three days later and joined others from their tribe under the direction of the Franciscans. She remembered seeing Junípero Serra strip himself to the waist and hold a candle flame to his naked flesh until it burned, and then whip himself with a scourge until his back was cut and bleeding, much like this boy's was now. Once, during one of Serra's self-mutilations, an Indian overcome with emotion had leaped up with tears in his eyes, taken the scourge from Serra's hand, and beat himself until he passed out. When the Indian died the next day, she remembered the Padre Presidente teaching that he had gone without a doubt directly to Paradise and was sitting at the right hand of God. Beatings were blessings, he taught, and so nobody should complain when they were beaten or put in the stocks for failing to hoe the garden or pronounce Latin properly.

Despite the padre's teachings, she hadn't truly understood anything about the mortification of the flesh until she had become a doctor, in the year after the missions closed. Then, although she was already an old woman, she had a dream in which she was dancing on the brink of the world, and she saw blood dripping from the seam between sea and sky. She saw someone dressed something like a padre, gray-robed, a child of the Mule, who broke off a piece of the horizon and gave it to her, saying, "The horizon is blood." It was like a sharp piece of ice, cold and bloody and sharp at both ends in her mouth. This was her first pain.

She was sick four days before she could control the pain. Then, with another doctor present, she craved something from the ocean. A piece of abalone was brought to her, and when she swallowed it, she felt nauseous. The other doctor said — Let it come out. And she vomited forth her pain, sharp-tipped and bloody. Then, at the other doctor's direction, she sucked it back in again, and was able to keep it in her body and control it.

As she took the path of curing, she was able to suck other people's pains out of them — sometimes bits of coyote fur, or grasshopper legs, or cougar whiskers, or small lizards — and when she could swallow them and control them, she became a more powerful and respected doctor. And as she gained in power, she began to understand the Padre Presidente, staring at a crucifix held in his left hand and whipping himself with a metal-tipped scourge. He had a pain inside him, a pain perhaps near the heart or near the groin, a pain he had never been able to control. He was trying to find the location of the pain, to make it come out, so he could take it back inside him and control it. But he had never been able to, and so he hated his body, because it had a pain inside it, incurable and uncontrollable. And he turned to trying to make his pain come out of others who did not have his pain, beating them for the relief of his hatred.

This boy, lying on the ground, had the same pain as Serra. She could see it inside him, glowing through the suppurating flesh. She placed the lambskin on the earth beside him, sat down on it, and took an eagle feather from her medicine bundle. She began to sing softly.

> Back well.
> Well back.
> You are well
> > on your way back.

Jimmy felt hands cool on his back, working some kind of poultice into his wounds, draping them with cobwebs. He revived, lifted his head up to see an old woman waving a feather over his back and singing softly. He saw her eyes note his open, and he felt her singing change, her song lines become questions asking for him to respond. The Doctor sang in her language —

> Good sun, I wish to get well
> Water, run not over me
> Open, cloud, my body
> Good sun, go down to the water

When she repeated her song, Jimmy responded —

Good sun, I wish to get well
> *I don't know where I was born*

Water, run not over me.
> *I'm tired of looking*

Open, cloud, my body
> *I want to be home at last*

Good sun, go down to the water
> *A place where I don't have to move*

The Doctor nodded. The sick should repeat what the doctor said, and so far as she could tell, he had in his own way. She took from her medicine bundle a bone tube and began to seek for the exact location of the pain in his body. The people around her and the boy leaned in, half afraid but fascinated by her medicine. She ran her hands over him, gradually centering on a spot that was hot and crawling. Her face stiffened, and she wrapped her lips around the bone tube, put the other end of the tube onto the spot on the boy's body she had found, and began to suck. She sucked ferociously at the pain, calling on all her allies, all the powers she had gained through chanting and dancing, all the other pains she had controlled and held inside her. Then she gagged terribly, retched out into her hand what she had sucked up from the boy's body.

It was a centipede, a hundred-legged beast, all of its legs still moving like lines of restless oars down its armored back, twisting and writhing, trying to march forward.

She held it up for the people to see, then she sat down, exhausted.

— Is the pain good? the Chief Man asked.

— The pain is good, she answered. But she looked at the curling unquiet life in her hands and thought that she could not swallow this pain, could not take this one into her and control it. This pain would kill her.

Jimmy F. Bush rose unsteadily to his feet. He asked if he could stay with them. Until his back healed, or longer. He was tired of moving.

The Doctor spoke in a tired voice. — Put him in the prayer lodge and let him sweat out more poison.

— Do so, the Chief Man said.

Jimmy let four men lead him gently underground, into the darkness, to become forever lost to his old mother and father, to his shipmates, to his ship the *National Intention*. The Chief Man looked at the old woman doctor, sitting still and exhausted, and he wondered if she knew the word from his dream, the word he had lost. The Doctor contemplated with awful severity the pain in her hand, that hundred-legged American pain that she would never control if it were in her body.

Chapter Two

How brilliant and green that October morn when Commodore Jones arose to ride over the newly conquered land, a ride that would ever be known as JONES'S PROGRESS.

This was the thought that played in the mind of William Waxdeck as he awoke the morning on which Jimmy F. Bush and Jack Chase went ashore on liberty. He let a dribble of green bile into the bucket at his head, then picked up his pen to begin the description of the *Democratium Ferens* carrying freedom and democracy into the further reaches of the territory, stopping on the way to dispense justice, right wrongs, satisfy grievances, mend injuries, and truly take possession of the land by winning the hearts and minds of the people. Although Waxdeck knew that he was to describe events that had yet to take place, he found that all the more reason to begin early. More than anything, Waxdeck feared events that were errant in the world, events that wandered vaguely without a proper interpretation. Waxdeck knew what should happen and, more important, he knew the meanings to be drawn from what should happen. Therefore, it seemed a simple task and indeed a valuable precaution to set events down in print before they occurred, so that no matter what occurred in the present, in the future his heroic couplets will have occurred.

He thought that it was an advantage never to have seen California, or anything he wrote about. Since he already knew the end of history, it was only right that he himself was outside of the history. And he felt, not unreasonably in his opinion, that even though only a few philologists might recognize it, he was the real Master of Monterey.

It was at this moment, with the description of the pristine morning and the gentle land welcoming its new leader ready in his head, that Waxdeck noticed the pages missing from around his feet. He bent up painfully to a sitting position and began to sort through the loose pages that papered his body. He knew some were missing, but he couldn't tell which ones. He tried to put the papers he had in some order, to discover what was missing, but it seemed that the missing pages were the very ones that were necessary to give order to the whole narrative, and without them it was impossible to even discover exactly what was missing. He began to sift through the papers in a frenzy, shifting piles wildly from his knees to his ankles to his thighs and back again, unable to find even the idea of order, unable to find even the beginning and the end, the first and the last indistinguishable.

Waxdeck felt the webwork that connected his words to events beginning to tremble and fray, and he wondered as he spread the papers in lapped piles who could have upset his hold on things. Was it an agent of one of the imperial powers that also coveted California, the Russians, the English, the French? Was one of the midshipmen, one of those to whom he refused to dedicate a canto, the traitor?

Then the ship's bell rang, and Waxdeck feared it was too

late. Eight bells. The Commodore would be setting forth at that very moment.

Commodore Jones arose that morning from his headquarters on land, one of the Presidio's blockhouses, and dressed with Hannibal's help in his finest dress blue uniform, eating and drinking nothing because he wanted to feel as pure in body and spirit as he knew Louisa Darling to be. When he stepped forth onto the parade grounds, they were waiting for him: Major McCormick and half a dozen marines mounted and ready to serve as an escort to protect his person from possible attacks from the rebel leader Bragas de León, and Míster Lurkin sitting a horse, again wearing a beaverskin hat low over his eyes and a thick gold ring on his right hand. Captain Rafael Rafael stood with the remaining marines in formation behind him, to hold the fort during the Commodore's progress, and a line of the leading men of Monterey had again assembled to see him off.

The Commodore mounted a cream-colored horse, and Hannibal took the seat of a gray mule with a notebook open on his lap, to record events for Waxdeck. In the back of the notebook, he had inserted his own prose narrative, in which he predicted the Commodore would be still seeking to establish possession as the *National Intention* foundered. In the rear, a bugle boy rode on a pony, leading a packhorse loaded down with biscuit and jerked beef. Then, with Lurkin at one side and McCormick at the other, and Hannibal just behind his horse's left flank, the Commodore rode out, to make a progress over the land, to establish freedom and democracy. Through the presidial gate he rode, to the bugle boy's sprightly version of

"Yankee Doodle" and the penetrating sound of snoring emitted by those still asleep from the previous day's celebration of the conquest.

Whether or not it was due to the wavering of Waxdeck's influence, the Commodore was even more pensive that morning, not entirely certain that he had taken possession of the land. The rumors that Mexico and the United States were not at war still buzzed around him, as well as the rumors of Micheltorena marching north with eight hundred troops in uniform. If both rumors proved true, the Commodore would not be defending his country from enemies; rather, he would be defending Mexico against the Mexicans. He found it all confusing, as confusing as the speech he had given, as confusing as the sign that should have assured him that his journeys were at an end, that he had come to the right place.

— Hannibal, the Commodore said, did you write an account of the speech?

— I wrote that the people danced with joy when you explained the goals of the *National Intention*. After Míster Lurkin's translation.

— Indeed, Míster Lurkin added, they were very gratified when they heard my translation.

— Perhaps we can send the account to the newspapers. So that one dear to me can hear how I acted in her name.

— Absolutely, sir. You've done everything just as Louisa Darling would have it.

The Commodore sighed. — You're a faithful man, Hannibal.

— Indeed, Míster Lurkin said. Most faithful.

Hannibal saw Míster Lurkin's shadowed face turn toward him, and he had the uncomfortable feeling that the Trader knew all about his own prose narrative, all about the way he undermined the Commodore with every word he wrote, even these notes for Waxdeck. He turned his eyes away from Míster Lurkin and repeated for himself the name of his lost beloved.

Míster Lurkin spurred his horse ahead and informed the party that their route would take them by some of the great California ranchos, by old Carmel Mission, and into the land of the lost people of Esselen. He first took them past an oak tree whose branches touched the water at high tide, the very place where mass was first said in 1603 by Ascención, and where mass was said again in 1770 by Junípero Serra, who raised a cross and claimed the land for his God *ad aeternum*, until the end of time and a millennium thereafter, while Portolá claimed the land for his King Felipe III by pulling up bunches of grass, and picking up stones and throwing them from one place to another, and thrusting his sword into the ground, and reading aloud the Act of Possession, which stated to the Native Californians in a Spanish that would make sense to the dullest lawyer that Jesus Christ was the master of the human lineage, and that his avatars the Popes had granted the American continent to the Spaniards, and that therefore the Native Californians would be made vassals of the Spanish king if they should accept this version of human history, and slaves of the Spanish king if they should not accept this version of human history.

— Whether any Natives were present to hear the declaration does not appear in the Chronicle, Lurkin added. —Yet when the party returned to Monterey after further explorations, they found the Cross adorned with feather-sticks, and arrows, and surrounded by offerings of clams and dried meat. The natives, it seems, reported that at night they had seen the cross shine with a light that overcame the shadows, and watched it grow so high that it touched the celestial sphere, and they brought offerings to the Spaniards' sign, which report confirmed the Spaniards in their belief that they now possessed the land *ad aeternum*.

Commodore Jones did some quick mental calculation, and realized that *ad aeternum* had only lasted some fifty years. He grew more sad and pensive, wondering whether the reign of freedom and democracy, initiated only the day before yesterday, would last any longer, and whether Louisa Darling would know of it.

They continued riding across the peninsula of Monterey, through the uplands used for sheep grazing, and Commodore Jones questioned Míster Lurkin on how best to win the hearts and minds of the people to the new government. He thought that the superiority of a realm of freedom and democracy was self-evident, but he was afraid that there were some who would stubbornly cling to the old ways.

— I'm afraid that freedom and democracy are foreign concepts here, Lurkin said. Concrete action and concrete benefits will do more in convincing the people that becoming American is an advantage.

Just then, they heard from a nearby hillside two voices, one that cried out in pain and the other that gave commands in a rough, rude voice. Commodore Jones turned his reins and directed his troop up the hill to where the voices came from. To his surprise and astonishment, he discovered as they approached that the voices spoke English.

— This will teach you to keep your mind on your work.

— I'm sorry, señor.

— And this will keep you from wasting time carving flutes.

— Sorry, señor, I will not lose a sheep again, I swear.

Commodore Jones found a red-bearded American who had tied a boy to a tree and was beating him with a leather belt. When the American turned around, he stood petrified at seeing an American naval officer riding a horse, accompanied by a troop of fully armed marines, an African, a merchant wearing a beaver hat, and a single bugler playing "Yankee Doodle."

— Who is this? asked Commodore Jones of Míster Lurkin.

— This is a sailor who took French leave of a merchant ship, John Cameron by name. He married into the Asunción family and gained a square league of their land grant.

The Commodore frowned. — And what has this boy done that you beat him here, outside of all established law?

— Sir, Andrés Segundo Sombra is a servant of mine, in charge of a flock of sheep. And he's so careless, passing the time trying to play music on the reeds that grow here, that every day that goes by, I'm missing another sheep.

Andrés Segundo, whose hands were lashed together, turned his head to speak to the Commodore. — Señor, he ties me to the tree and accuses me only to avoid paying me what he owes me.

— Untie the boy immediately, the Commodore ordered.

John Cameron, seeing the marines with their swords at their sides, untied him without a word.

The Commodore asked Andrés Segundo how much he was owed, and the boy replied nine months, at six reales per month. John Cameron swore it was not so many months, and that Andrés should bear the loss of so many sheep under his care.

— Let the beatings you have given his skin pay for the sheepskins he has lost you. That is just. And pay him immediately, because you are now in United States territory, the realm of freedom and democracy, and you are both now Americans.

— Right you are, sir, said John Cameron. As I was born there, I know that now that we're in the United States, you are in the right, and I'm in the wrong. And may I thank God that I'm once again in the United States, and not in the backward land where I've lived these past ten years. But I don't have any reales with me, and so Andrés will have to come with me to my house to get paid.

— Me go with him? ¡Mal año! Ya he leído esta historia. He'll beat me as soon as you're gone.

— No, he won't, said the Commodore. As he was born in the United States, and understands justice and the obligations of every citizen in a democracy, and as you are both now Americans, he will do what's right.

Andrés Segundo didn't look confident, so the Commodore took out his sword and pointed it at the sky.

— And if not, the arm of American justice will fall upon him.

John Cameron looked up at the point of the sword. — God

bless America, he said. The Commodore sheathed his sword, pleased at the response, and he turned his horse and rode back down to the river, where he and his troop continued their progress. As they went, John Cameron shouted after them, God bless America, while Andrés Segundo shouted with him, Viva América, Viva el juez honrado, Long live Commodore Jones.

They continued to shout until the troop was out of earshot. Then John Cameron sighed and turned to Andrés.

— Well, boy, as we're both now Americans, I suppose I'll have to do right by you.

— Long live the United States, Andrés said, if it means I'll get what I'm owed.

— Indeed you will, said John Cameron. And so saying, he seized Andrés and tied him to the tree again, and began to lay on with his belt with renewed fury.

— There, he said as he lashed the boy. That's freedom and democracy in America.

And he beat Andrés until his back was scrap, telling him with each blow that he would have plenty of freedom in the future to play reed flutes, since he would never again be a shepherd in *his* fields, and as much democracy as he could buy with a woeful tale, although democracy was usually easier purchased with coin of the realm. He finally let Andrés go, more from tiredness than from pity, and told him to go seek justice if he wished. Andrés departed, crying resentfully and swearing that John Cameron would have to pay him everything he owed him and more, because this was América, while John Cameron laughed.

Meanwhile, with praise ringing in his ears, Commodore Jones signaled the bugler to play a song. The bugler obliged with a proud rendition of "Yankee Doodle." The Commodore turned to Míster Lurkin as they rode.

— Concrete action and concrete benefits, he said. The people will get word of this, don't you think? And they will begin to be won over.

— No doubt, Míster Lurkin said. No doubt they will get word of it.

While the Commodore rode forward, Hannibal Memory heard a faint cry behind them, and he knew that Andrés Segundo was enjoying freedom and democracy exactly as much as he and his people did.

— I'll write this down, Hannibal said. And I'll remember it.

Commodore Jones was somewhat more optimistic while they crested a hill and came down to the valley of the Carmel River, where the crumbling walls of Mission San Carlos, the very site of the eternal possession of the land by the Franciscans, sat on a bluff overlooking the river and ocean. The whitewash had scaled off the walls in the nine years since secularization, and left great patches of bare clay, which disintegrated further with every rainstorm. The two great towers of the church were shrinking and shriveling, collapsing in on themselves, and most of the roof tiles of the neophytes' quarters had been stolen long ago, to roof, among other buildings in Monterey, Míster Lurkin's trading house. As Commodore Jones led the way down to the ruined mission, a single ex-neophyte sat on the stone steps and shouted in a voice that sounded like a lament.

— ¡Soy libre! Viva California Libre, mete la mano onde quiere.

The Commodore looked at Míster Lurkin for a translation.

— He's saying, "I'm free. Long live free California."

— Has news of our victory already arrived here? the Commodore asked.

— No, my good Commodore. This man has been saying the same thing since 1833.

Such was the case. When the mission system fell, and the reins of government were taken over by the enlightened men of European descent, the mission Indians were told that they were finally free of living in a priest-ridden society. Then they discovered that they were free to make over the mission land reserved for them to the enlightened men of European descent, and free to do most of the labor on that land, just as they had done for the Franciscans. Soylibre, for so the man on the stone steps was called, had been the personal cook for the Father President of the missions at the time of secularization. When he discovered after his former employer had sailed for San Blas that the only positions open to him were gardener, fat-boiler, or vaquero, so beneath the dignity of one who had as good a hand at salting piñole as anyone in California, he began to repeat the words *soy libre, soy libre* to himself in pure rage, determined to let himself die on the steps of the church. He announced to all that he would not leave the mission, that he had decided to die right there. And perhaps he would have if he could have stopped himself from eating. The Native Californians who worked in the former mission lands left him offerings of food, as though he were a holy anchorite, and so rather than dying, the martyr of secularization grew fat and sleek in the decaying church. The former cook had found a new position for himself. Some considered him *mentecato*, but Míster Lurkin claimed that, far from being crazy, Soylibre was the most intelligent of the Native Californians.

The band of horsemen galloped down to the weed-choked earth in front of the old mission, and Lurkin addressed Soylibre in Spanish.

— Have you heard of the change of government in California? This is no Chico for Pío Pico, or something of that nature. No, this time California will become a part of America.

Soylibre knew Lurkin, but the rest of the troop, from the fantastically curve-backed Commodore sitting high on a horse with his gold epaulettes hanging over his knees, to the turnip-faced McCormick pulling on his crotch, to the round-bellied African on the gray mule, to the single bugler they had brought along who even now was playing a sotto voce version of "Yankee Doodle" at this important point in Jones's Progress, seemed to him scarcely of this world. He looked long and hard at the Commodore, then spoke to Lurkin.

— I'm sure I can be as free under these as I have been free under the Mexicans.

Míster Lurkin translated for the Commodore, who then walked his horse up and down in front of Soylibre, gazing at the sleek old man with compassion.

— Tell him, the Commodore said, that we come not as others have come in the past. Rather, we come to bring this land into the realm of freedom and democracy. He is now an American. Tell him that California is entering into the great history of America, which is the inevitable progress of those ideals across the continent.

Míster Lurkin translated for Soylibre, who looked up at the Commodore in astonishment.

— Does he believe all that he has just said? he asked Míster Lurkin in Spanish.

— It appears so, Míster Lurkin said.

— And does he expect me to believe it?

— Without a doubt.

— Then he is crazier than I am, Soylibre said.

— What does he say? the Commodore asked impatiently.

— He's overcome by the news, Míster Lurkin said.

And to certify this report of his speech, Soylibre began to dance on the steps as though in celebration.

— Soy libre, soy libre, soy libre. Viva California libre, mete la mano onde quiere.

— Major, the Commodore said. Leave this man some of the beef jerky we've brought along, so that he can begin to know the fruits of liberty.

With that, he spurred his horse away from the mission and continued his progress upriver, toward the site Míster Lurkin said belonged to the lost people of Esselen. Major McCormick caught up after reluctantly leaving a few pounds of jerky for Soylibre while muttering to himself that he could just as well let people know about the fruits of liberty with his gun.

Hannibal recorded for Waxdeck that the *Democratium Ferens* had established justice where none had previously existed, and mercifully succored the needy who were clinging to the outmoded and bankrupt ways of the past. For himself, he wrote that the masters beat the servants here just as aboard the *National Intention*, and that servants' blood was the same color all over the world. He wrote that the former slaves of the missionaries are no better off now, and perhaps worse off. California already seemed to be too much the same place he had wanted to leave behind, and he wondered whether the woman he had written of, who could mend his broken story, was to be found.

Commodore Jones's optimism lasted only a couple of miles, and then he lapsed again into pensiveness adrift from Waxdeck's providential narrative, uncertain whether dispensing justice and helping the needy would really bring him what he sought.

The troop arrived at a flattened plain by the Carmel River, well into the range of the Santa Lucias. Commodore Jones marched his horse around, and he spoke in a loud voice. He spoke, trying to establish again the sense of his mission, which was wavering and tenuous.

— Let anyone who does not acknowledge the superiority of American arms, the goodness of freedom and democracy, the entry of this land into the great history of America, come forth. Or let it be acknowledged.

Hannibal didn't want to let the *National Intention* go unchallenged. He was the memory missing from Waxdeck's narrative. And yet, he knew that if he made his poetic insubordination public at this point, he and his line would be crushed, just as he had been beaten aboard the *Louisa Darling*.

In that moment, as Hannibal hesitated, a fantastical figure rode down out of the mountains on the other side of the river.

The apparition wore a velvet cape, a leathern hood crudely shaped like a knight's helmet with a buzzard feather sticking from it as a panache, and a cowhide shield on which was scrawled *Desheredado* — The Disinherited. He drew a sword, pointed it at the party on the opposite shore, reined in his horse so that it reared up on its hind legs, then turned and rode back toward the mountains.

— I know him, Major McCormick shouted. One of the raiders at the fiesta.

Indeed, it was Sergeant Vargas, imitating Ivanhoe at the Tournament of the Queen of Love and Beauty. The sergeant stopped at the verge of the forest and wheeled his horse around.

— The disinherited ones challenge you, he shouted in Spanish. Uds. y la gran puta que les parió.

— What does he say, Míster Lurkin? the Commodore asked.

— I think he's challenging you in the manner of Chivalric Romances.

— Permission to pursue, sir? asked Major McCormick. I can answer a challenge well enough with my gun, he added, pulling on his crotch.

— Go on, sir.

Major McCormick led his troop down to a ford across the river and then up the other bank, leaving behind the Commodore, Hannibal, Míster Lurkin, and also the bugle boy, who, truth be told, was something of a coward.

When Vargas saw the troop approach, he turned and rode up into the woods, following the plan of Don Bragas de León, the lionhearted one, who thought to lure the invading forces south, closer to the nine hundred crack troops that, according to rumor, were making a forced march from Los Angeles with Micheltorena at the head on a shining white stallion sixteen hands high.

Vargas joined Bragas de León and the three Ohlone vaqueros at the first redoubt. Bragas de León knew himself to be outnumbered and outgunned, but he hoped to fight a series of skirmishes, holding the enemy at bay and then retreating strategically to draw the Yanquis toward the jaws of Micheltorena, who would, no doubt, be arriving at any moment.

Major McCormick came upon the first redoubt, and spotted Vargas's buzzard feather poking above the breastworks. He drew his saber and shouted.

— Sabers! Attack!

Bragas de León was about to call for a withering fire to break the advance when he noticed that the three Ohlone vaqueros, who cared nothing about strategic retreats and less about glory, had already mounted up and were riding in the opposite direction. The lionhearted one saw the line of horse-marines mounting rapidly toward him.

— Retreat, he called loudly, to make sure that the Ohlones understood that they had been following orders.

At the second redoubt, where the Ohlones had not bothered to stop and regroup, but merely saved time and trouble by continuing to ride south, Bragas de León and Sergeant Vargas grew anxious and fired before McCormick's marines were in range. McCormick again pulled out his saber.

— Attack, he called.

— Retreat, Bragas de León answered.

At the third redoubt, the lionhearted one discovered as the horse-marines approached that the vaqueros had taken the pack animals with all the powder and shot, and he and the sergeant only had one shot left apiece.

— Retreat, he called.

— Attack, Major McCormick answered.

Constantly just out of range of each other, the two groups strayed further into the fastnesses of the Santa Lucía Mountains, where they found not the approaching forces of Micheltorena but rather brambles, stinging nettles, and mosquitoes with a taste for blood and a complete lack of discrimination concerning whether the blood came from American soldiers or the patriots of California.

Commodore Jones, in the meantime, had learned from Míster Lurkin what the device on Vargas's shield declared. He grew lonely, with his horse-marines away chasing the disinherited one, and no people of California here to thank him for bringing them into the realm of freedom and democracy. He wondered if the *National Intention* only advanced through disinheriting those who had come before, whether he could ever take possession of the land without dispossessing those who had come before. Louisa Darling came to his mind, the first virgin land he had dreamed of settling in, and he pondered whether any land could replace that one forever closed to him.

While Hannibal Memory and Míster Lurkin looked on, the Commodore dismounted from his horse. He tore up some tufts of grass, and picked up some stones and tossed them across the flattened plain. Then he took out his sword and thrust it into the ground. He looked around questioningly, hoping that Major McCormick would at that moment ride from the hills with the disinherited one, not held a prisoner but rather riding at his side, as brothers. But nobody appeared. He withdrew his sword from the ground, disappointed.

Míster Lurkin addressed the Commodore as though the Commodore's mind were clear as a pane of glass.

— Here also was home to some, he said, pointing at the ground.

— Here? the Commodore asked.

— This is a village site of the lost people of Esselen, Lurkin said.

Hannibal had been surreptitiously writing in his prose narrative that the horse-marines would find themselves bewildered in the mountains, but Lurkin's words caught his attention, and he paused, pencil over paper, ready to write down what was said.

— How were they lost? the Commodore asked.

Míster Lurkin explained that the missionaries and soldiers had saved the people of Esselen little by little, first by convincing some to attach themselves to the mission, and then by kidnapping a few children for the good of their souls, to persuade the parents to come in for the good of *their* souls. The rest had straggled in to be saved during years when food was scarce, even though they had to suffer through Latin and smallpox. After some decades, they were saved so thoroughly that they were utterly lost.

— While some lived, they would return here for the World

Renewal Ritual, Míster Lurkin said. An old man would flee the mission once a year to perform the ritual in the sweat lodge, to keep the world from decaying, and he would be put into the stocks when he returned.

— How long has it been since an Indian has been back? the Commodore asked.

Although the world's decay had yet to manifest itself in his account books, Míster Lurkin said it had been many years.

Then Hannibal began to write furiously. That the horse-marines would remain in the mountains. That the Commodore would investigate the sweat lodge, but never truly possess the land. That he, Hannibal, would escape as the *National Intention* foundered, to author his own line. California was not outside of history, he decided, but several histories seemed to be in contention here; his own line might find a place from which to struggle.

He looked at Míster Lurkin, to judge what kind of impediment he might be to escape. But he found Míster Lurkin already studying him from beneath the shadowy brim of his hat.

— Sir, Hannibal said. This is another opportunity for you to make history.

The Commodore looked at him uncertainly. — Do you truly think so?

— You've taken possession of California and brought it into American history. Now you can take possession of the prehistory as well.

The Commodore wondered about the old men who came to this place to renew the world, knowing that they would be beaten and put in the stocks.

— It would be the highest service you could render Louisa Darling, Hannibal continued. To make history out of something that is now barely a memory.

— Where is the sweat lodge? the Commodore asked.

The lodge had been dug into the side of the riverbank, and then a mounded roof of willow poles covered with tule brush and sealed with earth had been shaped over it. Now the mound was overgrown with wild grasses and the smoke hole at the center was only a depression, but the low entryway beside the river was still open behind some shrubs. Commodore Jones peered into the darkness, while Míster Lurkin warned him to be cautious.

— The central post not only holds up the roof of the sweat lodge, but some believe it also holds up the sky.

The Commodore had already decided to take possession of this last place. He hoped he could capture something that the old men knew, something that would make him feel less lonely. He hoped to find the true sign, the one that would tell him that his journeys were at an end, that he had come to the right place, that he was meant to be here. He had roamed the world in service of freedom and democracy, but now, even as Master of Monterey, he had not found what he sought. He had brought ideas to the land, but he had not found love.

— Hannibal, he said to his faithful Memory. You'll be certain to record what I've undertaken, so that it arrives at the ears of the one most precious to me.

— Aye, sir.

Commodore Jones slashed with his sword at the shrubs covering the entrance, which noise caused a number of crows to empty out of the old lodge. But the Commodore paid no attention to such ill auguries. He bent forward, a question mark entering into the most sacred space of the lost people of Esselen, while Hannibal urged him on with paeans to his courage, promising him that the very soul of freedom and democracy, the pure and chaste Louisa Darling, would hear of his exploit in carrying American history and ideals to the most dangerous and unknown reaches of the land. The bugler played a heroic rendition of "Yankee Doodle."

Then the Commodore disappeared completely into the darkness of the lodge, and nothing more was heard. At the end of five minutes, Hannibal shouted into the lodge, but there was no answer. At the end of ten minutes, there was no answer, and at the end of half an hour there was no answer. Whenever Hannibal looked over at Míster Lurkin, he found that Lurkin was already watching him, as though he knew exactly what Hannibal planned. There were just the two of them there, along with the bugler, who was beginning to complain that his lips hurt from playing the same song over and over again. Hannibal thought of simply mounting his gray mule and riding off, but he wasn't sure what Lurkin would do if he did, and he still wasn't certain, even though events had so far followed his narrative, that the *National Intention* was indeed foundering. If California were to become part of America, he would be thrown into chains as a deserter, for he knew that a round African man in California would not be hard to find.

Then, as though he had been waiting for this moment, Lurkin pointed to the crest of a hill. — Look there, he said.

A large woman in a white muslin blouse and black skirt was walking through the fresh grasses, surrounded by a bleating team of goats. The younger goats bumped their heads against her knees as she walked, or put their front hooves on her fleshy hips, as though reaching up with their tender and sensitive lips for her two breasts, which swung enormously from side to side with every step, promising nourishment and relief to half a world. She brushed the goats off laughingly as she led them up the hill to pastureland too steep for cattle.

— Is she of the people of Esselen? Hannibal asked.

— She is a *desterrada*, Lurkin replied. She doesn't own the goats she herds, or the land she pastures them on, or the shack she sleeps in at night. She owns nothing of value in the world.

— Nothing of value?

— Nothing you could exchange, the Trader replied.

Hannibal watched the woman bring the goats with her to where the grass was fresh and untrammeled. The goats followed along without dogs or sticks to guide them, as the woman laughed and lovingly cuffed the flanks of the ones closest to her. And Hannibal understood that she was the end of his writing. He had written of her, both as a way to mend his broken story and as a being in the world. But her overwhelming presence now was far beyond anything he had been able to express in words.

Lurkin's voice continued, low and insistent. — If you followed her, you would own nothing for the rest of your life. You could dance on holy days, and every other day of the year you could sweat building the wealth and property of somebody else. You would eat only at another's pleasure, and sleep at another's permission. Is that really better than being a part of the *National Intention?*

Hannibal looked at the shadowy face of Lurkin, then back up at the woman on the ridge.

— And at your death, Lurkin continued, you would leave your children naked and homeless.

— No, Hannibal said. I would leave them with life, and with memory.

— Oh, that woman might own her own memory. And you too might own your own memory. So might your children. But don't expect memory ever to make you Master of Monterey. Only writing can do that.

Hannibal kicked his gray ass in the flanks and turned toward the hill, away from Lurkin, away from the sweat lodge where Commodore Jones even then was seeking to take possession of the lost memory of Esselen to feel finally at home.

He had gone a dozen paces when he heard Lurkin's voice tell him to wait.

He turned around and saw the Trader with a two-shot derringer in his hand, pointed at him.

— If you're deserting, you'll have to leave the notebook.

Hannibal stared down the double barrels, round and open mouths.

— Not forty-four guns, Míster Lurkin said. But sometimes one is enough.

— The guns don't make the story, Hannibal said. It's the story that makes the guns.

— Oh, I know that well enough. And yet, a gun can determine which story gets told at any one time.

Hannibal looked up at the woman on the ridge. He understood he would never completely mend his broken story because of the unerasable intervening years. But he would love now, love what there is, and he would trust in his memory and the memory of his children to continue the story among other stories. It was the best he could do.

He threw the book at Míster Lurkin. It twisted in the air and knocked off the hat of the bugler, who had settled on a rock to nurse his sore lips. Hannibal turned toward the hill again and urged the mule up the hill toward the woman, who was disappearing over the ridge with her goats.

When he caught up with her, she stood with her hands on her hips as though she had been waiting for him, as though he had arrived late. Hannibal was shy and did not know what to say, as he had not been alone with a woman for twenty years.

The woman laughed and asked him if he were one of those from the ship, who were going to take over everything. Hannibal answered that he wasn't going to take over anything, and in fact had already given away everything except his memory. She laughed again and said she was certain he hadn't given away everything, because he had something to give to her. And she put her hand on what he had to give, which soon grew gift-like and pleased her so much that she shoved aside her sharp-odored goats to make room for the both of them to roll in. Together they engendered a new line of generations and enduring memory while they flattened half an acre of grass.

Chapter Three

After the Commodore had left to make his Progress through the land, the Captain locked himself in his quarters in the Presidio blockhouse, the crumbling tower on the fort's northwest corner. He left strict orders not to be disturbed unless Micheltorena's troops, which were now rumored to number fifteen hundred, were seen approaching, and he left special orders that he should under no circumstances be disturbed by women, especially those young and beautiful. This proved to be a necessary precaution, as more than one *hija del país,* and some who already had *hijas* at home, were drawn to the tower to seek an audience with the Captain. They sensed his Adamic gift, and wished to express personally their gratitude at his part in making California part of a brave new world that had such people in it. The aide-de-camp who stood outside the door was driven by simple pity to offer himself as a surrogate for the Captain, for which kind gesture he was rewarded with five slaps across the face, two boxed ears, and a nose twisted without a shred of mercy or remorse.

Rafael Rafael wondered whether he had ever been more content than when he had simply been able to look into his sister's face and forget the Dark Man. He remembered sharply, like a knife in his side, receiving her pledge of undying love and the news of her death on the same day, and he hadn't looked in a mirror for the twenty-plus years since that day out of the certainty that he would see the Dark Man's face laughing at him over his left shoulder. Now he felt Arcadia calling him, from a place where, Pearl Prynne had warned him, he could never arrive. He remained secluded in the failing tower, in dreamy doubt and anticipation, knowing unconsciously that these hours of sadness would prove to be some of the finest and happiest of his life.

Arcadia was once again confined in the room hung with the black webbings of her mournful trousseau under the watchful eye of Duenna Recta. From time to time, Arcadia looked through the heavy curtains out the barred window and saw old Don Ignacio sitting his stallion, sadly waiting for her to come to her senses. Outside the door, she knew that her uncle's trusted servant, Juan Canito, was sitting. She was trapped, and she sat back down to her loom to work furiously on what she called a funeral shroud.

When she had first been brought back from the fiesta by her uncle and aunt, she was told that she had behaved scandalously and endangered the honor of the family, which could have remained perfectly safe if she had only agreed to marry the eminently suitable septuagenarian to whom she was promised. There would be no more trips to church to hear mass, certainly not alone with Magda, who bore some blame for her behavior. If she needed the succor of the church, Fray Echevarría could come and give it to her in the family chapel, while also recounting to her all the blessedness women have brought to the world by saying yes, whether they wanted to or not. Otherwise, she could remain in her room, receiving no visitors, certainly not the blue-eyed *americano* whom she had saved.

Arcadia had declared to all, even as she was being carried away from the fiesta, that she would marry nobody, and when she was home she had sat at the weaving loom to work at a funeral shroud for herself, and she would speak with nobody about changing her mind until it was finished. She chose, however, colors inappropriate for a shroud: a russet background, the red of leaves falling, the burning orange of poppy blossoms, the green color of the sea close to shore, straw gold of hills at midsummer, rusty brown of redwood, blue of sky.

She saw Magda only when the old woman came in to change the *bacinilla* and bring her meals, and they had little chance to exchange words without Duenna Recta's sharp ears catching every word, but once Magda whispered to her quickly, *You must make your enemy your ally.*

How? whispered Arcadia.

By finding another enemy, Magda whispered.

The Duenna felt that the world had gone crazy. What had happened to the time in which she had been able to gain in respect simply by turning down every proposal of marriage that came her way? Things had made so much sense then! Since the invasion of the *americanos*, only two days ago, this young woman under her tutelage had refused a marriage that would lead her quickly into a peaceful and honored widowhood, the pinnacle of respect. Such a refusal would have been unheard of when she was a girl. Indeed, if Duenna Recta could have married someone at death's door, she might have done it herself. Arcadia had simply gone mad. The colors of the shroud proved it. And the Duenna was being blamed for it. She worked black lacework and looked disapproval at her charge.

When Arcadia finished a final warp and woof, she pulled the work from the loom and spoke with quiet urgency to the Duenna.

— Look, she said.

She wore her creation over her shoulder and head, and the Duenna saw her clothed brilliantly with the colors of the earth.

— That is no shroud, the Duenna stuttered.

— Of course not. It was a trick to say so. This is a shawl to be married in.

Duenna Recta rose joyfully to tell Arcadia's aunt and uncle that their niece had regained her sanity and wanted to marry a man five times her age, but Arcadia quieted her with a hand. She whispered to the Duenna that her marriage to Don Ignacio must be kept secret until after it was consummated, because she had heard rumors from the *desterrados* that the *americanos* planned to outlaw all priests and halt all holy Catholic weddings so that the *hijas del país* can be married, or worse, by heretics.

— My wedding must be a secret, she said, but I need your help.

The Duenna was ready to believe the worst of the *americanos*, heretics who spoke a rude and barbarous tongue, and she asked what she could do. Arcadia told her to tell Don Ignacio that he should wait for her until Pegasus was high in the sky. If she could sneak out, she would come to him and they would ride away together and so confound the *americanos*. He would know it was her and no heretical trick because she would be wearing the unique shawl-shroud. But if she had not been able to sneak out by the time Pegasus was beginning to fall, toward the west, he would have to come in silently and steal her away. He must remember to speak no word while he came for her. They would give Juan Canito aguardiente to make him sleep.

The Duenna whispered back that they should at least tell her aunt and uncle, but Arcadia whispered back that some servant would overhear, that the very walls had ears, and that the *americanos* would somehow get wind of it.

— You are the only one to whom I can trust my wedding, Arcadia said. I'm only now realizing how much I respect you.

She had found the key to Duenna Recta's heart. The Duenna was convinced that being respected held the same value as being in a state of grace with the Holy Catholic Church. She had been respected for so long by so many that she had never realized that respect for her retiring and virginal character had long since become respect for her age. Now that she felt that Arcadia understood the importance of being respected, she would do all she could to make sure that Arcadia would also have the opportunity to wear black for the last fifty years of her life.

At the dying of the light, the Duenna stole out from the Serrano rancho to where Don Ignacio sat his stallion. The falling sun turned the hills a mournful red, and the caballero's head drooped forward while his horse stretched its long neck down to graze quietly on the tender grasses. When the Duenna approached, the horse raised its eyes briefly, then, as if noting who it was, bowed down again so that the long muscle along its neck was a smooth arc under its mane.

Don Ignacio had sworn a great oath to keep watch over the woman whom he already considered his rightful wife, to protect her honor and his own from the invading *americanos*. He had remained all day, rounding the building with his stallion or grazing the horse in front of Arcadia's barred window, refusing to let even his sons spell him. However, now at the fading of the day, he found his honor was only with great difficulty supporting him on horseback, and that his honor would be much stronger if he could only take a nap. The memories of the twelve sons and eleven daughters he had already sired, the elk, bear, and cougar he had slain, the women he had known and the wives he had outlived, could not keep his head from slowly slumping forward every so often between his fine-boned shoulders like a larval creature ready to enter its cocoon.

The Duenna called Don Ignacio's name, but the Don did not answer. She called again. Again no answer. She could not touch him, because she had not touched a man in the forty years since her father died, and touching the stallion too was out of the question as it was, after all, a male creature. She finally picked up a stick and, holding it out at arm's length, began to tickle the horse under its chin. The creature finally raised up its long, sad neck and stamped around in a circle, and Don Ignacio shook himself into consciousness.

In the dim light, he saw with bloodshot eyes an old woman in black who was telling him fantastical things. His promised young bride was going to sneak out to meet him in a shroud. The shawl was all the colors of the earth. A secret wedding to confound the *americanos*. Hurry, because Arcadia wants to be respected, and few are as respected as a rich widow.

Don Ignacio shook his groggy head. — A shroud? he asked. A shroud?

— A shawl, le digo, I said a shawl.

Gradually, Don Ignacio recognized the Duenna and began to understand her message. He felt himself begin to sit taller in the saddle, walked his stallion around proudly. His bride was willing to defy conventions, steal out to see him, elope in a wedding shawl of her own weaving. He felt younger, more potent, and even while Duenna Recta saw in him a vehicle to save Arcadia from the covetousness of American heretics and to escort her into a respected widowhood, he saw in himself again the populator of the territory, the fountainhead, sire of a line of descendants who, when they took their place in the world, would look back on him and say, *There, he truly was Master of Monterey.*

He addressed a soliloquy to the barred, black-hung window where his desire resided. — Ho, Arcadia, come and meet your true groom, tu señor natural, the one who will keep you and guard you and render you happy and fecund.

A tear rolled down the old man's cheek. — To be loved like that. And to be sixty-eight years old.

Duenna Recta was scandalized, in part because of the talk of love and in part because she thought Don Ignacio was lying about his age. She was always intolerant of love, especially since she had, in a moment of weakness, found herself inclining toward it at the sound of this very man's voice only the previous evening, and she addressed him irritably, as she would a child or an old fool.

— Just watch for her tonight in her shroud and take her to the priest.

She marched away, empty and rancorous, while Don Ignacio called after her that it was a shawl, not a shroud, it was a shawl.

While Duenna Recta was gone, Magda had entered Arcadia's room to empty the *bacinilla*, and in the hurried seconds that they were alone together, Arcadia pressed the shawl to Magda.

— Too much to explain, she said. Go and take this to him.

Magda understood immediately who *him* was. While the light was fading, she took the shawl under the front of her dress, so that it seemed she was pregnant, and mounted a mule for Monterey.

Rafael Rafael reclined in the tower, his only companion Adam's sadness. He knew that Arcadia was not far off, and the feeling he had that she was the one he had been looking for all his life made him nostalgic and languorous, with a half-erection he was aware of only intermittently, disposed to wait and have her presence as a prospect and a potential. He wanted another go at Eve and the Garden, but he still wouldn't dare read through to the end of *Paradise Lost*, almost certain that even now it would end the same way it always did, and he wanted his own story not to have an ending, to remain in a sleepy middle outside of time. At least in *this* present, while the *National Intention* lay anchored and still, and while the restless and questioning Commodore was absent, he could wait in the dream that the wait could continue without ever reaching fulfillment or disappointment.

A knock on the door interrupted his reveries, and he gave his aide-de-camp permission to enter. The aide-de-camp told him that a woman had arrived who insisted on seeing him. Rafael Rafael sighed, not arising from his cot, and asked if she were young and beautiful like all the rest.

— No, sir. Rather older and stout.

This somewhat piqued the Captain's interest. — And why would she see me?

— She only speaks Spanish, sir. But she made it known through signs that I should show you this.

Rafael Rafael lifted his head and saw his aide-de-camp holding up the garment glowing with the colors of the earth.

Rafael Rafael sat up.

— Send her in, he said.

The aide-de-camp escorted Magda into the Captain's quarters, and immediately she began to exhort Rafael Rafael to go out and rescue Arcadia, and marry her, and make her happy forever. Magda waved her arms as she spoke with passion and tears, and she was so large that she seemed to fill up the tiny room with her fleshy odor of lilac and *estofada*. Rafael Rafael backed into a corner.

— I think I know what you are getting at, he said. But I can't abandon my post.

Magda, who knew the signs of a man's reluctance so well that she had no need of a common language, backed the Captain further into the corner and told him he was a very little man if he refused to go, a coward, a man *sin cojones*, which she sensed he was not. A man who was a man could do only one thing, which was rescue Arcadia from her plight. Captain Rafael Rafael, who also knew much of the signs of woman's persuasion and felt like he was understanding Magda without the benefit of bilinguality, asked her how he could be certain that this woman might be different from the other women he had known, those who had left him feeling empty and alone, with the face of the Dark Man leering over his left shoulder, anxious only to return to sea and read again the first half of *Paradise Lost* and the journals of Christopher Columbus. Hadn't he been called before, many times, only to be disappointed as many times, with women who waved handkerchiefs after him as his ship crossed the bar but who had understood only what he had in abundance, not what he lacked.

Magda replied that if he remained in this tower, he would regret it for the rest of his life. Arcadia waited for him and him alone to win her. If he had wasted his spirit in lust before, that was of little importance now, as now he should cast off his other concerns and regrets and follow his heart, now he had a choice between paradise or a hell of sorrow and remorse. To emphasize the point, she snatched the garment from the hands of the aide-de-camp, who had been boggled by the spectacle of a spirited debate between two people who didn't understand each other's words.

As Magda held out the shawl for the Captain to see, they both noticed letters woven into the underside, a message stitched by Arcadia on the only tablet allowed to her. The message was in Spanish, and Magda could not read or write. But

Rafael Rafael understood the first and last words of the message: Amor, Arcadia.

He also unconsciously understood that if he left, he would never return to that dreamy middle space of doubt and anticipation. But he rose to his feet.

— We'll find someone to read this for us, he said.

Magda hid the shawl again under her dress, and Captain Rafael Rafael ordered his aide-de-camp to keep the door to the vacant tower locked and guarded, as though he were still on the inside. Then they walked together down the path curving between the Presidio and the shore. Night had fallen, and the air was unquiet with the buzz of flying insects, and crickets calling, and the merciless frog watching with bulbed eyes, coyote grinning around the corners. In the sky, the constellation of Pegasus, the starry-winged horse, had risen in the east and was flying toward its zenith.

The light of Lurkin's trading house drew them in, as the Captain hoped to find a clerk who spoke both English and Spanish, and could read. To his surprise, he found Míster Lurkin himself there. He had assumed that the Commodore had made camp or found lodgings with some ranchero, and that Míster Lurkin had stayed with him. The Trader merely observed that he sometimes could seem to be in many places at the same time, not commenting on where the Commodore or McCormick and his marines were at present.

— A glass of pulque, Captain?

— And one for my companion as well.

Magda pulled the Captain's sleeve in warning. At the end of the counter, Fidel Segundón leaned over a drink. At his side, a young woman, a *desterrada*, was gazing with wonder at the white wedding dress hanging from the rafters beside the ploughshares, a glass of pulque forgotten in her hands. When Rafael Rafael looked over at them, Fidel asked him in Spanish how it felt to be rescued by a fourteen-year-old girl.

— What does he say? asked Rafael Rafael.

— He's wondering if you have recovered from your encounter with the bull, Míster Lurkin replied.

Then Don Ignacio's son aggressively asked Míster Lurkin who owed him more money, Don Ignacio or this petty *americano*. Míster Lurkin replied that he had the honor to be owed many thousands of reales by Don Ignacio, and in fact much of the Don's limitless lands were encumbered by debts, whereas the Captain owed him nothing at all.

— ¡Exacto! shouted Don Ignacio's son. Therefore, you must be friends to those who owe such a magnificent amount, not to the likes of this vagrant *americano*. Why do you even allow such a *fulano de tal*, such a *don nadie* to drink here, if it give offense to your friends?

— Ah, Fidel, Míster Lurkin replied. A trader must be a friend to all, and allow everybody to owe him money. Besides, I have hopes that one day, the Captain will owe me greatly.

— More than my father? Impossible!

— Sí, señor. Todo puede ser. But perhaps you should watch over your own companion, who is becoming altogether too friendly.

The young *desterrada*, after marveling at all the items for sale, had lighted upon the china-blue eyes of Rafael Rafael, and found the most marvelous item of all. Don Ignacio's son turned and found her gaping at the Captain, and after a moment of stupefaction, took her forcefully by the arm.

— Ya nos veremos, he said venomously over his shoulder while his companion managed to take out a handkerchief and wave it at Rafael Rafael as she was pulled through the door.

As the Captain was about to speak, a small gilded clock on a shelf behind the counter began to strike the hour. Míster Lurkin held up his hand for silence as the clock counted up the hours to twelve. Then he turned his back on Magda and Rafael Rafael and rearranged his clothing. When he turned back, though he still wore his beaver hat with a brim that shadowed his eyes and a heavy gold ring with a curious Egyptian symbol, he also now wore a white clerical collar above his shirt.

— It's Sunday, he said.

He explained that he was an ordained minister, although he seldom found anyone to whom he could minister, and in fact he presided over a congregation of one — himself. This, however, had its advantages. The congregation was always in perfect harmony with itself, there were never any schisms or differences of opinion, nobody ever gossiped or spread rumors, there was no badmouthing or backbiting, and everyone in the congregation was at perfect peace with their faith.

— I've become convinced, he said, that my congregation is precisely the right size.

Then Rafael Rafael thought he saw a special glint from under the Trader's hat.

— I can, however, perform marriages, he added. If two desire to become one.

Rafael Rafael felt in these words an offer to help him arrive at his dreamed-of Arcadia, but the offer was so plainly and forthrightly made that a shiver of terror went down his spine, and he wondered what price there might be that he did not yet understand. But he had left behind Adam's sadness, and he gestured to Magda to take out the garment. She drew it forth from under her dress as though it came from her womb and held it up for Míster Lurkin to read.

The Trader read through the Spanish, woven letter by letter into the pattern with heated desire. When he came to the end of the message, he smiled, and came around the counter, and placed the shawl around Magda's shoulders.

— You too have a part to play, he told her. Then he translated the message for them.

As Pegasus rode high into the sky, Don Ignacio felt his blood rise as it had thirty-seven years earlier when he had taken his first bride on horseback at the head of a wedding cavalcade back to his one-room ranch house for the feast and celebration, while his friends capered through the hills on horseback, performing tricks with their *reatas* or leaning down to pluck a wildflower at full gallop and then presenting it to him to pass to his new wife, who rode ahead of him in the saddle. Her name had also been Arcadia, and he could remember the way her breath moved her white dress in and out as she turned her head shyly and accepted the flower from him. He now expected, after two Marías, María José and María Jaime, to be once again with Arcadia, and his blood flowered within him as the stars turned round in the sky.

When he saw through the dark the marvelous shawl move toward him, he felt that his destiny was about to be fulfilled, the promise about to be kept, and he lifted his stallion's head up with the reins and galloped the short distance to his beloved, ready to lift her up onto the saddle in front of him and carry her off to the church, ready to become again señor of Arcadia, ready to sprout more branches from his old trunk, descendants who would hail him as Master of Monterey. But rather than lifting her up, he himself was carried off his horse and tumbled down into the grasses by an ancient and all-devouring hunger, and he felt himself dispossessed of any mastery, seized vehemently and despoiled even of his clothing. He had thought to discover a virgin ripe and hard as a walnut, but instead he was discovered by a wise covetousness that knew exactly what it wanted and where to find it.

Magda de-shirted Don Ignacio, and she threw his linen to the west, where she knew Captain Rafael Rafael would find it. But as she drew him down on the shawl, some of the freshness of Arcadia's desire was infused in her, and she remembered her own mad and vain search for the snake man, who had left her in Michoacán, the man who could drive her crazy just by touching her left earlobe. And while it was too dark to see if this man had truly the tattoo of a rattlesnake around his waist, she knew without reflection, in her long-toothed, autumnal way, that this was as close as she would ever come, and besides, as all cats are gray in the dark, this one could as well be the snake man as another. So she felt, as though it might be her last chance to feel, a precious delirium when his knobby hands of an old man touched her left earlobe and her right everything else, and she offered up to him all she had to offer, and wrested from him all he had to give, believing because she wanted to believe that she had found at last the man she had sought.

And Don Ignacio lay stunned with exhaustion on the shawl that was a shroud, understanding that he had not found Arcadia, but rather the third María, la Magdalena, and equally understanding, by the rosy ache in his heart that seemed to be leaking out his side, that he would go no further, that he would nevermore attempt an Arcadia in the rest of his yellow-leafed time on earth.

In the darkness, Captain Rafael Rafael was assembling himself into a version of the old Don, putting on piece by piece the clothing of a Californio, finally placing on his head the Don's yellow hat of the finest vicuña wool. It fit surprisingly well. He slouched to the rancho, walking like an old man, and found the main door open. He had no need of a guide to find his way to the door of Arcadia, as one room of the rancho glowed with a primeval heat, like the molten core of a globe suddenly showing through the thin crust, the likes of which he had not seen from all the women who had shared his Adamic gifts in his long seafaring life, never seen since that other night when he had stolen in on his sister in their father's mansion in Manhattan. The guard at the door, young Juan Canito, was as sleepy drunk as Duncan's watchers on aguardiente and distilled tobacco leaf. Captain Rafael Rafael stepped over him to the glowing threshold of Arcadia's room. He felt on the edge of the world, perhaps like old Columbus felt when he tacked into the great freshwater stream tumbling forth from South America, unable to make progress against the flood but certain that the river originated in the earthly paradise. He felt that he was on the verge of leaving forever the *National Intention*, leaving the sea that had led him wandering for the past twenty years, arriving at the place he had dreamed about and never again making history. He knocked quietly three times on the door as the message had instructed.

While Magda was rolling Don Ignacio in the shroud and the Captain was collecting the clothes that came flying off piece by piece, Duenna Recta was trying to convince Arcadia that the guard at the door was drunk, and that she should dress herself and go.

— I'm not ready, Arcadia said.

Secretly, the Duenna rejoiced that Arcadia was now hesitant about stealing away to a secret marriage, as she felt it rather unseemly in herself to be urging her on.

— Don't think of it as losing the jewel that no money can replace, the Duenna said. Think of it as gaining in respectability. Nobody is as respected as the wife of a rich gentleman, if it not be the widow of a rich gentleman.

— I don't feel ready, Arcadia said. To be so respected.

— Or think about protecting yourself from being married or worse by a heretic.

Arcadia blushed, and the Duenna was pleased at her maidenly shyness. Then they heard three quiet knocks. Duenna Recta stared sternly at Arcadia to warn her to be ready, then cracked open the door.

She was surprised by Don Ignacio's improved appearance. He seemed taller, and his shoulders were squarer, his carriage more erect. She wondered if this was what love did to men, and she stepped outside the door and closed it behind her. In that moment, she wanted to feel that she had been respectable for so long that she might be worthy of love.

— Arcadia is not ready, she said. For you to . . . respect her. But you can respect me.

Juan Canito on the floor snuffed loudly and let out a sleepy, relaxed fart.

Rafael Rafael, dressed in the clothes of Don Ignacio, couldn't understand what she was saying, but he knew from his long experience that the black-robed woman was offering herself in place of Arcadia. And knew that she would leave him still sad and empty and in thrall to the *National Intention*. When he stepped past her, she clutched at him with her clawlike, black-webbed hands.

— She's not ready. Nobody is as ready to be . . . respected . . . as I.

He opened the door. Arcadia was waiting, dressed in simple white, and held out her hand to him.

— Now take me, husband, she said.

As he took her hand, the Duenna's snatching claws knocked off the Don's hat of yellow vicuña wool. And she suddenly recognized that this was not Don Ignacio, this must be the *americano* from the previous day.

— ¡Socorro! she cried. Help, help!

The two lovers fled hand in hand past her grasp.

— Help, Duenna Recta cried, with ashes in her mouth as lamps became lit down the hallway. Help, she cried, calling out for them or for herself, knowing in her heart that she had been respected for so long, she was doomed to be respected for the rest of her life.

They mounted Don Ignacio's stallion, which Rafael Rafael had left at the outer gate, and they rode under the falling sign of Pegasus for Monterey, Arcadia behind Rafael Rafael, her arms wrapped tightly around his chest. She remembered praying to the Virgin Mary for love, and she thought now that the Virgin had granted her prayers. Because what she was doing was not so different from what the Virgin had done, in choosing and accepting a lover without her family's knowledge and approval, if the lover were as irresistible as a god. Riding rapidly over the hills she knew so well with her arms around her Captain, she felt as though she and the Captain had joined into one large being, a happy animal, strong as a centaur, running godlike through hills that were the very bones of the earth, as though they might run forever. And yet, the sign of Pegasus continued to fall as they rode, and Arcadia knew that they would not run forever, that they had a goal, a destination, which, once reached, would mark everything before it as different from everything that came after it. And she wondered if these hills would change tomorrow, once she was possessed of a husband, once her husband had possessed her. She tightened her arms around Rafael Rafael, searching for something in the steady gallop of the horse, smooth and lovely as the lapping waves of a calmed sea. But the hills had already begun to change in her sight, each rise passing like the tick of a clock, the click of a minute, measuring their progress toward Monterey.

Lurkin was making out a bill of lading, which proved beyond a shadow of a doubt to a prospective buyer that the barrels of salt pork and gunpowder that he had smuggled yesterday from the *National Intention* had actually been purchased at inflated prices from the brig *Pilgrim* in 1836. When he saw Rafael Rafael and Arcadia come, he stood up with a Bible in his hands, still wearing his clerical collar, his eyes shadowed by a beaverskin hat.

— So, you'll win Arcadia at last, he said.

Míster Lurkin read a ceremony in English and Spanish declaring that their union would be a paradise on earth, a garden of joy, a sweet succession of sunlit days and warm, comforting nights. No strife would ever trouble their golden world, no, nor would they ever know want. And when they truly joined together, they would have the power to suspend the passage of time.

Arcadia took her mother's ring and the splinter of filbert from around her finger and gave them to Rafael Rafael, who then unthreaded the ring, placed it on her finger, and put the splinter around his own neck. Lurkin had them both sign papers. Then, as they were about to leave, he drew the Captain aside and whispered into his ear.

— Whatever you do, don't look into a mirror.

— It's been more than twenty years since I looked into one, Rafael Rafael said.

— Yes, Lurkin said, but that was by your own choice. Now it's forbidden.

They rode together toward the crumbling tower of the Presidio, where Rafael Rafael had begun the evening in delicious despair. But at the cusp of a hill, Don Ignacio's stallion suddenly reared up in fright, and Captain Rafael Rafael had to wrestle with the reins to bring him under control. Facing them stood a massive bull, pawing the ground, its horns silvered by the setting stars. Arcadia felt the horse shiver with fear under them as Rafael Rafael fought to keep its head toward the path to the tower. She could see some ribbons spiked along the bull's back, and she knew from their fluttering that this bull had not just happened to come into their way; someone had maddened it and brought it on.

From the side of the path, a voice called out.

— Ea, Capitán. Now what will you do with the bull?

It was Don Ignacio's son, Fidel Segundón, who had spiked a feral bull and baited it with his horse into Monterey. He had seen the Captain ride out with Magda, and he knew that the *americano* would have to ride back to the Presidio sooner or later.

— ¡Capitán! Who will protect you now?

The bull watched the stallion struggle, and it lowered its butchering horns. As Rafael Rafael fought to keep from being thrown, Arcadia heard behind them the faint cry of those who had followed her from her home. When the stallion lowered its front hooves for a moment, she slipped from its back and landed heavily on the ground. Then she rose and placed herself directly between the bull and the plunging horse, and she held her hand out to the bull about to charge.

— Stay, toro, and don't charge.

She felt once more that she was reliving the scene of her father's death, and that this time she could change things, this time life alone might triumph.

— Stay toro, that all might live.

The bull lowered its massive head, pawed the earth, and threw itself toward her.

Arcadia scarcely had time to wonder at the loss of her charm, the loss of the power she had owned when she was alone and unknown, before she had fallen into the years of maturity. The bull's twin horns thundered at her, and she scarcely had time to wonder whether she had lost it in the moment she had seen and irresistibly chosen her mate, or in the moment she had taken the ring onto her finger, whether in the moment of choosing she had also decided all the not-chosen.

Captain Rafael Rafael leaped from the stallion, knowing he would be too late, knowing a single bullet would never stop a charging bull, as Arcadia stood in shock at her loss.

Then Fidel Segundón suddenly spurred his horse into the bull's path. He had recognized Arcadia, and in the moment of recognizing her had to protect her absolutely, as keeping her had been the motive of all his actions. He pulled back cruelly on his reins in front of Arcadia, punishing his horse's mouth, and then the innocent horse took the bull's charge in its ribs. The horse screamed like a human child as it was tossed side to side, spilling its rider and its intestines in the same helpless motion.

The Captain leveled his pistol at the bull's spinal column, and shot with sure aim and certain sadness, ending its madness and wildness with its life. Then he reloaded and shot the suffering horse as well.

Don Ignacio's son lay stunned on the ground at the feet of Arcadia. She thanked him, caressed his face as Rafael Rafael recovered the stallion. She told him that she must leave, as the torches of those following were coming closer, but surely they would care for him. But she hoped he would think well of Arcadia, not feel betrayed and think well of her.

— As well as one can think of someone who is lost to us forever, he said.

Rafael Rafael led the stallion to her and helped her on, then mounted before her, and they rode together under the setting sign of Pegasus for the crumbling tower. They found the Captain's aide-de-camp sleeping on a cot outside his quarters, cuddled up with a woman who had finally decided that since the Captain was absent, the aide-de-camp would do.

Captain Rafael Rafael woke up the soldier and told him not to let anyone into his quarters, nor disturb him for any reason. Then, as he and Arcadia were entering, he turned and gave one more order.

— Find me a mirror. Bring it here. Leave it outside the door.

Alone together. Arcadia had never been together with a man alone. And yet, despite her hot embarrassment, she was the aggressor because her sense of loss was so keen and recent. She despoiled him of Don Ignacio's clothing piece by piece, revealing for herself the first man, the first naked man she had known. Furred in parts like a stallion, yet the feeling she experienced was more intimate than any joy she had ever known at the getting of new life. Blushing but vehement, she discovered his Adamic gift, wondered at it, deciding at last that he was special and unique because he belonged to her, there was no one else in the world like him because he was her only husband, and she hoped that his abundance would make her no longer sensible to her loss.

Then he rose up and invited her to join him in nakedness, which she gladly did, and shame left her. He lifted her in a certain way, and sweat and blood broke from her skin, and she gave thanks to the Virgin for letting her find love, even as she understood in ecstatic pain that the woe one suffered in the search for love did not end with love's manifest presence, that loss could only be atoned for, never made good.

They tried to suspend the passage of time on seven separate occasions before dawn. But on each occasion, they did not quite manage to erase that darkish seam between them, and the sky to the east grew lighter. Time was moving despite their best efforts to truly join together, and in fact, Rafael Rafael felt that time was moving faster as he strove again and again to overcome the slight and inevitable space of separation between them, and he felt that if time ever had been suspended, it had been earlier when he had been brooding alone in this room. If anything, the suspension of time had been dissipated by a consummation that always left him falling from Arcadia and Arcadia falling from him, both of them at the mercy of the approaching sun.

When dawn broke, and Pegasus had finally flown beneath the horizon's rim, Rafael Rafael opened the door of his quarters and found himself looking into a mirror for the first time in more than twenty years, a large, oval-shaped mirror four feet tall standing in a cherrywood frame. Rafael Rafael looked, as he must, at the reflection over his left shoulder. There in the mirror was the face of the Dark Man, laughing at him, although now the Dark Man wore a beaverskin hat shadowing his eyes and a ring of Egyptian gold that glinted in the mirror as a wispy hand adjusted the brim of the hat.

Then Arcadia was behind him, her arms about his waist, her face showing over his right shoulder.

— Estoy embarazada, she said. I can feel it.

And although she spoke in Spanish, he knew exactly what she had said. He realized that they hadn't suspended time at all, and never would. He hadn't escaped from history by finding Arcadia, but rather had brought her into history, in a way that was now irreversible. He would never arrive at a place he could only dream about. Paradise could never be where you were, it could only be beyond, beyond a frontier, beyond the floodwaters of a great cresting freshwater river in the middle of the salt sea, unpossessed and forever free of possession.

He turned from the mirror to look at Arcadia's eyes, and he saw that she understood all that, and more than he would ever know. She was holding him in a wise way that both embraced him wholly and urged him back to bed. Perhaps the Father of Lies had not lied completely, perhaps this was as close to paradise as he could ever come.

— Ven conmigo, Arcadia said. Come, husband.

He went back with her to their bed, to try once more to the best of their mortal, entirely human capabilities, if not to suspend the passage of time then at least to beguile it, if not to find paradise, then at least to reconcile themselves to its loss.

If anyone had looked into the mirror, they would have seen the Dark Man, laughing still.

Chapter Four

→ → → ← ← ←

Three days after the Presidio had fallen to the superior strength of American arms, two days after the advent of freedom, democracy, and Jones, and the day after Jones's Progress, the bugle boy woke up cold and hungry at the village site of the lost people of Esselen, with a lump on his head from where Hannibal's book had hit him and sore lips from the nonstop renditions of "Yankee Doodle."

After tucking Hannibal's book under his arm, Míster Lurkin had abandoned him without warning. The bugler had simply looked around, and Míster Lurkin was gone. Major McCormick's troop hadn't returned from the mountain. And the Commodore, so far as he knew, was still underground. The bugle boy thought about making his way back to Monterey, but he hesitated because it might be considered desertion, and because he didn't have any real notion which way to go. Although he always rode with the leaders of any troop, animating all those who rode behind him onward to glory, he had no sense of direction and always relied on the leaders to point their horses the way that glory lay. Alone in the mountains, with no leaders left to follow, he spent a miserable night huddled in a grassy pit waiting to be eaten by beasts who knew nothing of glory but had a good idea what food smelled like.

When he awoke uneaten, with his bugle tarnished by the dew but otherwise unharmed, he went to the riverside and peered into the darkness where he thought the Commodore of the Pacific Fleet of the United States of America lay. He wondered, since Commodore Jones had been there so long, if glory were to be found in the darkness, and he briefly considered following the Commodore's lead underground. But one step into the entryway brought out a gang of crows shouting and roughhousing about his neck and head, and he quickly decided that the glory of this journey should, by all rights, belong to the Commodore and the Commodore alone, and it would be presumptuous for him to seek to share it. So he sat miserably on a rock by the river, watching the thick morning sunlight flash over the chuckling waters heading to the sea.

Then Major McCormick's troop of horse-marines descended from the mountains onto the village site, their uniforms torn and stained, their faces blotched and swollen with cold sleeplessness, their powder and shot exhausted. After following Don Bragas de León, the lionhearted one, and the *Desheredado* through the Santa Lucias, they succeeded in wounding the bark of several large oak trees and blowing an acorn out of the paws of a surprised chipmunk. The only blood drawn by the campaign had been by the numerous mosquitoes that lay in ambush near every pool of still water. Worse, they had been tricked by Sergeant Vargas into charging a hill where he had left his leathern hood with the buzzard's feather peeping up over a log as a decoy. While they attacked with sabers, Vargas and the lionhearted one had stolen the gray mule that carried all their food. Thus, the guerrilla force was now well supplied with beef jerky and hardtack, and could wait for Micheltorena and his two thousand troops to arrive, while the horse-marines trailed back to the river, bedraggled and dejected. The bugle boy noted that the mule was missing, and his stomach rumbled in despair.

— I can find food well enough with my gun, Major McCormick said. He did not pull on his crotch. — But I'm out of lead.

The Major asked the bugler of the whereabouts of the Commodore, but before the boy could answer, Míster Lurkin appeared suddenly on horseback, as though he had snuck up on the troop. He no longer carried Hannibal's book under his arm; he had traded it for a large sheaf of papers protected by a stiff parchment folder.

— Play "Yankee Doodle," Míster Lurkin said. The Commodore will hear you.

The bugle boy brushed his aching lips with his fingers, then lifted up his instrument to his lips. The pain brought tears to his eyes, and the tune sounded slow and mournful, like a dirge.

Slowly, out of the underground, Commodore Jones emerged. Little by little, his curved, seven-foot-long body came into the light of the morning. His face was pallid and his eyes wide and amazed as he blinked at the horse-marines and the Major, the bugle boy and the Trader who gathered around him in a semicircle. He closed his eyes as though trying to see once more what had occupied his senses in the abandoned sweat lodge. Then he opened his eyes again, as though in fright at the clarity of the morning.

— Did you discover something? asked Mister Lurkin.

The Commodore stood up to his full question-mark height.

— The pre-history of California? the Trader continued. The lost people of Esselen? Something else you intend to possess?

The Commodore spoke in a voice worked with stone.
— Oh, I have discovered. That intentions are never satisfied, they are only replaced, by other intentions. Even here, at the end of the continent there is no end.

He blinked once more and looked about himself, disoriented.

When Commodore Jones had first gone underground, he found everything to be black. Even the small light from the opening began to grow dim and shadowy, as though all the crows that had flown out of the abandoned sweat lodge were crowding back in. He felt his way in and groped for the central pole, which was thought to hold up the sky, but he couldn't find it. He waited, completely alone, pensive and melancholy, wondering whether Louisa Darling would hear of his labors to make the country grow and bring California into the realm of freedom and democracy, wondering still further whether or not his labors were futile, whether he could ever possess the pre-history of California, which now seemed to him to be the memory of California. Or whether he could only possess the future of California, and therefore the disinherited would always be disinherited, and he, Jones, would always feel alone, and lonesome, and homeless. He put out a hand to feel again for the pole that held up the sky and wondered about the

World Renewal Ritual, while a crow hopped up on his foot and he fell asleep.

When he woke, it was high noon. The sun was straight overhead so that he cast a shadow directly under his feet. He found himself in the midst of a large meadow, lush and verdant, crossed with trickling streams that ran in all directions, as though the sea could lie at any point of the compass from where he stood. The Commodore's stomach rumbled, a long distance down his curving spine from his brain, and told him he was hungry. He claimed the land for the United States of America, in honor of the ever-pure and undefiled Louisa Darling, and then he went off to look for some food.

A shot rang out, and then he heard a voice begin to sing. Jones walked toward the voice, for in truth he was completely lost and had decided that where there were gunpowder and a human voice, there would be food also. He came upon a man surrounded by three dogs, wearing a long-fringed hunting shirt made of linen, a breechcloth, and a coonskin cap. As Jones drew nearer, he noticed a stench of rotting flesh rising from the cap on the man's head.

The hunter lowered his rifle at a herd of buffalo, and Jones paused quietly, until his stomach roared so loud that several patient animals lifted their heads in mild surprise. The hunter cursed under his breath and squeezed the trigger. A long pause ensued, filled only by the growling of Jones's guts, and then the rifle fired, dropping one buffalo like a sack of rags.

The hunter looked over his shoulder at Jones, but before he could speak, Jones expressed his pleasure at meeting him, his regret at having broken his concentration, his delight at not having spoiled the shot, and the earnest hope that they could soon dress and devour the flesh of the fine specimen he had just so skillfully killed.

The hunter stood up slowly, supporting himself on his long rifle. — If I could, he said, I would put the beast together again piece by piece, joint by joint after every shot, so that I could kill the buffalo and have it remain buffalo, shoot the elk and see it become again elk. But this game is not for you and me. It's for those who come after.

When Jones looked back to where the buffalo fell, he saw that a train of ox-drawn wagons, the largest of them twelve feet tall, had stopped by the kill, and a gang of wolfish men and women descended, butchering the animal with their bare hands, spattering themselves and their wagons with blood. One woman in an apron bit into a woolly leg as though it were a watermelon.

— Hurry, said the hunter. We'll flee while they're busy.

— Which way? asked Jones.

— West. The hunter began to hobble off, and Jones held a handkerchief to his nose and followed, though his rumbling stomach wished him to be back with the bloody crew. He noticed that the hunter was missing his left foot and had to use his rifle as a makeshift crutch.

When they had fled a certain distance, the hunter slowed down to a walk and began to sing again:

Of the great names which in our faces stare
      The General Boon, back woodsman of Kentucky
Was happiest amongst mortals any where;
      For killing nothing but a bear or buck, he

Enjoyed the lonely vigorous harmless days
Of his old age in wilds of deepest maze.

Jones stopped, astonished, suddenly recognizing the squatty, broad-shouldered man beside him. — Are you really Boone, that selfsame man who brought freedom and democracy across the Appalachian Mountains, opened the road to a land of milk and honey for a million fellow citizens, and brought Kentucky into American history?

The hunter barely paused to squint back at Jones. — Keep moving, he said. Who is it wants to know?

Jones declared himself the Master of Monterey, who was seeking to bring California into American history, and the hunter groaned. — So it's reached there, has it? Don't talk to me about history, for I've no use for it. What has history done with me but make me into a cardboard poppet, spouting off about hating the Shawnee and loving commerce. History has called me a Big Man and dressed me in buckskin and stuck this rotting hat on my head, a kind of dress I despised in life. What of the thousands of acres once in my name in Kentucky, what became of them if not taken from me by those damned Yankees that history and I supposedly escorted across the Cumberland Gap? Even in death, they won't leave me in peace, digging up my body from Missouri and moving it back to Kentucky, except for the bones of my left foot, which they left behind by accident, leaving me to limp through eternity. There I lay, a reliquary saint of the West for those speculators and men of commerce who came after me for their own profit and my loss. History has made me into the first of *them*, when all my heart's desire was simply to be myself, always new in a new world, a state I found only when I was most completely alone.

They continued walking across the confusing green meadow, while the hunter asked Jones questions about his conquest. He could scarcely believe that the frontier had moved so far so rapidly, and he asked aloud where a man of his kind would ever find space enough to live.

— The Yankees will be in California soon, he said. The same lawyers who followed me into Kentucky. You mark my words.

When Jones asked him if all those who lived down here were dead, the hunter cackled.

— Well, there's some dead, and some ought to be, and all of us are somewhat bewildered. Then there are those who come after, those buffalo-eaters, who I've heard will never ever die.

— Are we still headed west? Jones asked, as he had the impression that they were walking in circles.

— Every direction is west, the hunter said, limping along on his makeshift crutch.

Jones began wondering about the efficacy of his claiming this land for the United States, whether he could claim land if he were lost and had no way of distinguishing it from any other land, or would even be able to tell how many miles it was from St. Louis and in which direction, and he wondered whether he could bring freedom and democracy to the dead, and whether they had any need for it. His stomach rumbled and he felt queasy at the same time, almost seasick with disorientation.

— There's a son of a bitch ahead who is dead and ought to be, the hunter said.

Jones saw ahead of him a knight in armor, scanning the infinitely distant horizon that lay ahead of them. His armor, even though it was battered and pocked with rock marks, still glittered, and he wore a helmet with a crested plume, though the plume was scraggly and mud-stained.

The hunter, without warning, picked up a stone and threw it at the knight. The rock pinged hollow off the knight's backplate, and the knight turned around in terror until he saw who was there.

— Hijos de puta, he said.

The hunter laughed. — You still looking for your seven cities of mud? he asked.

— And I will find them, the knight shouted. Before you find your beloved Kentucky again filled with elk and buffalo and empty of white men.

When Jones asked why he had cast the stone, the hunter explained that the knight had invaded Pueblo country, and had been stupid enough to wear gilded armor during every siege, which caused every damned Indian in the place to throw their rocks right at him.

— He must have gone simple after being hit in the head during the first siege, the hunter said. — Or he wouldn't have kept wearing that damned stupid armor.

The knight strode to them and addressed Jones with great dignity. — Do not pay attention to him, señor. He is jealous because I still have a hope of finding what I seek.

— And what do you seek? Jones asked, while the hunter laughed cynically.

— When I saw that the city of Cíbola was indeed a city of

earthen brick and mortar, as this *desgraciado* will gladly tell you, I ventured on, still following tales of a land where the chief anointed himself in perfumed oil and was then sprinkled with gold dust, and who then dove into a sacred lake where the gold remained: *el dorado,* the gilded man. But I found only the endless herds of buffalo, and those peoples who live by the buffalo and do not cultivate the ground. After two years, I turned back, sick and weary, with all the peoples I had brought under Spanish rule turned against me. But one brother, Fray Padilla, remained behind, still to seek the seven cities of Antillia, cities founded by seven bishops driven out of Spain by the Moors hundreds of years past, the first cities where the reign of Our Lord has been established on earth. We were in the midst of grasslands so vast and flat and featureless that even the natives could only find their way by shooting an arrow toward the horizon at dawn, when they could take a bearing from the sunrise, following the arrow and shooting another over it when they came to it. But Fray Padilla claimed that faith would guide him, and I left him there in the trackless wilderness. Would that I had remained with him, to seek the seven cities of God, not the seven cities of Gold.

The hunter jeered. — What makes you so sure he found them?

— If he had not, the knight replied, he would be here with us.

— He's food for buzzards, the hunter said mockingly.

— Even if that is true, he is happier destroyed by what he sought than you, who were the instrument that brought destruction to that which you most loved.

— Why you damned Conquistador, the hunter said, stung. You destroyed everything you looked for more than I did.

— Did not.

— Did so.

— Weren't you the one who surveyed the land in Kentucky, splitting it up into lots that could be bought and sold? Weren't you the one who despoiled the land of its primeval wholeness? And now you complain that you yourself were bought and sold in turn, when you brought it on yourself.

— And you, you were named Captain-General of the provinces of Acus, Cíbola, the seven cities, Quivira, and any other lands you might discover, and all the people who were there, or had been there, or would be there from now until the end of time. What did you do but put pueblos to the torch and burn Indians at the stake, and make sure the ones who were left would never want anything to do with Spain, and return home without a gold doubloon to show for two years.

— Even though I failed, at least I was recognized by the king for meritorious service, and was given burial in a crypt in a fine church near the Zócalo of Mexico. What did your countrymen do for you besides pack your stinking body from one hole in the ground to another? And not all of it, either, he added with a smirk.

The hunter began to hobble toward the knight. — Come here, you damned foreigner. I'll put another dent or two in your armor.

The knight stayed just out of range, taunting the hunter, who swung his rifle butt at the bedraggled plume in the knight's helmet but hit only air.

Commodore Jones looked on, astounded. The hunter was yelling at the knight that all he ever really wanted was to rip gold from the bowels of Indians or the Earth, whichever was quicker, and ship it back to Spain, with one fifth for the king, while the knight called the hunter a child of nature, if child of nature meant one who was untutored, unlettered, naive, stupid, rude, barbaric, and ignorant of the ways of the world, as though one could blaze a trail and not have anyone follow. He was a boob, a simpleton, a lowbrow fool, and moreover his hat smelled.

— Gentlemen, please, called Commodore Jones. It had become obvious to him that these two argued frequently. Could I ask you to pause and answer a question?

The two men stopped and looked at him, aware of his existence again for the first time in a quarter of an hour.

— Has either of you ever seen or heard of the pole of the lost people of Esselen, the one that holds up the sky? the Commodore asked.

The hunter and the knight looked at each other, and then the hunter laughed.

— No wonder he's shaped like a question mark, he said.

The Commodore's stomach rumbled, and he heard the sound of weeping. He turned and saw a giantess walking with her face in her hands, towering over the confusing green meadow. She was dressed like a Greek goddess, in a long flowing robe that fell to her bare feet, but her feet were muddy. Her tears trickled constantly between her fingers, feeding the little streams that ran out in all directions from where she passed. While she didn't stop walking, she lifted her face once from her hands and looked at the Commodore with a glance of awful recognition, then lowered her face to her hands again.

The Commodore felt a shiver run all through his curving spine. The giantess's face was sallow and drawn, and her teeth stuck out of her mouth, and her eyes, though purplish as the evening sky, were sunken into her face and rather close together. Yet despite the fact that decades had passed since he had seen her entering a church in Boston, the Commodore recognized without a doubt that the giantess was indeed Louisa Darling. He wanted to run after her, tell her of his feats, his exploits, his bringing of freedom and democracy to California, all in honor of her. But her strides covered furlongs, and she was distant from him before he could take a step.

— Allí anda, said the knight. Pursued by her memory.

— She don't look too good, the hunter added. Must be the morning sickness again.

Unbelieving, the Commodore looked at his two companions, then back after Louisa Darling, who in his mind could never have sickness of any kind. And then he recognized, harrying Louisa's steps, his own steward, Hannibal. He rubbed his eyes and looked again, but he could not mistake the round African who had been at his side for more than twenty years.

The hunter sighed. — I almost wish I'd a shot her when I had the chance.

The hunter told the story of the firehunt, when he was holding a firebrand aloft in his left hand and his rifle in his right, hunting deer hypnotized by the flames through the bright reflection of their eyes. One night he had leveled his barrel at a pair of eyes and was about to shoot when he realized that those shining eyes weren't quite like the eyes of any other deer he had ever seen. He hesitated, and the eyes cut and ran, and when he followed he found a panting maiden, and he knew then and there he would have to love her the rest of his life.

Jones protested that the woman was Louisa Darling, the woman *he* loved, and his two companions laughed.

— We all see her as we must, the knight said.

— Look out! the hunter shouted. The bloody wagon train was drawing near them, and now the crew had slaughtered the oxen, themselves pulling the wagons like handcarts while ripping apart the limbs of their loyal, vacant-eyed beasts.

— Head west! The hunter was hobbling away using his long rifle as a crutch. Head west!

Jones, his stomach rumbling, followed the other two as they moved away from the murderous wagons.

— They'll be at each other before long, the hunter said.

— Who are they? Jones asked.

— Don't know. Some say it's the party of Ishmael Bush, still crossing the Prairie. Others say it's the party of George and Tamsen Donner. Nobody dare ask.

— Do they ever stop following you?

— Never, the hunter said.

— Look ahead, said the knight. It's the tomb of the Marquis of the Valley.

They came upon a marble sarcophagus, with a stout carven figure lying on top of the tomb and a small dog resting below his feet. But when they drew nearer, Jones realized that the figure was not carven stone but rather as much flesh and blood as his two companions. He seemed to be merely sleeping, dressed in courtly Spanish finery, a ruff collar and doublet and breeches. And he gave one sure sign of being alive, as his breeches were filthy with excrement, which dripped down the side of the tomb, that earthiness that would soon become part of the earth, although the body itself would never touch the earth.

The knight explained that they never knew when they would come upon the tomb, as they never knew where they were in relation to it. Jones said that the pole of the lost people of Esselen must rest in a constant location. Surely that could orient them.

The hunter sighed. — None of us have ever found the lost people of Esselen, or their pole, although we have all tried.

As though in response, the stout body of the Marquis of the Valley began to speak, although his eyes remained closed as in sleep. — When I sacked the beautiful city of Tenochtitlán, I restored the one true faith among a people who had never known they were wanting it. I won titles and riches and undying fame for myself, souls for the church to harvest, and peoples and nations for the Emperor's all-uniting rule. Still, I could not rest. Only when in action could I feel Providence acting through me. I wrote the Emperor, asked him to send farmers with seed, brood mares, devout priests, and no lawyers whatsoever. Then I mounted an expedition to the virgin lands of the west.

— He always says the same thing, the hunter stuck in.

— When I came to the sea, my men and I built two ships, to seek out the rich island that was said to lie just beyond the horizon. But we found only a dry and hostile land, where brutes scrabbled among rocks for grubs and crabs, and no trees like those that flower in Castile can be seen. Sick and embittered, I believed I had lost the direction of Providence, and I named the island California, as a jest, after the marvelous land that Montalvo described where there is no metal save gold. I left the Captain Hurtado to seek further, and I returned to Mexico. There I was soon entangled in the suits brought by the lawyers who had arrived despite my pleas, and I was mocked for having wasted my wealth to discover profitless lands.

— Damned lawyers, the hunter said.

— I saw the city rebuilt, as I had directed, but I realized that I had destroyed the most beautiful thing I had ever known. The Captain Hurtado and his men were never heard of again. From that time until the day I agonized upon my bed in Spain, I envied the captain's fate.

— You see, the knight said. It is better to be destroyed by what you seek.

— No, the Commodore said. Good sir, no. Providence still guides the course of the land you named. Hear my intentions. California will become a realm of freedom and democracy, to join into the progress of those ideals across the continent, to become part of American history. California will be a true golden land, a beacon to all those who dream and would make their dreams live.

The Marquis of the Valley spoke, and his voice sounded dry and distant, like dust motes in the sunlight down a long, arcaded walkway. — Your intentions are noble. Will remain noble until the moment you attempt to fulfill them. And madness will follow.

Then Hannibal appeared at Commodore Jones's side, although the Commodore hadn't heard him approach, and said that he had a message from Louisa Darling. The Commodore begged him to give it without delay.

— She would like you to deed over to her a little land, Hannibal said. Just enough for her to live in peace, without intention or memory.

— Madness, madness, the Marquis intoned.

The Commodore said, — I would I were a surveyor or a land commissioner. For of all the land I've conquered in her name, I don't have title to a single acre.

— Even all would not be enough for Louisa Darling.

— Hannibal, the Commodore said. Don't you recognize me?

— No, the African replied. I don't *recognize* you at all. And he laughed and whirled away, again shadowing the tracks of the weeping woman, quickly distant from the gaping Commodore.

— Madness. Madness follows.

As though summoned by the Marquis, the bloody wagons again approached. The hunter shouted to head west, and they scrambled away. Then the Commodore heard the faint strains of music, "Yankee Doodle," being played.

— Follow the music, he called. The direction of the music.

But his two companions fled elsewhere. The Commodore looked over his shoulder and saw that the wagons were following him, and that now there didn't seem to be any people with the train at all, but only a rolling head with a gaping bloody mouth.

The sound of the music grew louder, and the Commodore clawed after it, now down on all fours in the confusing green meadow.

Then, slowly, he seemed to be crawling upward, and the light changed from the constant noon of the meadow to the tin light of morning.

He blinked, and the music ceased, and he saw the horse-marines and the Major, the bugle boy and the Trader, gathered about him in a semicircle.

— Oh, I have discovered, he said. That intentions are never satisfied, they are only replaced, by other intentions. Even here, at the end of the continent, there is no end.

He looked around, suddenly confused.

— Where is my faithful Memory? he asked.

Míster Lurkin shook his head. — Gone. Ran off with a goatherd. To be free to remember things he believes to have consequence.

The Commodore felt lost and abandoned, alone in the world and with no notion of where he was to go, or why, or for whom. — I knew it. For now he will haunt *my* memory, and all my memories of her.

Míster Lurkin took the papers out from under his arm. — Another American ship came into port last night to join your squadron. The *Dale*. The latest news from Mexico and the United States shows that the rumors were false. War hasn't broken out. The two nations are at peace. Except here in California.

The Commodore looked up at him in torment.

— What will you do, Commodore? The history you would

have written has become smoke and air. Or will you have it written that you determined to turn your disappointment into malice, will you hold California against Micheltorena and his two thousand five hundred troops, will you make it so, will you still be Master of Monterey?

The Commodore knew that all he had done had been futility, done in the name of someone or something that was not a name for what moved him. And he knew that relinquishment itself would be futility, because those who come after would still come after. Yet he knew he would relinquish, now he would relinquish, even though he would forevermore know himself alone and homeless, because he could no longer believe naïvely, no longer believe without standing beside himself and willing himself a believer.

— What will you do, Commodore?

The Commodore drew himself up to his full, question-mark height to answer.

— I shall relinquish, restore the land to Mexico, and take the *National Intention* back around the Cape to Hampton Roads, where the voyage began.

While Míster Lurkin perhaps smiled, the horse-marines began to mutter, and Major McCormick, saluting, asked permission to speak.

— I can take over land well enough with my gun, he said. But I can't see myself giving any back.

The Commodore touched him on the shoulder. — We will have to learn to see ourselves in a different way.

Chapter Five

Commodore Jones mounted a roan horse and turned its head back toward Monterey. Míster Lurkin rode at his side, the sheaf of papers that declared the reign of peace firmly under his arm, while the tired and bruised Major McCormick and his horse-marines trailed behind. At the very rear of the sad procession rode the bugle boy, who, as he was not asked to play anything, wished he could exchange his bugle for a sausage.

Jones led his troop back across the same land through which they had triumphantly progressed the day before, stopping once at a rise to look back on the village site of Esselen. He would relinquish California, return Monterey to those who had previously possessed it, although he sensed that they had never really possessed that which they desired, that they, like the hunter, had forever altered that which they would grasp and clutch to themselves by the passion they had to grasp and clutch. The Commodore could never possess what the ex-Governor had possessed, nor could Alvarado possess what the lost people of Esselen had possessed, nor could those who came after possess what he, Commodore Jones, had imagined himself master of for such a brief term. Everything had changed.

They rode down the Carmel River to the ruined Mission San Carlos, where Soylibre still sat on the church steps, regaling himself with beef jerky. All the men looked hungrily at the sleek ex-cook, who smacked his lips and made a great show of relishing the food they had bestowed upon him. He told Míster Lurkin that thus far he was enjoying the realm of freedom and democracy, and that he hoped it would long continue.

— But it's over, Míster Lurkin said. California will once again belong to Mexico, and Micheltorena will govern.

— ¿De veras? I am sorry for it, as this was the tastiest jerky I have ever had.

— What does he say? asked Jones.

— He is sad that American rule ended so soon, as he was already enjoying the fruits of liberty.

Soylibre sucked on a piece of jerky and nodded sadly at the Commodore.

Although the Commodore felt bereft of all faith, he asked Míster Lurkin to tell Soylibre to keep the ideals alive inside him, as he didn't want to destroy the Indian's simple credence. Soylibre asked Míster Lurkin if he could get any more jerky by keeping the ideals alive.

— Doubtful, Míster Lurkin replied. In fact, they are more likely to ask you to return some of that they gave you yesterday.

— Then I won't keep the ideals. I'll keep the jerky instead, until the Americans come back. Then I'll believe whatever they want me to believe.

— What does he say?

— He is waiting and will be waiting for your return.

The Commodore turned his horse away, wondering if he would ever return, wondering how many others he would be leaving behind who craved freedom and democracy. Soylibre, free temporarily from the realm of freedom, called after them.

— Soy libre, soy libre.

They rode up the hill to where Commodore Jones had saved Andrés Segundo by establishing American law. He hoped to see the boy peacefully watching over his sheep, content and grateful. But there was nobody on the hilltop. One yearling sheep, separated from its flock, bleated pathetically and rubbed its woolly side against the tree where Andrés had been tied and beaten.

Commodore Jones pointed to the ground. — Here, at least, though my command was brief, I did some tangible good.

— Indeed, said Míster Lurkin. Though it seems sheep can still be lost.

— Sir? Major McCormick saluted. I was wondering, since none of the men have eaten since yesterday and it's still a long ride to Monterey, whether we couldn't just have a bit of fresh mutton.

The Commodore hesitated, and in the moment of hesitation, the sheep's throat was cut and it was flayed, spitted, and turning over an open fire.

— Very well, the Commodore said, as the flesh bubbled. We'll just leave some scrip tacked to that tree. To conform as best we can with the law.

They rode from the hilltop down into the pueblo of Monterey, through the whitewashed adobe dwellings that lay scattered on the green plain, past women dressed in black walking slowly to church to hear the midday mass and men spurring out toward the great herds of cattle. In the enclosed courtyards behind the white houses, they heard the rhythmic *pit-pat-pit*, like a bird's heartbeat, of Ohlone women kneeling in a circle and forming tortillas between their fingers and palms.

When the Commodore led his troop into the plaza of the Presidio, he had the odd sensation that he was exiting a dream, and that he had to exit through the same dreamscapes by which he had entered. In the plaza, the same line of dignitaries stood in the same order as they had two days previously, and his soldiers stood in ranks just as they had when he had taken possession. The ex-Governor Alvarado stood at the head of the line, flanked by Comandante Silva and the leading landowners, although the Commodore noticed one subtle change, the absence of one elderly landowner named Castro. He noticed a change in his soldiers as well, as some of them were now dressed like Californios, had exchanged their brass-buttoned blues for magenta and orange serapes and broad-brimmed wool hats. In the crowd that had gathered to witness, some of the men were wearing sailors' straw boaters, or the short-billed caps of the marines, and women wore the shiny black neckerchiefs of sailors over one shoulder.

The Commodore found prepared for his signature a document, in Spanish and English, renouncing the conquest and rescinding the surrender, returning California, including those parts of California that had never been seen and only existed in legend, tall tale, and hearsay, to Mexican rule forever and unto eternity. His hand shook, but he signed it Thomas ap Catesby Jones, Commodore of the Pacific Fleet of the United States of America. He handed the document over to the ex-Governor, and although cut off from Waxdeck's words, he felt compelled to give a short speech.

— Our occupation was brief, our possession a mere passing wind. We return to you your lands, cattle, and households, to be once again Mexico. And yet, though our stay was brief, understand that our sadness, for the beauty of California which we will never again know, will endure throughout our lives. *Et in Arcadia ego.*

Míster Lurkin immediately offered a translation, in which he stated that all was as it had been before, that they were still the rightful owners of their vast tracts of land measured in leagues, and would be throughout the lasting reign of peace that had begun like a golden age between the United States and Mexico. Míster Lurkin further proposed a fandango to celebrate the peaceful outcome of the conquest of Monterey, which had ended without a single casualty, and his proposal was greeted with shouts and applause.

Fray Echevarría began to weep with joy when he heard the news, certain that the strange turn of events had taken place in answer to his prayers that California be returned to God, and that all heretics and apostates be banished from the land with a burning sword. He wondered now whether the rest of his prayers would be fulfilled, as he had beseeched the Lord to return the Franciscans to supreme power throughout California, there to await the Second Coming as soon as they had fulfilled the last prophecy by converting the savage tribes to the north, who were part of the lost tribes of Israel, to the holy Catholic faith.

The ex-Governor Alvarado, who was more of a cynic and halfway a heretic himself, accepted the document of renunciation from Commodore Jones's hands. But he expected to see the Americans return eventually to this isolated, sparsely populated outpost of old Mexico. He only hoped that Micheltorena would arrive by then, and he wondered whether it would be possible to resign the post of ex-Governor, since the governors sent up from Mexico tended to last only six months and there was a good chance he would be called on to surrender again if he were still ex-Governor.

Commodore Jones ordered the band to run down the American flag and run up the Mexican flag over the Presidio, and to play the Mexican National Anthem. The band began to talk amongst themselves, and finally the bugle boy came over to address the Commodore.

— Sir, the only tune we know how to play is "Yankee Doodle."

The Commodore was astounded. — You don't know the National Song of Mexico?

— We've never had to take down our own flag before, sir.

— Well, somebody in the band must know some other song. Have them play that while the flags are exchanged.

The bugle boy saluted, and after some more muttered discussions amongst the band members, a tuba player began to lower the flag while the bugle boy did a solo rendition of "Froggy Went A-Courtin'."

With the music still playing, Commodore Jones turned his

horse toward the gate of the Presidio to begin the ride down to the harbor. Then he reined in suddenly and turned to Míster Lurkin.

— Where is the Captain? he asked.

— You'll see him, Míster Lurkin assured him. They continued through the gate as the Mexican flag was run up, followed slowly by soldiers on foot dressed in multicolored serapes, the band, and finally the horse-marines, with the bugle boy in the rear, still playing "Froggy Went A-Courtin'." When they had all finally cleared the gate, the Californios brought out their own guitars and flutes and began to play a jota under the restored flag of Mexico.

In that moment, el señor Don Bragas de León, the lionhearted one, stormed into the Presidio accompanied by Sergeant Vargas and three Ohlone vaqueros. Fortified by salt pork and hardtack, they had decided on a lightning strike at the fort to throw the occupying force into confusion until Micheltorena arrived, which should be tomorrow or the next day. The guerrillas swirled into the plaza on horseback, and then stopped dumbfounded as they found their countrymen dancing to guitars under a Mexican flag.

— What has happened? Bragas de León shouted. Has Micheltorena arrived?

The dancers paused and laughed at him, while he asked repeatedly what had happened, growing flustered and red-faced when nobody would answer his shouted questions. Bragas de León turned back toward the gate and saw, on the road to the harbor, the hind ends of a dozen horses swishing their tails at him. Then the music resumed, and the dancers continued to laugh at him, Don Bragas de León, he who would be Master of Monterey.

On the slow path down to the harbor, Commodore Jones saw two wedding processions going by toward the Presidio church. He asked Míster Lurkin who they were, and the Trader explained that an old landowner, Don Ignacio Castro, was on his deathbed and had finally given permission to his twelve sons and eleven daughters to marry. They all planned to do so within the month and apply to Mexico for land grants to found great estates, all except the second son, Fidel, who had declared that he would never marry, but would rather take orders as a friar and go among the Indians.

— He prefers to wait for the end of the world, with Fray Echevarría, Míster Lurkin said. But with twenty-two siblings having children, he'll have a long wait.

Míster Lurkin invited the Commodore for a glass of brandy at his store while the barge was made ready. The two tied their horses outside, and the Commodore ducked to enter the adobe building. Inside, a clerk was in earnest discussion with a ranchero about a list of debts and liens against his land.

Míster Lurkin dusted off a heavy decanter and polished two beveled glasses. — This is from France, he said.

The Commodore looked around the store, saw the wedding dress hanging from the roof beams alongside the iron ploughshares, and the barrels of seed corn on the floor. But he also noticed that many of the items, the tins of biscuit, the rolls of marline, the picked oakum, barrels of gunpowder, and boxes of lead shot, seemed to have come from the *National Intention*. As the Trader handed him a glass, he looked more closely at the clerk behind the desk and recognized his own yeoman, the round-faced Keyes, now dressed in the same dark coat and beaver hat as Míster Lurkin. The Commodore demanded of him what he was doing there, in that outfit.

— Helping further the aims of the voyage, sir, Keyes replied. Freedom and democracy means freedom of commerce as well. Don't you think? Free circulation of belt buckles. Every lead ball . . . equal . . . to every other lead ball. And freedom for the individual to pursue his own self-interest.

— Indeed, my good Commodore, said Míster Lurkin. I've recognized the purity of this man's venality, and I've taken him into my employ.

The Commodore noticed that the ranchero had turned away his face and pulled down his broad-brimmed hat, and had ducked his chin into his serape. But the merest glitter of blue eyes allowed him to recognize the man seated opposite his yeoman as his captain, Captain Rafael Rafael.

— And you, sir! What are you doing here? At such a time, in such an attire.

The Captain smiled, but there was great sadness in his voice.
— Commodore Jones, I wanted so badly to sail over a horizon and never come back, to go back to a place in the past I remembered, or arrive at a place I only had dreamed about. And now that I have gotten exactly what I wanted I've found that it's not exactly what I wanted, or no longer is, because I have it, because the horizon is still out there. But it's the best I can do, suddenly beshitted with debt though I may be, better than to go on endlessly questioning. I'll sail no more.

And Commodore Jones, who was no longer Master of Monterey and could compel nothing ashore, drank and left the trading house, while Keyes continued to explain to Rafael Rafael that his land that was Arcadia's land was already entangled in debts, dating at least since the visit in 1836 of the brig *Pilgrim*, as could be seen plainly from the documents before him, but that Lurkin's trading house would gladly extend him credit against next year's hides and tallow.

The Commodore's barge was at the landing, with a mixed crew of oarsmen, some sailors wearing sombreros and serapes, and some Ohlones wearing Navy uniforms. The Commodore turned his horizontal gaze out to sea and saw that his ship, the *National Intention,* was down by the head and listing to starboard, and he realized that it must be taking on water and that the pumps needed to be manned. He was about to board the barge and tell the crew to lay on the oars, when a voice he recognized called from the road.

— Señor Jones! Señor Jones! ¡Juez honrado! Wait! ¡Espérese!

Andrés Segundo was running down the cart path toward the landing in bare feet. He had been looking for Commodore Jones since John Cameron had beaten him and let him go, trusting that the Commodore would bring the arm of American law down upon his former master, now that they all lived in the realm of freedom and democracy. The Commodore saw the boy's bloody clothes, the shirt turned to rags, the swollen face, and he knew what had happened.

— Señor Commodore Jones. You must come with me, to punish John Cameron and make him do what is right. For he still owes me fifty-four reales, and I haven't eaten anything since yesterday. ¡Viva América!

— I'm sorry, lad. But this isn't the United States of America.

Andrés looked at him, confused. — This isn't América?

Commodore Jones shook his head sadly.

— You mean, this isn't the realm of freedom and democracy?

— No, it's not.

— This isn't where all men's rights are protected and respected?

— No, said the Commodore. Perhaps it will be, someday. But now, I can't help you. For I'm no longer Master of Monterey.

He boarded his barge and turned his question-mark body back to sea, and at a sign, the oarsmen began to row lustily toward the *National Intention*.

Andrés watched the barge depart from shore in disbelief, which, as the Commodore grew more distant, changed into pure rage. He shouted after the Commodore, — If you ever do come back, to establish the realm of freedom and democracy, and to protect all men's rights . . . leave me out of it!

The barge, followed by other liberty boats, pulled alongside the ship, and the Commodore climbed aboard and immediately gave the orders that had been lacking for three days.

— Man the pumps! Prepare the ship for sea!

Chips, at that moment crawling up from the bilge with another bucket of salt water to dump over the side, groaned in relief and agony at the orders. He had, little by little over the past day and a half, stolen paper from Waxdeck's quarters, soaked it in tar, and dived down into the bilges to plug leaks with epic verse. And while he had used up most of the epic, he had only slowed the leaks, and he knew the *National Intention* was in danger. Yet to hear that the ship was getting ready for sea meant that the green land would remain unconquered, the village of white-walled houses and red-tile roofs scattered like seeds on the plain below the forest would remain undestroyed, that peaceful world that Chips hated and envied and would be revenged upon would remain peaceful to torment him. As the ship's crew climbed back aboard and the ship hummed into activity, Chips looked out at California and raked his pale face with his nails until blood ran into his black, tangled beard.

— Here, now, Chips. The red-capped boatswain came by and cuffed him on the shoulder. Down into the bilges with you. Didn't you hear? We've got to get the pumps out!

Commodore Jones raised the first lieutenant to the rank of Captain, as he never expected to see Rafael Rafael again, and he appointed a round-shouldered, bald-headed man who wore thick spectacles nicknamed "Old Revolvers" to take Keyes's position as yeoman. The new yeoman quickly made a good bargain with representatives of Míster Lurkin to buy up some oakum the Trader had by chance obtained in 1836. The leaks were stopped, and the verse that had temporarily stayed the water was discarded and left to drift in the sea.

When the bilges had been emptied of enough water to put the ship on an even keel, the Commodore gave the order to weigh anchor and loose sails, and seamen manned the capstan to lift the heavy anchor by its cable and cat it home, while

Merry Jack Chase, on the maintop, directed the unfastening of the gaskets and the unfurling of the sails. The two Mexican trading vessels, the *Paz y Religión* and the *Don Quijote*, had been released from seizure and they dipped their flags in salute. Slowly, the *National Intention* tacked past Point Pinos and headed south with the current and the prevailing westerlies.

The Commodore looked vaguely among the men working on deck for seaman Bush, but he was nowhere to be seen. Still, the ship had gotten under way without a flogging, and perhaps there need be no flogging with the ship headed back to where it had begun . . . homeward bound, whatever home might mean now.

He looked out, still horizontally, as California receded in the distance, and the pueblo of Monterey was slowly occulted from view, one building at a time, by the curving bluffs and tall trees.

There were Rafael Rafael, and Hannibal, and Keyes. Each one trying to realize some intention on the grounds where they now stood. There were also the knight, and the hunter, and the marquis, forever wandering, their intentions thrown out before them like shadows they would always chase, and Louisa Darling, whom each one saw as he must. And there were those who came after, those who would sooner or later devour the sum of each individual's intention and subsume it into the national intention.

Suddenly, Midshipman Waxdeck appeared on deck in the ship's waist, just below where the Commodore stood on the quarterdeck. He wavered pale and unsteady, thin as a line, dressed in white skivvies, a spot of green bile at the corner of his mouth. Despoiled of all his papers, his ink run dry, he had finally staggered up the ladder to the main deck, and now saw California for the first time as it began to fall below the horizon.

Major McCormick came to his side to steady him as he stood on his own two feet for the first time since the ship had left Hampton Roads.

— Here now, dear boy. Let me hold you.

Waxdeck looked upon the land he had written about, the land he had attempted to put into an epic narrative of conquest, a narrative centered on the culture-hero, the restless and questioning Jones who leaned on the rail above him. A tear came to his eye and he wiped his mouth and watched California disappear.

— It's so much more beautiful than words, he said.

Up in the rigging, Merry Jack Chase danced above the loosened sails. — Well said, lad, he laughed. Well put. Perfectly expressed.

Commodore Jones lowered his head, covered his ears with his hands.

Belowdecks, eloquent and inchoate, Chips groaned.

EPILOGUE

Fond Reader:

There are some facts left to relate, in which the Author hopes you will retain an interest, although it is far from clear how these facts will influence the interpretation of what has gone before. Would it illuminate matters to know that Micheltorena, with his three hundred troops, had not been approaching Monterey at all? In fact, he had retreated twenty miles to Los Angeles, where he remained unheroically garrisoned, even while writing to his own Secretary of War and Marine that he wished himself a "Thunderbolt to fly and annihilate the invaders." After the relinquishment, Micheltorena demanded compensation for fifteen hundred complete infantry uniforms ruined in a forced march to Monterey, and also payment for a complete set of musical instruments, as imaginary marches cannot take place without music.

The unending reign of peace declared by Lurkin in his translation of Jones's final speech ended four years later in 1846, as other players enacted the roles our characters had attempted. Commodore Sloat occupied Monterey, again without a shot. At the same time, in Sonoma, a band of drunken trappers and ex-sailors rudely painted a beast on a petticoat offered by one of their wives and raised it up a flagpole, establishing a republic. The beast was intended to be a bear, but later viewers have judged that it most closely resembles a rooting hog. The conquest became official in 1848 with the Treaty of Guadaloupe Hidalgo. Later that year, gold was discovered at Sutter's Mill, and gold-seekers, mythified as Argonauts, were en route to California.

Would it make this history more understandable if you were to know that, despite the guarantees of property rights in the treaty, most of the Californios' land grants were worn away by squatters and litigation, and much of the acreage ended up in the hands of the same Yankee lawyers who had followed the hunter into Kentucky? Or to know that the last independent indigenous people in California, the Modocs, were driven into a mountain fastness in 1873, and fought against rifle and cannon for months until starvation drove them out? That the last native speakers of Ohlone are believed to have passed away sometime soon after the year 1900?

You may wish some notice of the individuals in this history, although much of what follows can only be based on hearsay and conjecture. Hannibal Memory went to the gold fields with his mate and his children. He was not allowed to work a claim because of the color of his skin, but he made and kept more money than most of the miners by setting up a cook house and serving hot meals in the evenings. His specialty was stewed goat. Jimmy F. Bush has been lost to history, although it is known that the site of the polyglot village where he ended up is now occupied by the Casa de Coffee and Pancakes. His mother and father finally crossed the Sierra Nevada in 1848, saw the American flag flying over Sutter's fort, and wondered if they had arrived at the same place they had started from. They eventually owned an apricot ranch in the Santa Clara Valley, still occasionally counting their children and wondering if they had lost one or two on the rush across the continent. Andrés Segundo Sombra left California after it again became the realm of freedom and democracy and went to Argentina, where he became a famous gaucho.

The ex-Governor Alvarado sold the Mariposa land grant to John C. Frémont right after the conquest, thinking he had made a sharp deal on a grant of dubious legality, and then was chagrined to find that one of the richest gold-producing veins in California ran right through the heart of it. He was reduced to a petty, debt-ridden existence after 1848, but he never escaped from his title, and for the rest of his life he was forced to hear creditors dun him in the most polite and galling phrases: Señor Don ex-Governor, honorable Mister Alvarado, could you manage to pay the five cents you owe me for washing and ironing your collars? Señor Don ex-Governor, I fear to impose on your honor, but has it come to your worship's attention that you are two days behind on the rent?

McCormick and Waxdeck set up a Bachelors' Hall together in Norfolk, Virginia. While Waxdeck resigned his commission, McCormick continued to go to sea, coming home between voyages to regale Waxdeck with tales in the great oral tradition. Waxdeck for a time continued to write, with an eye to immortalizing McCormick's feats for the edification of future generations. But he soon gave it up, finding that cooking was easier and more immediately gratifying than writing ever could be, not to mention more appreciated by McCormick, who would die unable to sign his name. With some practice, Waxdeck learned to make the burgoos, lobscouses, and dunderfunks so dear to McCormick's heart, and have them taste just as though they had been made on a ship that hadn't touched land in months.

Arcadia and Rafael, along with many other Californios, gradually lost their land, but they managed to keep a house in Paso Robles. While continuing to try to make time stop, they had seven children. In later years, Arcadia made and sold preserves from the fruit orchards that were beginning to be planted, and Rafael took up the pen to become a poet, and made acquaintance with Helen Hunt Jackson, Edwin Markham, Frank Norris, and "Pres" Presley among the California literati. His theme was always trying to return to a place he remembered in the past, or trying to arrive at a place he could only dream about — goals that he thought he had renounced, but that he still tried unsuccessfully to achieve in verse.

Míster Lurkin became a successful dealer in real estate. After the conquest, he foreclosed on his creditors, gained control over vast tracts of land, subdivided it, and sold it so quickly that he scarcely seemed to have owned it at all, though he was always master of the profits from it. He left behind several historical memoirs, including one called *The Affair at Monterey*, which includes a never published appendix written in a different hand than his and entitled *The Book of Memory*. The original manuscript was left in the hands of H. H. Bancroft, and can be found in his library to this day.

As for Jones himself — after being relieved of his command, he received the mildest of reprimands from the Secretary of the Navy, along with assurances that he would soon again receive employment commensurate with his rank and abilities. Curiously, his disillusionment did not lead him to change his life in the least. Indeed, he served again as Commodore of the Pacific Fleet, although after Sloat & Stockton & Kearney & Frémont had already garnered what glory there was to be had in the conquest of California. He spent the rest of his days restless and questioning, even though bereft of all his former goals, an empty questioning for he knew not what — because contentment was not and never had been part of the national intention — without anyone to write his epic except for the Author of this sad, tragic, and absolutely true narrative who now, at last, puts down his pen.

FINIS

ACKNOWLEDGMENTS

This novel owes much to the many friends and fellow writers who read the manuscript and gave generous and invaluable guidance. I would like to thank especially Joanne Bloom, Alison Bond, Pam Carlquist, Franklin Fisher, Deborah Foss, Howard Horwitz, Teresa Jordan, David Kranes, Ron Molen, Kristen Rogers, Dorothy Solomon, and Steve Tatum. I would also like to thank the many librarians at the Bancroft Library and the Special Collections Department of the J. Willard Marriott Library for their wonderful and professional help, and I extend a special thanks to Lisa Christiansen of the California History Center.

While writing this novel, I received generous assistance from the National Endowment for the Arts. I also received help and support from the Writers at Work writers conference, the Utah Arts Council, the Red Rock Writers Guild, and especially from all my friends in Southern Utah.